If you have a home computer with internet access you may:

- request an item be placed on hold
- renew an item that is overdue
- view titles and due dates checked out on your card
- view your own outstanding fines

To view your patron record from your home computer:
Click on the NSPL homepage:
http://nspl.suffolk.lib.ny.us

North Shore Public Library

A BAD DAY FOR MERCY

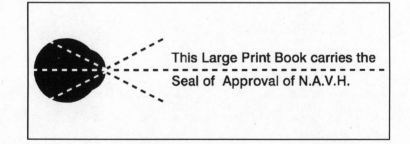

This Large Print Book carries the
Seal of Approval of N.A.V.H.

A BAD DAY FOR MERCY

SOPHIE LITTLEFIELD

THORNDIKE PRESS
A part of Gale, Cengage Learning

GALE
CENGAGE Learning·

Detroit • New York • San Francisco • New Haven, Conn • Waterville, Maine • London

GALE
CENGAGE Learning®

LIBRARY OF CONGRESS CATALOGING-IN-PUBLICATION DATA

Littlefield, Sophie.
  A bad day for mercy / by Sophie Littlefield.
    pages ; cm. — (Thorndike Press large print mystery)
    ISBN 978-1-4104-5050-0 (hardcover) — ISBN 1-4104-5050-3 (hardcover)
  1. Hardesty, Stella (Fictitious character)—Fiction. 2. Murder—Investigation—Fiction. 3. Middle-aged women—Fiction. 4. Large type books. I. Title.
PS3612.I882B27 2012b
813'.6—dc23   2012019216

Published in 2012 by arrangement with St. Martin's Press, LLC.

Printed in the United States of America
1 2 3 4 5 6 7 16 15 14 13 12

For K-kins

CHAPTER ONE

Jogging home from the Freshway at sunset on a sultry evening in late May had been a fine idea. Trying to carry home a box of frozen taquitos, a carton of pistachio ice cream, a family-sized bag of Fritos Scoops, a tub of French onion dip, two cans of vegetable soup, a three-pack of Dove Beauty Bars, and a bottle of Johnnie Walker Black in her backpack had not been a very good idea — even if the pack was a BlackHawk Raptor model, cleared for special ops use. The heavy load bounced and jostled against Stella Hardesty's spine as each step brought her closer to her little white house on Poplar Street.

She hadn't had much of a choice, anyway — her Jeep was in the shop for a suspension problem that she suspected was the result of too many fast drives down too many bumpy dirt roads, an ill-advised habit that she enjoyed to an unseemly degree for a middle-aged woman.

Stella considered slowing down to a walk, but she'd decided to train for the Bean Blossom Half Marathon in Casey, which was less than three weeks away, and that meant she had to stick to a strict and grueling schedule. Today's entry read "5m run + strength," and while Stella had given herself a two-mile advantage due to the added weight she was carrying and credited herself for assembling a Quilter's Dream 2140 cabinet using only hand tools, she figured that fiftyish ladies burdened with a few extra pounds were probably not good candidates for creative tweaking of the recommended regimen.

Not to mention the fact that she was planning to take the day after tomorrow off to observe a certain minor milestone. Or ignore it. She wasn't certain yet, and she wasn't entirely sure that an extragenerous serving of junk food and whisky would be exactly clarifying, but either way she wasn't about to put herself through any contortions of the physical fitness variety on the day she began her fifty-second year on earth. Besides, her daughter, Noelle, was coming over to give her a birthday mani-pedi, and she didn't intend to risk messing up the polish by putting her sneakers on afterward.

No, she definitely needed to get her huffing and puffing and muscle augmenting and stamina building in today, or it would be that much harder to pick up the pace on Sunday, when she was due to go for a leisurely nine-mile jog around Homer Reservoir with Camellia Edwards, her good friend Dotty's energetic half sister who was pursuing an associate's degree in exercise physiology and would surely know if she'd been slacking.

A startling little tremor at her waist caused Stella to break stride until she remembered that she'd tucked her phone into the pocket of her shorts. Stella didn't like to be without the device, since one never knew when a potential client might call, and Stella's clients weren't the sort one wanted to leave hanging too long. She dug the phone out and was pleased to see her sister's number. Never, in the quarter century since Gracellen had moved to California, had she missed Stella's birthday.

"You're a couple days early," Stella said by way of an answer. "Not that I'm complaining."

"Oh eee ep!"

"I'm sorry, Gracie, I can't much hear you," Stella interrupted as her sister's faint voice blipped in and out of static. "Y'all up at the cabin?"

Gracellen and her husband, Chess, owned a cabin up near Lake Tahoe that was about twice as large as Stella's house and ten times fancier. It had fake log rafters and wall hangings featuring bears cavorting with moose — despite the fact that Stella was pretty sure there were no moose in California — and a leather sectional sofa and a fifty-five-inch wall-mounted TV, but for all that you couldn't get a lick of cell phone reception. Chess liked to say that he'd paid extra for the phones not to work, since he was so besieged by underlings and customers and whoever it was he dealt with on a daily basis that he had to drive three hours just for a moment's peace.

Chess had been a stuffy red-faced soft-palmed overdressed young executive of thirty-two when he happened on Gracellen waitressing in a St. Louis pub. Over his parents' strenuous objections, and despite the eleven-year age difference, he'd whisked her off to Sacramento a week later, stopping briefly in Vegas to get married. Now Chess was a stuffy red-faced soft-palmed overdressed middle-aged executive of fifty-eight, and Stella never could find anything to talk about with the man, but he kept her sister in designer duds and nice cars and cabin weekends, so Stella couldn't help but overlook his incredible boringness, especially since her sister didn't seem to mind putting up with him too much.

"Yes ut err ett!" Gracellen's voice, at least the little bits of it that came through, seemed highly excited.

"Mmm hmm, darlin', thank you so much for calling, but how about you call me when you get back to town where the phones work?"

"Onnn aim uh —"

"Nice talking to you, too, sweetie," Stella said and snapped off the phone. She loved her little sister, but a conversation with Gracellen was likely to go on for hours, and Stella figured it was just as well not to have it in the middle of Hickory Street with her ponytail stuck to her sweaty neck and her running shorts riding up her behind.

She gave her shorts a little tug and tried in vain to shift the contents of her pack to a more comfortable position, but as she set out down the street again it felt as though the soup cans were fighting for space against her vertebrae, and she had just allowed herself a lengthy stream of colorful curses when a car pulled over and idled along next to her, maintaining her pace.

11

Not just a car, Stella realized with a flush of embarrassment as she glanced over to see who was acting as her pace car — BJ Brodersen's tricked-out Ford 250. Even without the custom curlicue sparkly decals in a sort of vaguely cresting-wave design along the side, Stella would have recognized the big, sleek truck — there weren't too many folks in Prosper, Missouri, who had the ready cash to spend on fog lights and a winch mount and sport exhaust and fiberglass bed cover. But BJ's bar did a steady business, and since he lived behind the bar in an old garage that had been converted into a tidy bachelor apartment, his expenses were low, so he had the money to spend lovingly tending to his prized possession.

"Evenin', Stella," BJ said, his bulky forearm resting on the driver's side window. "How are you?"

Stella rolled her eyes and tugged at her shorts again, wishing she'd worn the cute ones that Noelle had given her recently to replace the ragged ones Stella usually wore and was in fact wearing tonight. The cute shorts were folded carefully in Stella's drawer, waiting for Stella to lose just a few more pounds, along with the darling matching fitness top.

Stella knew about how she looked. She

had put in half a day at her shop, Hardesty Sewing Machine Repair & Sales, assembling the Quilter's Dream display table and stocking a shipment of Gütermann thread while her assistant, Chrissy Shaw, hunted down an error in the billing from the Viking folks and harangued their customer service department into making it right. After lunch she'd paid a visit to a gentleman over in Harrisonville related to her other business, the one she did under the table and outside the shadow of the law and, whenever possible, out of earshot, and while the gentleman was far sorrier than he had been when he woke up in the morning, Stella had pulled or twisted or otherwise abused a muscle in her shoulder and broken a couple of nails and smudged her makeup in the process of settling their differences. A big chunk of her hair had escaped her ponytail and hung in her face, and her T-shirt was several sizes too big and bore the phrase ONLY MY HAIRDRESSER KNOWS, an obscure reference to a hairstyling product carried by the salon where Noelle worked.

Not expecting to run into one of the few appealing and eligible bachelors in Prosper, Stella had thrown on not only the butt-crack-wedgie shorts but an old pair of socks that came up over her ankles and made her

13

legs look shorter and dumpier than they actually were. Still, she managed a pained smile and a little wave. "Evenin' yourself, BJ."

"Now what-all are you up to?" he asked, as they continued their slow process down the street. BJ was not a thickheaded man, only painfully polite and rather shy, so Stella resisted pointing out that his query belied the obvious.

"Oh, you know, out for a little run."

"You're lookin' real good there, Stella," BJ observed without actually meeting her eyes, his gaze focused carefully and politely somewhere around her collarbones, well above any regions that might be considered inappropriate or lecherous. BJ was about a thousand times more gracious than the average customer in his bar, who tended to include folks who weren't well dressed enough or flush enough to drink anywhere else and who rarely bothered to filter or censor their conversations, especially as the evening wore on. He didn't hold anyone else to his mild-mannered standards, welcoming all comers with equanimity, which Stella appreciated. Among the lessons of middle age was an abiding distaste for folks who thought their bank account made them better than other folks, especially as Stella's side business seemed to prove over and over that aside from the minority of folks who were genuinely and irritatingly and sometimes profoundly mean, most people were basically just as flawed as everyone else no matter how many zeroes were on their paychecks.

"Why, thank you, BJ," Stella said. "You're looking, um, very nice, too."

Only then did she take a closer look at him, slowing down to a halt at the sight of his rather surprisingly shiny shirt, which in the slanting last rays of sunset appeared to be a bright pink. His name was stitched in a fancy script over his pocket, with tiny hearts instead of periods after each initial. While the shirt did look nice against his neatly combed salt-and-pepper hair and smooth-shaved, square-jawed face, it was an unexpected fashion choice for a man whose taste usually ran to faded golf shirts and Levi's belted a little lower than his gut.

As she watched, BJ's surprisingly boyish face took on a hue not unlike his shirt. "I. Um. This. You see . . . I'm going bowling. League Night."

"Oh." More polite nodding. Tuesdays and Fridays, the Prosper Bowl did a brisk business with the many club teams from all over the south half of the county, since the only other bowling alley in Sawyer County was up in Fayette.

"Yeah. See, the little gal from Seagram's . . . she . . . er . . ."

"Oh," Stella said shortly, suddenly feeling even more self-conscious. While she was far more buff than she'd been a few years ago when she devoted her time to basic housewifery, she was still a robustly shaped woman of a certain age, and no amount of sugarcoating was going to allow her to compete with the sort of tight little package that was the domain of most females who hadn't yet counted out three decades.

"Junelle . . . why, she's like a little niece or something."

"Oh," Stella repeated, brightening.

"And she and her girls, they weren't going to be able to compete in this tournament if they didn't come up with a fifth, since one of 'em's out having a baby. So now I got Jorge helping out nights, I figured . . ." BJ gave a sheepish little shrug that looked positively adorable. "Which is why I'm now a Seagram's Sister."

For a moment they beamed at each other, BJ peeping out of the corner of his eyes and Stella sneaking yet another tug at her offending shorts. There was something about a bashful man — she half wanted to pat his

16

brush-cut head, and half wanted to . . . well, enough of that.

Stella had been carrying a torch for a particular man for over three years. Unfortunately that man was the local sheriff, a fellow by the name of Goat Jones. He was about as bashful as a firecracker, as hesitant as a bull, as unassuming as a July marigold. While it was evidently a permanent condition that Stella ran out of both breath and inhibition around the man, she was a little tired of the way their careers conspired to keep them apart. Him being a lawman, and her being . . . well, a lawless woman. By necessity of course, and for the good of the downtrodden . . . but all the fiery principles in the world didn't much help when one of them was trying to observe the capital-L Letter of the law and the other of them, that being Stella, was trying to thread her way through it like silk through a straw needle.

A while back, Goat had brought her a gift that other women might not have found romantic, it being a waterlogged photo of Stella beating the shit out of a local loser who'd abused his wife once too often until Stella got wind of the situation, but to Stella it beat a big box of candy and a truckload of roses. There was nothing that said "I Heart You" like destroying evidence that

17

could send a person to jail.

She'd hoped that little keepsake might be followed up by some vigorous hay-rolling, or at least a night at the movies, but Goat had been keeping his distance. Stella supposed she could understand: After all, the man had broken his most solemn oath by handing over evidence. Still, she was getting a little restless waiting for his conscience to settle itself down enough for him to indulge his inner bad boy in her direction.

"Say," she said, aiming for an offhand tone. "The tourney play don't start until later in the evening, isn't that right?"

BJ blinked at her from under long fringy lashes. "That's so."

"Well, I was just thinking, I mean I understand you might have dinner plans already, but I could fix us a little something, I mean nothing special but —"

"Yes," BJ said quickly.

Stella smiled, deciding she wouldn't point out that she hadn't got around to actually laying out the terms of her invitation. A gentleman's enthusiasm in the face of one's flat-out womanly mysteries was a powerful thing.

BJ's blush deepened. "Lemme do a U-ie and come around so you can hop on in."

"Don't be silly," Stella said, as she crossed

18

daringly in front of the truck, not even trying to dislodge the tight Lycra fabric from her ass and adding a little sway to her step.

CHAPTER TWO

Half an hour later the taquitos were in the oven, the onion dip upended in a pretty Fiestaware dish, the chips mounded in a salad bowl, and Stella was fresh out of the shower and subtly spritzed with White Diamonds. She emerged from her bedroom to find BJ peering at the latest *Redbook,* a pair of half-moon specs perched on his nose. The gin and tonic Stella'd mixed sat nearly untouched on the coffee table.

When BJ noticed Stella he hastily snatched the glasses off his nose and stuffed them into his embroidered shirt pocket.

"Those glasses look nice on you," Stella said, plucking her own drink — a neat slug of Johnnie in a tumbler — off the counter and joining him on the couch. She chose a spot that left a foot of chintz between them. Far enough apart for decorum . . . but close enough, she hoped, to signal a world of potential.

"Oh, now, Stella, don't be mean," BJ mumbled, ducking his chin down practically to his pearly pink collar.

Stella reached out before she had a chance to think and hooked a finger under his strong, bristly chin. She tipped his face up so his wide brown eyes were aimed directly at her and caught her breath to note the equal parts longing and uncertainty all mixed up in their depths.

"But I meant it," she whispered. "Just about anything looks nice on you, BJ."

After that followed one of those moments that you wish you could dip into acrylic and plate with gold and mount on a stand with a gilded plaque with the date and a thousand exclamation points — the kind of moment that even when you're in it you know will be playing on the pull-down screen in your mind on your dying day. Here was a man who wanted her, who — unlike Goat — offered nothing more complicated than a sweet lusty romp, with maybe the potential for something even more sweet and uncomplicated to follow.

BJ's hand traveled all slo-mo like up to Stella's, and he wrapped his warm fingers around hers and drew her hand around his neck. She closed the distance with a happy little sigh, and when her lips landed squarely on his she was only a little surprised at the rather generous and fleshy nature of his tongue, the funny way he patted at her waist as though he were shaping dough into a loaf — so unlike Goat — before a wave of pure animal lust came crashing from sources unknown and Stella figured she'd just throw caution to the wind and go with it.

Stella was very familiar with the contours and curves of her pink chintz sofa, having fluffed its pillows and vacuumed its crevices about a thousand times in the past decade, so she was able to drag BJ down on top of her with no fear of smacking her head on a sofa arm or dislodging a stray throw pillow. For his part, BJ seemed fine with the whole animal attraction approach and swiftly maneuvered a knee between her willing and pliant thighs. A nagging little voice in the back of Stella's mind whispered reminders of the way Goat's hands — callused and wind-weathered and strong as steel — felt when they tugged her hair or grazed a nipple, but even that voice dimmed as BJ's sweet doughy lips trailed a path across her cheeks, under her ears, down her neck, settling with a happy sigh between her breasts.

"Erm bermferm," he muttered, giving her soft little kisses while his hands stole shyly to her hips, where they settled tentatively, almost reverently.

"Come again?" Stella said contentedly, letting her eyes flutter shut and throwing her head back so her shoulder-length hair, recently colored a shade somewhere on the red side of auburn by Noelle, could spill luxuriously over the edge of the sofa.

BJ lifted his head from her breasts and gave her a heavy-lidded gaze, his cheeks flushed dark with exertion and, Stella fervently hoped, lust. "You're beautiful," he clarified, before diving back into his happy task, and that gave Stella the extra assurance she was looking for. She put her hands on his and gave them a little push, willing BJ to surge past tentative to, say, willful and unstoppable, or at least untamed and demanding, or even needful and greedy. For one wild and headstrong moment he slid his hands under her rear and squeezed, but then he retreated, his hands coming to rest once more in the no-combat zone of her general waist area while he continued his gentle exploration of the valley between her breasts.

Stella tried once more, giving his hands a less subtle shove in a downward direction, but he resisted, adding a polite little moan — and a memory came unbidden into Stella's mind: Goat, here, on this couch, during a makeout session a few months ago. He had not been tentative. He had not been polite. He had been all wanting and taking and insisting, and the thought of the way he'd nearly thrown her down and grabbed great handfuls of her soft and willing flesh caused a moan of her own to escape her lips.

BJ froze.

Stella's eyes flew open and she found herself staring at BJ's chin, and she had time to note that he'd missed a little patch with the razor before he was scrambling off her as fast and furiously as though he had discovered he'd accidentally mounted a prize boar. Before Stella had a chance to protest or demand an explanation, she looked past BJ and saw the source of his consternation, and suddenly she was racing BJ in an effort to look as though they hadn't just been doing precisely what they had been doing.

"Is that — Mr. Brodersen, is that *you?*" Todd Groffe asked with unprecedented awe, his fourteen-year-old jaw dropping impressively.

"Hello, Todd," Stella said briskly, standing and dusting off the front of her capri pants as though she'd been doing nothing more exciting than pulling a few stray weeds from the flower bed. "Say hello as though you were not brought up in a barn."

"Does the sheriff know he's here?" Todd stage-whispered, never taking his eyes off BJ, who was making furtive adjustments to his trousers while crossing his legs and sliding as far away on the couch as he could.

"He's not — I don't — what are you doing here, anyway?" Stella managed to get out. "Don't you and your hoodlum pals have a date to smoke crack behind the Arco or something?"

"We done smoked it," Todd said, his voice settling back to his too-bored-to-be-bothered register now that the excitement had waned, along with BJ's ardor. "And we also knocked over Dumfree Liquors and all got blow jobs and burned us up a flag, so you can just hold on to your lecture, Stella. It's too late for savin' me."

"Is that right," Stella said, getting her composure back. She picked up a throw pillow that had fallen victim to the recent lust storm, fluffed it, and placed it primly between herself and BJ while Todd sprawled in the easy chair. "What did Chanel think of that business?"

She noted with satisfaction that Todd's smart-ass smirk disappeared in a flash of sweet and tender adolescent self-doubt.

25

Todd tugged at the collar of his T-shirt, which inexplicably bore an image of a duck with a human skull and a cigarette hanging out of its beak.

"I said, how is your young lady friend?" Stella repeated smugly.

"She's fine, I guess," he mumbled.

"And her mother?"

"Fine, prob'ly." Todd slid further down in the chair until his bony butt hovered off the edge.

"And old Mrs. Tanaka? Out at Crestview Care?"

Todd scowled. "How'm I s'posed to know, Stella?"

Stella beamed with triumph. Winning a round with her young neighbor gave her all manner of satisfaction, especially now that he was getting older and cagier. His romance with the hottest girl in eighth grade had been given a boost not long ago when Noelle gave him a makeover, which he had assiduously kept up with gallons of goopy hair product. Noelle, who apparently had decided that Todd was a perfect substitute for the little brother she never had, bought him ridiculous T-shirts and baggy plaid shorts and overpriced jeans at the mall over in Coffey, thirty miles away, where she lived. When she came for her weekend visits, the two of them talked music and movies and school while they did Noelle's laundry.

Todd was family, even if they didn't have a box for that particular relationship on the U.S. Census Bureau form.

"Oh, I don't know," she said, "only I'm thinkin' that little mark on your neck didn't exactly get there all by itself, see what I'm sayin'?"

Todd's hand flew to the hickey that peeped up over his collar like a smudge of ketchup and blushed a furious purple. Good. They were even, and she could count on the boy's silence — for now, at least.

"Mr. Brodersen was just about to —" Stella began. Then she was interrupted by the phone again. She pulled it out and squinted at the display. Gracellen. She didn't much feel like listening to the static, so she returned it to her pocket. "Mr. Brodersen was about to go to his bowling night. And I imagine you were on your way someplace important, too, right, Todd?"

"Bowling don't start until seven thirty," BJ said helpfully. "I might could stay a bit longer."

Stella gave him a thin-lipped smile. Now that that first wave of lustful feelings had been forced off the road by Todd's untimely arrival, a measure of uncertainty had crept

27

into her mind. Things had been moving awful fast — after all, she and BJ had never even been on a proper date — and also too slow, if that made any sense. She needed some time, some solitary time, to review in her mind the dance of passion that BJ had been performing on her and figure out if they were hearing the same tune, so to speak.

His tongue had been . . . just so darn *fleshy.*

Stella felt her face warm at the thought and fixed a glare on Todd, who was sifting through the bowl of mixed nuts that Stella had set out, picking out all the cashews and tossing them into his mouth.

"Let me say it plain, Todd," she said. "Time for you to go on home. Your mama's gonna be home with the girls by now."

Todd had adorable seven-year-old twin sisters and a mother who attempted to keep up with three kids and a job and a house and a stack of bills that would make a weaker woman weep, as well as an exhusband whose life had recently become a bit more interesting, though Sherilee didn't know it. Alongside the sewing machine shop Stella had inherited from her dead son-of-a-bitch husband, she had her second, secret business that involved straightening out all

28

manner of abusers and deadbeats and worthless husbands and boyfriends. Ordinarily a fee was involved, a sum tailored to a woman's means, but in Sherilee's case Stella was doing a little pro bono work.

After all, Royal Groffe was hardly the worst offender Stella had ever encountered. He'd just let late payment of his child support become a habit since moving from up near the northeast corner of Missouri to Kansas City, where there was more call for experienced pipe fitters — as well as a lot more nightlife to spend his paycheck on. Sherilee was not the complaining sort, so it had taken several months of late payments — months in which she lay awake nights trying to figure out how to stretch a paycheck to cover food for her children while still keeping the lights on — before she'd let slip to Stella how worried she was.

Stella had driven up to Kansas City, where she visited the job site where Royal was employed. From what she could tell, sitting in her Jeep Liberty and nibbling Junior Mints to pass the time while she observed him through her Zhumell short-barrel waterproof binoculars, a pair she favored because they fit easily in her purse, he was a skilled and dedicated worker. That was a check in the plus column, the way Stella saw it, since that meant he was likely to stay steadily employed. Still, Stella met him in the parking lot after work and gave him a manicure with a 30-watt woodburning tool plugged into the power converter she kept in the Jeep and ran off its cigarette lighter, to explain that his lax attitude about sending support payments constituted a check in the minus column.

Since then his checks had arrived early.

Todd's scowl deepened, and he tossed the last of the nuts into his mouth and chewed glumly. "Mom said stay outta the house while she fixes dinner."

Stella's ears pricked up at that. Sherilee never sent Todd out of the house, with the exception of Sunday nights, when he came over to watch TV with Stella while Sherilee took her girls out for ice cream or a movie or to feed the ducks at Nickel Pond. Until recently she'd had a standing date with her son on Saturday nights, but now that Todd was weighted down with a girlfriend as well as a flock of equally hormonal and sullen friends, he generally made his own weekend plans, which made Sherilee all the more determined to spend as much time with her boy as she could after work. As for Todd, as much as he complained about his pesky little sisters and his mother's draconian discipline, he took his man-of-the-house role seriously enough to make Stella's heart ache.

So whenever Todd seemed determined to stay away from home, Stella had learned to be suspicious. She reached for the backpack Todd had tossed on the rug and dragged it close before Todd could stop her.

"Hey!" he protested. "Ain't no call to be goin' through my stuff, Stella!"

"Shouldn't bother you none, if you ain't got anything to hide," she said placidly.

"That's illegal search!" he protested, and looked like he was going to launch himself at Stella, but when BJ glared and lifted himself an inch off the chintz cushions, Todd sank back in the chair. BJ was six foot three in sock feet, and Todd hadn't yet finished growing.

"Aha!" Stella crowed, finding a can of Krylon International Harvester Red paint in the bottom of the pack among the broken pencils and empty Cheeto bags and crumpled papers. "At it again, are you?"

When Royal Groffe had undertaken a renewed effort to deliver his support payments on time, he'd apparently been so swayed by Stella's visit that he'd begun bringing the checks in person. Sherilee had marveled that he stayed on the porch re-

31

spectfully cooling his heels, his hair combed carefully and his hands clasped in front of him like a Sunday preacher. She'd asked him in out of good manners more than anything else, and while his daughters peeped curiously around the corner at this man who was barely more than a memory, Todd remembered enough about his father to be plunged into a fit of burst illusions and broken promises and forgotten birthdays.

To say that the boy was bitter would be an understatement. The second time his father had come inside for a glass of sweet tea, Todd snuck around to where Royal's silver Mazda was parked alongside the curb and hastily tagged it on the driver's side. When Royal came out of the house after his fifteen-minute visit, he was greeted by foot-tall red letters along the driver's side that spelled out

I AM ANA

— which caused him no end of confusion until he rounded the corner and discovered that the cryptic message continued around the back end of the car, clear across the license plate and bumper:

SSHOLE

. . . which pretty much cleared it up.

Royal had begun to make a fuss about tanning his son's hide and taking the cost of repairs out of his support payments. When his ranting turned to threats and yelling, Sherilee called Stella with a desperate plea to come get Todd before he launched his scrawny teenaged self at his father and got himself into even more trouble. Stella wandered down in a pink velour jogging suit and gave Royal a sweet smile. If Sherilee was surprised to see her ex swallow his temper and drive meekly away, she hid it well.

Still, Stella wasn't sure she'd be able to save the boy a second time. She did a swift calculation: Friday was payday, but the support check came only twice a month, and she couldn't remember whether this was a pay week or not.

"Todd Groffe," she said, "what have you done now?"

"Nothing! I swear, Stella, that's just in there from last time. I ain't got around to putting it back in the garage, is all."

"Young man, I best not discover that you are lying to this fine lady," BJ said, his arms crossed over his broad chest.

Todd made an unintelligible sound, staring at the carpet with his hands jammed in his pockets. Stella suppressed a smile and allowed herself to enjoy BJ's simmering glower before she turned her attention back to Todd. "So if I go look out the picture window, I won't see your dad's car over at your mom's?"

Todd managed a look of grievous injury. " 'Course not!"

Stella, however, knew better. She sighed and pushed herself off the couch.

"Less by 'over at Mom's,' you mean, like, parked out front or something," Todd added hastily. "He, uh, *might* be visiting, I guess."

Sure enough, Stella spied the outline of the car in the quick-falling evening.

A passing car lit up the street with twin beams, and Stella was already turning away when something about the vehicle caught her attention, and she turned back.

A *sheriff's* vehicle. Specifically, the squeaky-clean cruiser operated by the top law enforcement dog of Sawyer County, none other than Goat Jones himself.

CHAPTER THREE

Stella practically leaped back from the window. Was he spying on her? Surely not . . . well, she'd been known to cruise past the sheriff's department herself, from time to time, hoping for a glimpse of his long-legged form, but that was different, wasn't it?

Though the idea that he might be making a check on her gave Stella a little thrill that was tempered by the thought that this particular trip over to her side of town would have netted Goat an eyeful of BJ's truck in addition to a nice view of her sugar maple in full leaf.

Maybe Goat wouldn't recognize it.

Right. There was no one in a thirty-mile radius who didn't know damn well that the only such truck around belonged to BJ.

Stella gave the drapes a frustrated yank, drawing them closed across the picture window. Then she had second thoughts, wondering if closed curtains would make Goat think she was up to some sort of hanky-panky, and yanked them back open.

She rounded on Todd, catching herself before she unleashed the full force of her irritation on the boy.

"So that *is* your dad's car I see out there."

"But I *swear* I ain't done nothin' to it. Promise." Todd gave her a look of such tremulous conviction that Stella's doubts receded a little. Maybe the boy had learned his lesson last time. Maybe Royal truly was trying to be a better man. Maybe there was a chance, if not for reconciliation, at least for a thawing of relations between father and son, and that was nothing to sneeze at. A boy needed a father figure, after all.

"All right," Stella sighed, wondering if she'd regret it later. "But you leave now and get your ass home and make sure you please-and-thank-you your way through your dad's visit, hear?"

Todd nodded vigorously. "Yes, ma'am."

He slipped out the door before Stella could wonder too much about that particular leave-taking comment. She didn't remember Todd Groffe ever uttering another "yes ma'am," a discrepancy that bore further investigation. Now wasn't the time, though — when the phone rang for the third

36

time and without even having to glance at it Stella knew it had to be Gracellen. Her sister was persistent, and there was no better way to get her ire up than to ignore her, which Stella had spent much of their childhood doing, the four-year difference in their ages being just long enough to make Gracellen a constant pest.

"Do you mind if I take this call?" she asked as demurely as she could manage. "I won't be but a second."

"Why sure, Stella." BJ settled back against the sofa and regarded her with a little smile that implied that watching her talk on the phone was his idea of top-notch entertainment.

"Hello, Gracie," Stella said pleasantly.

"Stellie, Chip's ear's come in the mail!"

There was no static this time, but Stella took the phone away from the phone and stared at it, confused, before trying again. "What's that you said?"

"In a little box like what might hold a necklace, wrapped up in plastic, it's his *ear!*"

Her sister's voice dissolved into a tremulous wail. Despite many decades among wealthy Californians, all it took was the first trace of upset and the Missouri returned to Gracellen's voice in full force.

"Gracie, have you been drinking?"

"Stella, I have just drove us all the way down the durn mountain cause Chess's got one a his tension headaches on account a the ear and I am right clear at the end of my wits here and I would appreciate if you would —"

"Okay, okay, Gracie," Stella said. "Let's take this step by step. Now when you say Chip, you mean Chester the third, right?"

Gracie's husband Chess was actually Chester Papadakis the second, and his son — by a first wife — was Chester the third. With all those Chesters running around Sacramento they'd had to be a little creative with the nicknaming.

"Yes, yes, of course that's who I mean."

Stella squeezed her eyes shut and took a breath. She pressed the phone against her shirt and composed herself before opening her eyes and smiling sweetly. "BJ, if it's all right, I might just take this . . ."

"Sure, sure, sure," BJ said, beaming even more broadly, as if she'd announced a plan to do a striptease rather than take a private call.

Stella hurried down the hall to the most private room in the house. Once she got the bathroom door locked, she hissed into the phone. "So Chip's ear . . . you mean his, um, actual —"

"The thing he *hears* outta," Gracie wailed with renewed grief. "Or used to hear outta anyway, 'cause now I reckon he's hearin' outta a hole in the side a his head seein' as he ain't got a *ear* anymore."

"I'm still having a little trouble here, Gracie. What makes you think that the ear is, you know, Chip's?"

"Oh, Stella, you know how he had those piercings that made Chess so darn mad?"

Stella knew well. The relationship Gracie's husband had with his son was stormy, to say the least. After fathering the boy and subsequently leaving his mother, Chess had spent a number of years pretending to have forgotten the two of them existed, not unlike Royal Groffe's treatment of his children, except for the check-writing part. Chester the first had built up a considerable fortune in the nut business, buying up orchards all around California's Central Valley before Chess was five years old, so that by the time he was an adult his father's pecans had supplied him with a nearly endless well of cash to get him out of scrapes.

His son's marriage to wife number one — whose name was Iola — was viewed by Chester as a misstep. A serious one, certainly, since the divorce cost him a great deal of money. However, that was nothing

39

compared to what Chester considered his son's greatest mistake of all: discovering a two-bit cocktail waitress in a St. Louis bar while bringing Must-Be-Nuts to the Midwest, and then compounding the error by marrying her.

There was talk of disownment, of tossing Chess right out of the family business. Stella was a young wife with a baby back then, and she received Gracellen's cross-country phone calls with a great deal of sympathy but little in the way of advice, having never dealt with wealthy Greek-American in-laws. Gracie did her best to be a good stepmother on the weekends when Chip visited, and a respectful and helpful stepdaughter at Sunday dinners at her in-laws' house. Eventually her sweet nature swayed the old man and a sort of détente was reached, especially when Chess's mother took ill and Gracie, who had not returned to work once she was ensconced in the enormous family ranch, cared for her until she died in the bed Gracie had moved under a window so the old lady could look up into the blossoms on a wisteria vine that clung to an arbor outside. The old lady blessed her before she passed, and Chester the first tearfully declared her the daughter of his heart at a funeral service that went on for nearly two hours and was attended by every member of Sacramento's Greek-American community.

Everyone, that is, except one. Iola stayed away, the years of being ignored by Chester having drained any warmth Iola might have retained for her ex-father-in-law. It made no difference that, after his wife passed, Chester had a change of heart and decided he wished to enfold his grandson back into the family, especially since Gracellen and Chess had no children of their own. By then, Chip was a sullen teenaged ne'er-do-well, the sort whose misbehavior rarely rose above brawling and bad grades and speeding tickets but certainly did not leave a lot of room for heart-warming reunions with estranged relatives. To an invitation to visit his grandfather, the source of the child support checks that were about to come to an end, Chip extended a colorful variation on "No thanks."

Iola, on the other hand, sensed an opportunity of the financial sort. Her own support payments were due to go into a dramatic slump, given that Chip was practically an adult, and, perhaps aided by a listlessness that was enhanced by her prescription drug habits, she had never bothered to find a job or an alternate source of income. Iola beseeched her angry son to find it in his heart to forgive his father; instead, the boy took the last of the support money and lit out for Wisconsin, where he intended to live simply but promptly got himself embroiled in a gambling habit instead. In the decade since, Chip's ever-changing schemes to support himself alternated with desperate pleas for money, made through calls that skirted his father and went straight to his source. Chester Senior finally had what he wanted: a grandson who was pleasant to him — at least when he wanted money.

"I do remember those piercings," Stella said cautiously. "I believe he had more than most *ladies* I know."

Every two years Chess and Gracellen sent Stella a plane ticket to come spend Thanksgiving with them, and if Chip happened to be in one of his cash-poor episodes, he could be found at the holiday table. This last visit, his head had been practically shaved and his ears had been studded like a leather club chair; he glowered at the end of the table and said very little to anyone.

"Yes, and then he went and got these little bitty rings through the cartilage, three on each side — oh, it was just terrible looking, Stella. But at least that's how we know it's his. Although it's awful wrinkled up and stale and it has a smell on it — *oh*."

"So let me get this straight — a box with Chip's ear in it came to the cabin? Was there a note?"

"Well of course there was, Stellie, that's how we know Chip's gone and done it this time, they're going to kill him if we don't send them thirty thousand dollars!"

Stella sucked in her breath in dismay. "Gambling again?"

"Of course it's gambling. That boy ain't never knowed a card game or a roll a the dice he could pass up. He used to bet on what color dress his teacher was going to wear and was the mailman coming before noon and how many saltines in the package would be busted. Used to be kinda cute till we figured out it was going to be the ruin of him."

"Well, can't you just call Chester and have him send the money?"

"He don't have it, Stella!" Gracellen was wailing again.

"What do you mean, Chester's loaded!" The one time the Papadakis family patriarch had deigned to come to the holiday dinner, he'd arrived in a glowering snit and looked around the table at all the fixings as though he were looking for country mice to come dancing down the table waving little bitty

43

pitch-forks. Stella was pretty sure the diamond in his pinky ring cost more than her car, and the gold weighing down his wife looked like it would topple her over at any moment.

"Well, that was then and this is now. You may a heard the economy's in the crapper."

"Yes, Gracie, news does still reach these parts now and then," Stella said wearily. The decades her sister had spent on the West Coast had unfortunately drained any affection she had for her home state, though Stella had observed on her visits that Sacramento seemed to have its share of the same chain restaurants and ugly-ass strip malls that Kansas City did. "They bring it in on the Pony Express, so we're a bit behind, plus since we're still trading in shiny rocks rather than cash —"

"Don't make fun of me," Gracie snuffled, then burst into full-scale sobs. "Folks aren't buying pecans like they used to. Everybody's all over the almonds now that the stupid California Almond Board's going around saying they can cure cancer and make you more regular and what-all. Never mind that a almond ain't even a proper *nut,* it's a seed, but you never hear them talking about *that!* It's false advertising, is what it is!"

"But Gracie, there's got to be money —"

"Oh, Stella, you wouldn't even believe it. Our house ain't worth what we paid for it, so there's no way Chester Senior's is, and besides, he took out a second mortgage a while back on the ranch."

The "ranch" was a god-awful rambling affair that Chess's parents had built on a fifty-acre patch of land outside Sacramento, complete with fountains and a brick circular drive and enough arches and columns and porticos to make its architectural inspirations murky at best.

"And there's something else." She hiccupped gently and snuffled a few times, trying to get enough composure to continue.

"Aw, Gracie, what could be so bad?" Stella asked, her heart squeezing up with fear, because she knew firsthand that a bad situation could always get worse. Still, her role in the sisterly dynamic was to be the optimist. Even after she herself had taken out her husband, Ollie, with a wrench three years back after decades of abuse, she broke the news to Gracie from jail by saying that they had some "things to work through."

"Chester Senior's being investigated for fr- fr- . . . for fraud. Chess's got to meet with them federal people tomorrow. He's so nervous he threw up in the Olive Garden parking lot — and that was *before* we ate."

45

"Chester and Chess have been ripping off their own company?" Stella demanded, incredulous. "Don't take this wrong, sugar, but how the heck do you even cook the books when you're just moving nuts around?"

"I don't know," Gracellen wailed. "It was all Bill's doing, before Chess had to fire him. You know I never get involved in the business side of things. But they absolutely cannot have even a hint of Chip's gambling problem getting back to the investigators. How's that gonna look? And how can you even *think* they're guilty, it was that stupid Bill and the problems in the warehouse, only they sent this team down here don't got any kindness in 'em at all, Chess says they never even take off their *jackets* and plus one of 'em's a *vegan,* wouldn't even try one a my turtle brownies I sent in to the office."

"You sent brownies to the office? To what, make them change their minds?"

"Well a'course I did, Stella, times like this we all got to pull together, everyone has to do their part. Which is why I'm calling you! We got until Sunday and then they're gonna start chopping off more pieces of poor Chip!"

"Who's 'they,' anyway? Chip's bookie?"

"I don't know, Stella. The note ain't signed, there's just instructions where to bring the money. It's got to be dropped off in person. Chip ain't picking up his cell phone and we don't know what he's been up to, we actually thought he was doing better, he told us he hadn't touched a card game in months, he was even talkin' about tryin' them meetings they got, you know, the Gamblers Anonymous people —"

"Okay," Stella sighed. Things *were* bad, but letting Gracie carry on this way wasn't going to help. "Let's take this from the top. You got a note and an ear. The ear's Chip's. No one can get ahold of Chip, and unless someone brings thirty thousand dollars up to Wisconsin, they said they're going to mess him up some more. That about right?"

"Yes," Gracellen said meekly. "There's a address that I Google Mapped, looks like a warehouse-type situation. The note says leave the money in a white barrel with black letters that's gonna be out by the door anytime between now and Sunday night at midnight and if we do, won't nothing bad happen to Chip. Oh, Stella, he must be so scared, and what if he didn't have his tetanus shots, and plus just think how he's gonna have to wear his hair now to cover up where his ear used to be —"

47

"Calm down, Gracie," Stella snapped. Her sister had always tended toward the hysterical, but usually when they were together there was nothing more vexing than an overdone turkey or mud tracked into the powder room. "If we're gonna get through this, we've got to stay focused and smart."

"You'll do it, then, Stellie? You'll take care of Chip?"

In her sister's wobbly, teary voice Stella heard echoes of every childhood scrape they'd ever got into. She'd stuck up for her baby sister on the playground, told mean girls to back off, taken a swing at the boy who first broke Gracellen's heart, patched her cuts and bruises, helped her study, and shared her chores. She'd always been there when it counted, and that wasn't about to change now.

"What exactly do you want me to do?" Stella asked carefully. Gracie knew very little about her off-hours activities, and she hoped to keep it that way.

"Just, if you could go fetch him? And maybe bring him down to stay with you a while until we figure what to do next? Chess is going to go talk to the bank, see maybe about the retirement money —"

"But Gracie, if these fellows are pros, don't you suppose they have their eye on

48

his place? How do you suppose they're gonna feel about me driving him away like we're off on a Sunday picnic? Plus also what if he doesn't want to come with me?"

"No Stella, see, that's what makes it work, is who's gonna think twice about *you* showing up? In that old car a yours, wearing some old jog suit, why, you could be the cleaning lady."

Stella bristled at the wide swath of insult her sister had just painted, not bothering to point out that washed-up gambling addicts didn't generally employ domestic help. "Yeah, okay, fine, I'll do it." She sighed. "I'll go get your boy. Speaking of those brownies, you still make 'em with the cream cheese and the pecan toffee bits?"

"Oh, yes," her sister said, relief flooding her voice. "I'm gonna go mix up a batch right now. I'll have Chess take 'em to work for the UPS. Why Stella, they'll be waiting at your house soon's you straighten out this thing with Chip."

After she wrote down all the details and hung up the phone, Stella reflected that there had been many occasions when she'd dived into danger for far less than one of Gracellen's brownies, which had taken the blue ribbon at the Sawyer County Fair in 1972, beating out even Flora Meldercone's coconut three-layer cake, which had been rumored to be the foundation of all three of her marriages.

CHAPTER FOUR

It didn't take nearly as long for Stella to explain the latest turn of events to BJ as it had for Gracellen to lay it out for her, especially as she stuck to a streamlined and not entirely accurate version. For instance, she steered clear of the "fraud," "gambling," and "severed ear" aspects of the story, saying only that her sister's stepson had got himself into a bit of a jam and she needed to make an unexpected trip north to Wisconsin to straighten things out.

Stella was accustomed to doctoring up the versions of the truth that she doled out to those around her. That practice was made necessary by the nature of her work, which had the disadvantage of making her a candidate for arrest and jail and even, if folks believed some of the rumors going around in certain circles, the prospect of a long stint in the section of the prison from which folks never returned.

Yes, there were some who believed Stella Hardesty was a cold-blooded murderer. Technically, she supposed she was, given the whole Ollie thing, but both the Sawyer County judge and her own conscience — and popular opinion in town as well — had long since let her off the hook for that one, given the thirty-year spate of bruises and loosened teeth and sprains and black eyes and concussions she'd put up with from the man before the incident with the wrench.

She'd been happy to be let off the hook, but once she started helping other women out with their abusive men, she discovered that there were advantages to cultivating a certain mystique. When Stella corralled a wife beater and straightened him out with any of the many tools and props of her profession, she had found that it often helped to imply that other wrongdoing men had met with even greater misfortune. Since the terms of Stella's "agreements" with her clients' abusers, who she thought of as parolees, often involved them leaving town and staying gone, it was an easy enough thing to imply that they were the six-feet-under kind of gone rather than the two-states-over or staying-with-a-cousin variety.

It wasn't like this fiction traveled very far. Her parolees were generally more than happy to keep to themselves the fact that they'd had the shit kicked out of them by a 5'6" 160-pound fifty-year-old woman. Stella's clients were usually experts at hiding things, too, given the fact that most had been covering up injuries and insults and threats for years, even decades, before they'd finally had enough and sought out Stella's help. Sure, there was an underground network among abused women. One of the sad truths of this sisterhood was that no one could convince an abuse victim that it was time to leave before her time. Stella wished she had a nickel for every time some dumbfuck said something along the lines of "If things is so bad why don't she just leave?" In fact, Stella would enjoy sticking all those nickels into a sock and swinging it at the idiots who made further assertions that "*I'd* leave the minute he looked at me cross-eyed" or "She must be getting something out of the abuse, she's probably just codependent."

Getting beat up as long as Stella had tended to make a gal a little cranky about this sort of analysis.

Anyway, Stella figured the best thing she'd done in life besides raising a beautiful and kind daughter was to be the person who said *I will* when an abused woman looked around at her personal hell and the so-called justice system and concluded *No one can help me.* For her to keep doing her work, though, she had to maintain the fiction that she was nothing more than a mild-mannered sewing shop owner with a Bow-flex and a bad attitude.

"So anyway, I guess I better hit the road," she said, with regret that she hadn't had to manufacture. Despite the confusing specter of Goat Jones and the consternation and compunctions and second thoughts that came with it, things had been trundling along from steamy well on their way to mind-blowing. Stella was tired of being a reclaimed virgin — she hadn't had sex in something like five years, a fact that she avoided dwelling on since it depressed the hell out of her — and she was ready to start wearing the rubber off her treads again. Sure, it would have been nice to carve that first notch with the apple of her eye, but a woman could only wait around for so long. Goat's law career had proved a maddening obstacle, both because of the fact that his little three-man-plus-one-woman shop stayed busier than ticks on a hound trying to keep a lid on crime in the county, and because both he and Stella were still so wary of an entanglement that brought with it so much built-in potential for disaster, given their respective professions. With one of them upholding the law and the other breaking it, a doom scenario seemed likely, which wouldn't stop Stella in the heat of the moment, and given how close they had come on several occasions seemed like it wouldn't maybe stop Goat either, but their red-hot romance had been sidetracked by so many obstacles that Stella was getting impatient.

"I guess I better call Chrissy and see if she'll lend me her car," she sighed. "Potter said the Jeep won't be ready until tomorrow, earliest."

BJ's eyebrows rose in alarm. "You're gonna take the Celica?"

"Oh, she don't need it, she only works across the parking lot." Chrissy lived with her four-year-old son in a tiny apartment at the back of the China Paradise restaurant, which shared a parking lot with Hardesty Sewing Machine Repair & Sales. If Chrissy needed anything while Stella was gone, the Freshway was only a couple of blocks away. Plus, Chrissy — ordinarily loose-lipped about her many and varied romantic entanglements — had been seeing some mysterious new suitor who evidently couldn't get enough of her. Stella was well aware of

Chrissy's powers of persuasion, and it was entirely likely that she could get the man to drive her around in a stretch limo, feeding her strawberries dipped in chocolate, if she wanted to.

"No, it's not that, it's just —" BJ balled his hands into a fist. "Damn it, Stella, I don't want you heading up the tarnation to Wisconsin in that thing. Why, it ain't even safe."

Stella had to smile. The '96 Celica wasn't much to look at, it was true, but Chrissy's extended family included a variety of brothers who weren't great at hanging on to conventional employment but who were masters of innovation when it came to doing a lot with a little. Whether it was coaxing hardscrabble crops out of the family's poor clay-plagued acreage, or convincing women that underneath their skinny and unspectacular frames purred high-test engines of love, or fixing up broke-down cars with bits and pieces lifted off the abandoned vehicles parked all over the back field, the Lardner boys generally got the job done. "That old car could take me around the world, BJ. I imagine it could probably drive right across the oceans, just like Chitty Chitty Bang Bang."

BJ seized her hand, a stealth move that

caught Stella by surprise and started her heartbeat on the increase again. "Take my truck, Stella. I'd just feel better."

Stella's jaw dropped in astonishment. "Your truck?" She couldn't have been more surprised if he'd offered to carve out a kidney with his pocketknife and hand it over. It was well known around town that there was nothing BJ Brodersen loved more than his truck — not his stack of medals from the first Gulf War, not his popular bar. Its origins as a humble red Ford 250 had been disguised and augmented with thousands of dollars of upgrades and custom options, and on weekends BJ could be seen in his driveway, lovingly scrubbing and polishing and drying it. He gave local kids rides around the block just for the sheer joy of tooting the horn at crossroads; he drove it with a bevy of young lovelies in the back for the homecoming parade.

"Well yes, Stella, it's a damn sight more likely to get you where you're going. I mean no offense to Chrissy's vehicle, but if you encounter any trouble —"

"What, like a snowy mountain pass or something? A swamp, maybe a tsunami up there near the Canadian border?"

"Don't be smart, Stella," BJ said, frowning, but Stella noticed that he wasn't mad

57

so much as truly concerned. In his soft brown eyes — like a doe, she thought, noticing how they had little flecks of gold dancing through the middles — there was unmistakable worry. "I was thinking more like a blown tire or if you hit a skid or, or, you know you can't control them other drivers, what if they's drinkin' or typin' on them damn cell phones —"

"All right," Stella said impulsively. He was awful hard to resist in this state. She leaned in and planted a chaste peck on his cheek. "I accept. I would love to borrow your truck, Big Johnson."

His relief was even greater than Stella had expected, if she were to judge from the way he grabbed her and pulled her in for a more substantial lip-lock to seal the deal.

It took her only a few minutes to throw a couple of changes of clothes and some toiletries into her trusty backpack. The ice cream, forgotten in the midst of the BJ visit, had leaked a little onto the patented Nytaneon fabric, but a quick swipe with a damp cloth took care of that; Stella made a mental note to go on the BlackHawk folks' Web site and leave an appreciative comment. Apparently most of their customers used the packs for jungle combat and such, given their advertising images, so they might not care much about the easy upkeep, but you never knew.

She wasn't sure what to expect once she got up to Wisconsin, and she was deliberately not overthinking it. Thing was, this was a whole new kind of trouble, and Stella knew from experience that the best approach was to just go figure out the lay of the land before making any judgments. Still, she was glad she'd taken her equipment out of the Jeep before sending it in for repair. The guns she stored in the steel box bolted to the Jeep's floor were in an old tackle box that had belonged to her father, and the essentials of her trade were stored in a few large Rubbermaid totes and Tupperware containers. BJ helped her load all of this into the truck's generous jump seat; he had a custom cover over the truck bed to keep a load safe from the elements, but Stella didn't fancy the idea of her equipment — particularly the items that were loaded — sliding all over the back of the truck. BJ didn't comment on the tackle box or the heavy containers, and she gave him credit for that: As her father, Buster Collier, used to say, a smart man lets a lady have her secrets. In his case he was referring to Stella's mother's extrafirm-support girdle and her salon touch-ups, but Stella figured the rule extended to a modern lady's habits as well.

Then it was time to say good-bye.

"You need me to show you how to work the GPS?" BJ asked, fretting like a mother hen as he leaned into the cab to show her all the features and doodads and adjust the seat and steering wheel to her form, which was considerably more petite than his solid six feet some-odd inches.

"No, BJ, I think I can figure that out," Stella reassured him, enjoying the way he pressed against her, nearly pinning her to the cold hard driver's side of the truck, a stance that led to all sorts of delicious images. "Noelle's got one in the Prius and I've used it some."

"You'll call me, let me know you're safe?"

"I promise." Stella gave him her best smile. She was glad she'd added a subtle spritz of White Diamonds under her snug knit top while she was packing. Just because she was likely going to have to drive all night and bust some ass when she got up there didn't mean she couldn't smell irresistible while she did it.

BJ evidently agreed, because he leaned in and inhaled a big fraction of the air around them. "Oh, Stella, you do worry me."

60

He took one of her hands in his big, meaty one and pressed it to his chest. Stella could feel his heart beating under his waffly cotton shirt. It felt nice.

"Don't fret," she said softly. "I got my own special guardian angel lookin' out for me."

"She damn well better," BJ said throatily before he gave Stella a last kiss, one ardent enough to remember.

CHAPTER FIVE

For the first hour of the eight-hour trip, once Stella made the pleasant adjustment to the incredibly smooth ride supplied by the OEM suspension lift that had her riding an extra foot or two off the ground, she amused herself by thinking about her guardian angel. Stella had no doubt she possessed one — how else to explain the fact that she was three years into her second career and hadn't spent so much as a single night in jail? That she usually came out on top from her one-on-one encounters with nothing worse than a rope burn or a pulled muscle or, in one memorable case, a hell of a bruise when the sledgehammer she was using on a man's pinky finger slipped out of her grip and fell on her instep?

Stella figured her guardian angel probably looked a little like her. For that matter, Stella wouldn't be surprised if the gal's angelic personal history shared a few parallels as well. She probably got lost in the back of the angel crowd, being shorter, dumpier, and older than the ones you always saw depicted on Christmas cards and First Communion knickknacks, the blond, blue-eyed willowy variety who somehow managed to keep their robes and wings pristine despite the strenuous demands of angelhood. Plus they probably all had lovely names like Grace and Chastity and Faith, while Stella's was probably saddled with a name like . . . Bertha. Bert for short. Yeah, her name was Bert, she was soundly middle-aged, she'd arrived at the pearly gates dressed in the stretched-out sweats she saved for gardening, her upper arms jiggled, and she couldn't see her toes past her tummy. She'd been afraid to speak up in Angel Orientation, so she probably got the shoddiest quarters, the ones by the air-conditioning unit and closest to the Dumpsters, and none of the hot man angels ever asked her to dance at the mixers.

Then . . . this thought arrived as Stella passed through the twinkling lights of Jefferson City, giving the stately capitol building a jaunty two-finger wave . . . then one day Bert got pissed. Maybe it was discovering that they ran out of ambrosia just as she got to the front of the line.

63

Maybe it was because the holy calisthenics instructor had designed all the exercises for angels with long slender limbs and flexible spines and bottomless stamina. Maybe it was getting her wingtips stuck in the doors of the chapel once too often, making all the other angels cluck judgmentally at how long it was taking her to get the hang of folding them prettily on her back.

Whatever it was, on that day, Stella had no doubt that Bert snapped. "Listen up, y'all!" she imagined her girl shouting, gnawed-nail fists on her hips. "I am sick and tired of being treated like a second-class citizen of Heaven just because I can't fly straight or do laps around the cloud bank or recite all of Psalm 119. I'll tell you what, I have something that the rest of you girls are only just getting started on. I've got experience, I've got some hard miles, and most of all, I've got balls."

That word, "balls," would have echoed shockingly through the celestial chamber while, all around her, flaxen-haired beauties fainted and pressed their hands to their hearts. Then Bert would have announced herself done with training and taken herself straight to the Job Board and picked off the most challenging case she could find.

Stella.

Stella laughed out loud, imagining that day. It was probably the same day that Ollie found himself laid out like a sheared sheep on the kitchen floor, a nice big dent in his woman-beating skull. She hoped she'd kept Bert busy and entertained. She *knew* Bert had made the Big Guy proud.

Stella prayed to the Big Guy every day, far more often than all those years when she'd shown up faithfully every week in church. She had never said it to another living soul, but she was pretty sure that the Big Guy walked beside her everywhere she went. Sure, there were a hell of a lot of people in the world who'd object to the particulars of her one-woman religious philosophy, but Stella figured that since she didn't go around telling Baptists and Presbyterians and Jehovah's Witnesses and Buddhists and Muslims what to believe, they ought to just learn to keep their opinions to themselves as well.

By the time Stella stopped at the turnoff for Hannibal for a pee break, the novelty of the trip had worn off and the drive had grown monotonous. Night had fallen, a star-studded sliver-mooned warm sort of a late-May night, and Stella got herself a big Diet Coke and a full tank of gas, suffering heart palpitations when she discovered what kind of cash it took to fill up BJ's tank. Before starting the engine she transferred one of the guns from the tackle box to her purse, just in case, and helped herself to the CD holder she found stowed neatly in the glove box.

She discovered that she and BJ shared a few favorite crooners, and settled on Shane Yellowbird. When the first track came up "Pickup Truck," she figured it was a sign, blew a kiss to Bert, and settled in for a cruise and a listen:

Somewhere around the bend
I know we'll have better luck in my pickup
   truck

Yeah, somewhere around the bend, indeed.

A little before two in the morning Stella came up on Rockford, Illinois, and figured she ought to get out for another pee break and a swift jog around the parking lot of an all-night QuikGo to keep her awake for the final stretch. She had no intention of going to the warehouse, or whatever it was, where she was expected to leave all the cash that she didn't have, and that evidently her sister's husband's family had let slip through their fingers like so much of that colored sand you could stuff into bottles at the carnival. Snagging Chip unawares wasn't much of a plan, especially if he didn't care to accompany her to Missouri, but Stella was pretty sure she could talk him into it. It might have put Gracie's mind at ease to know about Stella's considerable resources, since for all her sister knew, the only weapons in Stella's arsenal were a sassy mouth and a hefty store of maternal concern.

In the not-very-clean bathroom of the QuikGo, Stella dabbed at her face with a wet paper towel, trying to wake up. She peeped in the cloudy mirror and immediately regretted it; the purple circles under her eyes were decorated with the mascara that had gotten dislodged in those final moments of mashing with BJ, and she'd left all her lipstick on the rim of the Diet Coke tumbler. Oh well, she wasn't headed for a beauty contest.

She picked out a roll of SweeTarts — "tart" sounded like it might enhance alertness — and got in line behind the QuikGo's only other middle-of-the-night customer, a skinny youth who, from behind, bore a passing resemblance to Todd, with his too-long hair and shorts three sizes too large for his skinny hips. Even the T-shirt was remarkably similar —

"No, sir," the boy mumbled, pushing a stack of loose change across the counter and stifling a yawn as the clerk put a pair of impossibly tall cans of some sort of sports drink into a paper sack. "One's for my Gram. She's old and all but she likes 'em and the caffeine keeps her going."

That voice — Stella would know it anywhere. She'd first heard it when its owner was a towheaded six-year-old who was pedaling his bike as fast as he could after the neighbor's cat. She'd heard that voice snuffle and sob when its owner's daddy left for the last time. In recent years she'd heard it changing, cracking and wobbling as it started to turn into a man's voice — though it was going to be a while before that happened, and that was if its owner survived the whuppin' that was about to be unleashed on his skinny ass.

"I'll take that," she snapped, reaching out a hand and snatching the paper sack, grabbing one bony shoulder and giving it a spin. "Todd Groffe, as I live and breathe, what the hell are you doing here?"

The clerk, a fortyish fellow with a Penske cap pulled low and an unlit pipe clenched between his teeth, gave Stella a squint-eyed once-over. "You're his *granny?*" he de-

68

manded, letting go of the sack and scooping change into the drawer. "Time's been kind to you, I'd say."

Stella couldn't help taking a moment to process the compliment. One never knew where one was going to find them, just like Popeye's restaurants when you were on a trip; you had to get your biscuits — or sweet words, as the case may be — whenever they came along. "He ain't mine, but I suppose I'll take him off your hands," she said sweetly, adding a little toss of her hair.

Still, a fellow who worked the late shift eight hours away from Prosper wasn't exactly a promising candidate for a dating relationship, so Stella gave him a regretful smile and dragged Todd toward the door.

"Now I'm gonna ask you a question," she hissed into his ear as he squawked in protest, oversized sneakers dragging along the floor. "I imagine you already know what it is. And I'ma tell you right now I ain't interested in anything you got to say but the truth and quick, too."

"It wasn't like I done it on purpose," Todd said crossly.

"Done *what?*"

"Fell asleep in there."

Todd pointed across the parking lot at BJ's truck. Stella saw that the tailgate had been

69

left down, the black fiberglass cover still in place.

"You been in the back of BJ's truck this whole time?"

"Well yeah, Stella, I cain't even get my permit for another four months —"

"I wasn't suggesting you'd be *driving* up here —"

"Well, hell, Stella, look around, you see any other way I'd end up here? What state are we even in, anyway? We going to Florida?"

Stella's eyes widened with disbelief. "You came along because you figured I was headed for *Florida?* Now why in . . . never mind. You just stand there lookin' like you fell off the turnip truck while I call your mom."

Night had rolled in humid and warm, and Stella enjoyed a faint little stirring of the night breezes that carried with them the fresh scent of the row of spruces that bordered the QuikGo. Somewhere in a field beyond, a dog's bark was answered by a whistle. She pulled the phone out and speed-dialed Todd's mother, the long-suffering Sherilee Groffe, wishing she didn't have to wake the poor woman up in the middle of the night. Since Sherilee did the job of several people every day of the year

70

— she was mother and father and breadwinner and dispenser of both justice and kisses, with no time for herself except the hours when her head hit the pillow — it didn't seem fair to add to her burden.

Still, Stella knew a mother's worry, the way each morning dawned with thoughts of one's offspring before anything else, with a prayer for their safety and an entreaty to the Big Guy to hold them gently for one more day.

Which was also why she answered the way she did after Sherilee's sleepy hello.

"Todd's fine," she said quickly. "This is Stella. Don't you worry."

"Oh, nooooo," Sherilee moaned. Stella could hear some rustling as she came awake. "What's that fool boy done now? I should've known he wasn't over to Taylor Spokes's house. Why, they barely been speakin' since that thing with the gym lockers."

Stella covered the mouthpiece and glared at Todd. "You told your mama you was sleepin' over at the Spokeses' place, didn't you."

Todd shrugged, an elaborately indifferent roll of the shoulders that was meant to signal boredom, but Stella didn't miss the way his fingers picked at the collar of his shirt. The boy felt bad. And that was good. Todd was an ingrate, but he was a sweet one who hated to pain his mother.

She thrust the phone at him. "You tell her how sorry you are, boy," she stage-whispered fiercely. "Make it the performance of a lifetime."

Todd ducked his chin and kicked at the pavement and heaved a giant sigh, but he accepted the phone. "Mom, I —"

Even from a few feet away Stella could hear most of what Sherilee had to say. The woman had an impressive pair of lungs and she used them to bellow and scold without leaving a single gap to get a word in until she'd had her say — and then the silence hung oppressive and thick, and Stella almost felt a little sorry for the boy.

"I'm really, really, really sorry," Todd mumbled. Stella saw the shimmer of un-spilled tears in the moonlight and felt herself relenting a little. "I shoulda known better, I didn't mean to —"

"Gimme that," she said, snatching back her phone and knocking Todd on the head with it before turning her attention back to Sherilee. "It's me again. Look, I'm going to take good care of him, I promise."

"Is he over at your place?"

"Uh . . . well, not exactly. In fact we're

sort of out of town. It's kind of complicated."

"Oh no, you ain't up at Fayette, are you?"
Fayette, the county seat, featured the county
jail, among other things. The sheriff's
department's temporary holding cell in
Prosper had been fashioned from an old
Dumpster enclosure, so most suspects
didn't cool their heels there for very long
before being sent north.

"No, no, nothing like that. Todd ain't done
anything illegal that I know of." Although at
that moment Stella remembered seeing
Goat's cruiser — which she had foolishly
believed had been evidence he was looking
out for *her* — but could easily have been a
pursuit-type situation involving *Todd.*

"You mean, 'cept what he done to Royal's
car. Oh, that man was spittin' nails." Stella
could hear the frustration in Sherilee's
voice, and she had the thought that having
to be the go-between between one's son-of-
a-bitch ex and one's own kids was yet one
more layer of hell that a single mother
didn't deserve but was often stuck with
anyway.

"He's still mad about that? Didn't insurance pay to repaint?"

"Yes, but I'm talkin' about what Todd
done *today.* Royal come over after work to

73

drop off the check and practically invited himself in and what am I gonna do about that, the girls are so excited to see their daddy, so I set out some cookies and what-all and didn't even give it a thought when Todd told me he was headed over to Taylor's. Keepin' him apart from his dad seemed like a good idea, in fact. And then when Royal saw what Todd done, and right on that fresh paint what he paid extra to get the waterborne finish —"

"Oh, no," Stella said, her heart sinking. She stared at Todd, who realized he'd been found out. Rather than slinking further into remorse, though, he stood up tall and jutted his chin angrily forward, sparks practically flying from his long-lashed eyes. Yes, he'd done it for sure — and he wasn't sorry.

That was a whole other type of problem, one she'd best sort out away from his mother.

"What did he write this time?" she asked heavily.

"Well, it was kind of like last time when he run outta room," Sherilee said. "From the driver's side it said I SUCK in big old red letters but then you round the corner and it said . . . uh, something else."

Stella bit her lip, deadly curious but not about to pry, not with the sort of night that

74

poor Sherilee was having.

She didn't have to. *"BALLS,"* Sherilee whispered. "That's what was wrote across the back. I SUCK BALLS. Oh, that sure did make Royal mad. He called the sheriff up straightaway, even after I offered to pay for it."

"Oh, Sherilee," Stella said, adding a couple of tasks to her ongoing to-do list: Deal with Todd — and then deal with Royal next. Maybe he needed to send his checks Certified Mail for a while. Stella was all for boys having their fathers in their lives — and she'd go so far as to say that an imperfect father was better than none at all — but a cooling-off period seemed like it might be in order. "Okay, look. I'll talk to Royal, and the sheriff too, but it's going to have to wait a day or so. In fact I need to keep ahold of Todd for a bit. That okay with you?"

"Sure, you can keep him," Sherilee said without hesitation. "Only where are you-all at?"

"Well, see . . . we're headed up to Wisconsin."

"Wisconsin!" Sherilee exclaimed, as though Stella had said Rome or the North Pole.

"Yes. I have a little . . . business thing up here, shouldn't take me too long. I'll keep

75

Todd in sight every minute, I'll promise you that. That sound okay?" Stella wasn't sure if she was making promises she could keep, but there would be time to worry about that later.

"Oh my yes," Sherilee said, sounding only marginally relieved. "That'll give me a chance to work on Royal, see if I can get him calmed down some."

"Could you maybe look in on Roxy for me?"

"Sure thing, the girls just love that dog. We'll bring her over here until you get back."

"Thanks, Sherilee. I promise we'll check in with you."

"All right. And Stella . . ."

"Yeah?"

There was a pause, and then Sherilee coughed delicately. "See he gets some sleep, will you? And eats something that ain't all sugar? And . . . maybe give him a kiss when he ain't lookin'?"

Stella turned away from Todd so he couldn't see her smile. "You got it, Sherilee."

She pocketed the phone and got her scowl back in place before turning back around. Todd followed her meekly to the truck and clambered into the passenger seat. They weren't half a mile down the road before he was asleep, tucked against the door with his arms crossed across his chest, and Stella couldn't help hoping his dreams were sweet ones.

Chapter Six

By the time they reached the outskirts of Smythe, Wisconsin, Stella was wishing she could pull over and sleep, too. However, the vague plan she'd cooked up over the course of the nearly five hundred miles she'd covered in BJ's truck hinged on making her move while it was still the middle of the night — or, more precisely, 3:46 A.M., according to the clock on the dashboard.

The way she figured it, her best source of information was bound to be Chip himself. She had the address that Gracellen had given her, a rented house that her sister had assured her was "right in the thick of things," as though keeping close to the pulse of this eight-thousand-person town would make the place any more exciting for a young single man. Missing ear or no, there weren't that many places a man could hide, Stella concluded as she drove down the shuttered streets, passing a single grocery store and half a dozen churches and a war memorial that rose a couple of stories tall in the moonlight.

When the eerie, disembodied voice of BJ's GPS assured Stella she was on the right track as she pulled a U-turn at a dead end and stopped in front of a very small cinderblock house wedged between a couple of aging wood-frame ranchers, Stella wrinkled her brow in consternation. She let the truck idle at the curb while she dug out her reading glasses and the ancient address book she'd had for several years. Stella was itching to get herself an iPhone so she could keep everything on it, but the little address book had been the last gift her mother had given her before she died, a little "just-because" gift because Pat Collier had spotted the sunflowers on the cover and, knowing her daughter loved sunflowers just about more than any other flower, had wrapped it up with a little bow and brought it over with a pan of homemade lemon bars.

Maybe it was because it was nearly four in the morning and she'd been up all night. Maybe it was the stress of volunteering for what looked like yet another messy, potentially violent escapade in a year that had already featured several. Maybe it was the heightened responsibility of having a sprawling, lanky, ripe teen in the car, one who was unpredictable on the best of days and who was going to be in her care for the foreseeable future.

Whatever the cause, when Stella squinted at the address book in the dome light of the borrowed truck, music playing faintly in the background so as not to disturb Todd's slumber, she felt a pang of sadness that she hadn't felt in a while. Not only missing her mother, who'd passed a number of years ago, but also missing having someone know the special things about her. Someone who remembered she loved sunflowers and lemon bars, who knew she had double-jointed toes and an astigmatism in both eyes and liked to nap in front of a fire on rainy days and read the comics first and sprinkle her grapefruit with sugar.

"Now stop that, Stella," she whispered to herself, wiping a tear away with the back of her hand and blinking several times. "You got more'n most folks."

That was true in spades. The older Stella got, the more she realized that a single good friend was a precious gift that lots of people couldn't hang on to, whether it was from a lack of trying or bad luck or people dying out from under you — and she had several. While none of them might know everything

80

about her the way her mama had, put them all together and they took darn good care of her. Chrissy sometimes knew Stella better than she knew herself, and she didn't put up with any whining; the girl kept her on top of her game. Jelloman Nunn was the closest thing to a maternal figure Stella had, which was kind of funny since he was ten years older than her tops, and a *man,* not to mention one with a long gray ponytail and a beard down to his Adam's apple and a thriving weed business — but he could be counted on to fuss over her and bake for her and set her up with a pile of blankets and a chick flick in front of the TV if she so much as got the sniffles.

Then there was Dotty Edwards and Sherilee and Jane down at Hair Lines and Roseanne Lu and all her clients. Stella shook her head and clucked in impatience; she didn't have any right to fuss. In the back of her mind was that other thought bubble, the one that occasionally bloomed into a fullfledged craving to have all those fine qualities rolled up into a single person, more specifically a male person who was reasonably attractive and equipped for an assortment of bedroom-type activities. Okay, okay, a *boyfriend,* not to put too fine a point on things. It was no kind of mystery why her little pity party had gone in that direction, since she was sitting here in a man's truck, the very same man who'd only hours ago been working his big strong manly hand downward toward her tender nethers, one who'd been hinting for a while now that he might be available for a variety of leisure-time activities.

Heck, Stella had both a problem and a ready-made solution. Only, why did it all have to come to the surface now, five hundred miles from home, when she had a job to do and — as usual — an imperfect set of resources to do it with?

Stella opened the address book to the *P* page and ran her fingers down the list until it landed on "Papadakis." Chess and Grac-ellen had the most robust entry, not only because they'd moved into the huge fancy tract home recently, but because Stella liked to keep a variety of facts on hand for gift shopping, like their sizes and colors and the fact that Chess was allergic to latex and rooted for the A's and Raiders. For Chip, who she did not know nearly as well, fewer particulars were listed, but one of them was his address, and it took only a second to confirm that she was, indeed, parked in front of it.

Which was a curious thing. It wasn't that

Stella couldn't picture the young man in this humble little house despite his family's considerable if recently diminished wealth — she knew how any kind of addiction, including the gambling sort, could send one's quality of life plummeting.

No, what caused her some consternation was the way he'd seen fit to decorate the place. Even in the not-optimal light cast by the streetlights and the truck's aftermarket xenon headlights, Stella could make out clumps of faux flowers in the window boxes, bunches of plastic geraniums and roses and daisies with festoons of ivy trailing over the edges.

It wasn't the most manly decor Stella had ever seen, and it didn't quite jive with Stella's memory of the boy, who had been sullen and poorly groomed and not really giving off a whole lot of indication that he had a softer side that might show itself in outward displays of floral exuberance, even if she wasn't one to judge about such things.

She turned off the truck and put the back of her hand gently to Todd's cheek, which was warm from sleep. She rested her hand there for a moment, feeling him breathe, a habit that went back to the night she brought Noelle home from the hospital, a mother's need to confirm for herself that her children were well and thriving. Even if Todd wasn't exactly *hers,* well, she'd given his mother a promise to care for him, and that meant "as if he were her very own."

Todd didn't stir when she shut the door and trudged up to the house. She knocked gently, not wishing to wake the neighbors, and given how close-set the houses were and how flimsy the construction looked to be, that was a real concern.

Inside she heard some shuffling and muttering and then a thump and some more urgent muttering and then silence. Someone was up, even at this hour, and from the sounds of it, there was more than one someone. Which might, come to think of it, explain the flower boxes, especially if the other someone was female — though for the life of her Stella didn't recall Gracellen ever mentioning Chip having any romantic interests.

She waited a while and knocked again, but when even a soft pounding failed to raise anyone to answer the door, she went back to the truck. As gently as she could, she opened the driver's side door and rooted around the jump seat, collecting the Tupperware that contained her breaking-in tools. Not that she anticipated any trouble from Chip or any ladies he might be entertaining, but this had gone from a straightforward rousting from bed to a slightly more complicated scenario, and Stella made it a policy to meet complications appropriately armed.

Todd had moved slightly, his arm now flung up over his head, his soft snores as gentle and sweet as a puppy's growl, and Stella gave him a little pat before heading back to the house. She made quick work of the flimsy mortise lock on the door and pushed it open, finding herself in a dim living room that contained some mismatched furniture and a few silk flower arrangements and an overarching scent of potpourri with notes of cleaning products and something organic and unpleasant. Stella was trying to suppress both nausea and a sneeze when she heard rustling from the back of the house and found herself unable to announce her presence due to what felt like a sudden asphyxiation by Crystal Rain scent.

When she followed the source of the sounds into the kitchen, Stella beheld a scenario that took a few minutes to comprehend, the various parts so at odds that they almost threw a switch in her tired brain. A man resembling Chip, except twenty pounds closer to a healthy weight and with a sheen to his feather-cut brown hair, was bent over the table holding a wicked-looking blade and a large meat fork. Whisking away draining fluids with a rag was a pretty dark-haired woman with a voluptuous build that was barely covered by a tank top and an apron, her extraordinarily pale shoulders and long legs visible underneath. And between the two of them, sliced and piled and trussed like a thanksgiving turkey, was what was left of a man — specifically, about three-quarters of the upper half.

CHAPTER SEVEN

"Oh!" the woman shrieked, taking a step back.

"Good heavens," Stella exclaimed, nausea surging with renewed vigor.

"Aunt Stella? Is that *you*?" the young man who evidently actually *was* Chip asked, setting down his blade but holding on to the meat fork, which he'd been poised to poke into the exposed innards of the unfortunate torso on the table. The body's head was resting on a folded dish towel, its mouth slightly ajar, its lids only half lowered, appearing to watch the procedures with something like bemused patience, as though he supposed he'd be a sport and put up with this unexpected interruption to his dismemberment and maybe even offer a beer from the fridge if only his hand was still attached.

"What — how —"

Stella discovered that she was pointing her little SIG at the strange tableau. She didn't

87

recall pulling it out of her purse, but even in her state of shock and disgust she had the wherewithal to be pleased that her reflexes were so finely tuned.

Although it wasn't clear what she would shoot, or what effect shooting might have.

"Chip, what on *earth* are y'all up to?" she managed.

"Oh, this looks bad, I know," Chip said, "but I can explain. Here, watch you don't slip, there's . . . urr, *stuff* on the floor." As though she were holding a sandwich rather than a gun, Chip grabbed a fresh rag and got down on his knees and set to mopping. "This here's Natalya Markovic, by the way. My girlfriend."

"Hello," the woman said in heavily accented English, bobbing her head up and down enthusiastically. "I am very pleased to meet."

On closer inspection Stella realized that there was something a little off about the woman. Her mouth and chin were swollen on one side, as though she'd been hit with a baseball. Also, she was older than her initial impression. Fine lines bracketed her expressive brown eyes. She was still a real looker, though, possibly of the Eastern European variety, and she made Stella self-conscious of the fact that any makeup that had survived the mashing with BJ had long since melted into the wrinkles and under her eyes.

"I'm Stella Hardesty. Um, what are you two doing cutting up this . . . this person?"

"Oh, Chip is cutting, I am *cleaning,*" Natalya clarified. As if to illustrate the difference she seized a bottle of Crystal Rain Windex and gave the table an energetic spray. "I say we must be very clean."

"Natalya kind of has a thing about keeping things neat and sterile," Chip said, straightening and tossing the rag in the sink, where a pile of rags was collecting. "If you knew her background you'd understand. Uh, I'd give you a hug but . . ."

"That's okay," Stella said. She felt sort of silly with the gun in her hand, as it didn't look like either one of them had any imminent plans to slice her up, too, so she slid it back in her purse. Then followed one of those awkward moments when she didn't know exactly what to do with her hands; she clasped the purse handle in front of her and felt even more out of place, as though she were about to sing backup for a particularly realistic-looking stage show of a murder musical. "I'm, um. Sorry to bust in on you this way, but you didn't answer the door."

"You made sure it shut after you, didn't

you?" Chip asked. "Maybe I better go check."

"We must stay very careful," Natalya piped up. "There can be more trouble."

Stella found that her head was starting to swim with the oddity of the situation. "Who exactly are you worried about?" She pointed delicately at the remains of the gentleman on the table. "I mean, if you're willing to do something like this, and I assume you figure this guy had it coming —"

"Oh, we did not kill this man!" Natalya said, her eyes widening in surprise and indignation. "We are come home from movies and here he is, on porch. We are dragging him inside before anyone can see."

"Wait," Stella said. "Who — look here, can you start from the top for me? Because I'm kind of confused."

"Well, is Chip night off, but he is always working overnight shift so we are all the time staying up very late. So we go to movie at theater and is after midnight when we come home, because we are getting drink at Best Western bar, is open late and having good price, so he is show here after, hmmm, maybe is after nine o'clock and before one o'clock."

"Uh, thanks, but what I meant is, just who is this guy?"

Chip, who had jogged to the front door and tested the knob, sidled back into the room and surveyed his handiwork, shaking his head sorrowfully. "Aunt Stella, what you're looking at there is a bad man."

"Well, part of him, anyway," Stella observed.

"Oh no, we got the whole shebang." Chip pointed to a corner of the kitchen. On a plastic sheet lay a neat pile of jumbo-sized Ziplocs, most fogged with moisture that obscured their contents; the top one, however, contained what certainly resembled a chunk of human flesh, possibly a forearm. "We're just, you know, making him easier to dispose of."

"Where you fixing to do that?" Stella demanded. "And if you didn't kill him, how do you figure it's your job, anyway?"

"Oh, I know," Chip said, nodding in fervent agreement. "It totally *sucks* that we got to do this, but who else are we gonna get?"

"Um . . ." Stella hesitated for a moment, wondering if her stepnephew-in-law had gone seriously around the bend. "If what you're telling me is that you came home and found this person laid out dead on your porch all unexpected-like, you mighta called up the cops, for a start. I could be wrong, but I'd figure they might be interested enough to take a break from their traffic stops and whatnot to come take a look, even up here in Wisconsin."

"Oh no, that is terrible mistake," Natalya said. "Man who is killing him, he is desperate. He is maybe killing us, too."

"Who wants to kill you? And what is the warning about? Look, Chip, I don't mean to be rude, but is this connected to your gambling issues?" Only then did a thought strike her. "Wait a minute — what the hell! You've got both your ears! I can't believe I didn't —"

She shook her head in disgust. Talk about a lapse in deductive detecting skills. Chip's ears were definitely both still attached to his head, though they were missing the multiple studs and little hoops that he was wearing the last time Stella saw him.

"Oh, that," Chip said, coloring. He touched his ear self-consciously, as though he'd been caught out in the process of naughtily regenerating it. His face colored the deep red of shame and embarrassment. "I guess Gracellen told you, huh."

"Well yes, Chip, your stepmom called me just about out of her mind when she got a fucking *ear* in a fucking *box*," Stella said.

"Oh no," Natalya exclaimed, her face

turning a similar deep red shade.

"Uh, Stella," Chip said sheepishly. "Could you . . . uh . . . Natalya don't like that kind of language. Our home is a profanity-free zone."

Stella stared at him in disbelief. "You want me to fu— to, uh, watch my *language* when you two are in the middle of reenacting the Texas Chainsaw Massacre here?"

Natalya squeezed her eyes shut and pressed her hands to her ears and began humming, a soulful, wistful sound that immediately made Stella feel like she'd stepped on a baby bunny.

"Aw, hell," she muttered, before tapping Natalya gently on the shoulder. "I'm sorry, Natalya. Sometimes I speak before I think. I'll try to be more careful."

"Thank you," the woman said. A second later she nearly knocked Stella over with a hug whose strength belied the woman's dainty build. She smelled of a generous dousing of perfume overlaid with notes of bleach and Windex, and she sniffed delicately into Stella's shoulder. "Oh, is so good to meet family of Chip."

Stella hugged back, feeling an oddly maternal inclination. Stella was five-six but could tuck Natalya comfortably under her chin. "China doll" popped into her mind.

She remembered the one time Chip had brought a girl to Thanksgiving dinner; she had been a vacant-eyed, gum-chewing girl with more eyeliner than conversational skill. Natalya was an improvement, at least in the grooming and enthusiasm departments. Stella gently disentangled herself from the hug and scowled at Chip. "So what gives with the ear thing?"

"Oh. Well, it wasn't mine."

"Yeah, I think we established that."

"I, uh, got it at work. I was just trying — I mean, I get that I overstepped, it was wrong, blah blah blah. But Jesus, Stella, my folks are loaded, I mean Gramps practically shits cash, it's not like they'll even miss it —"

"Chip!" Natalya gasped.

"Sorry, sorry, sweetie —"

"What did you need thirty thousand bucks for anyway?" Stella demanded, deciding to leave aside her newfound knowledge of the Papadakis family's precarious financial situation for the moment.

"Thirty thousand!" Natalya squawked. "Chip! You said —"

Chip took on a pained expression and held up a palm. "Stella, if you could just — ah, hell, Natalya, I'm sorry, I might have given you ummm, a slightly —"

"But you said —"

"I just didn't want you to worry, honey," Chip said miserably. He jammed his hands in his pockets and assumed a hangdog expression. "If I'd told you the truth, I mean you were saying it was hopeless already and all . . ."

"But you say Benton wants five thousand dollars only!"

"Natalya, believe me, if it was only five thousand dollars, it would have been done by now," Chip said passionately, cupping her face in his hands. Stella had to suppress an "ewww" moment, considering where his hands had recently been, but Natalya gazed upon him with a fiery combination of anguish and adoration. "I'd've sold my car, my — my plasma, my *sperm,* whatever it took!"

"Wait just a second here," Stella demanded, resisting the urge to pry the pair apart to get their attention. "What exactly was the thirty thousand bucks *for?*"

"It's this ass— uh, this guy," Chip said, pointing a finger at the mess on the table. "It's all his fault."

"He is husband," Natalya sniffed, nodding.

"He's your *husband?*"

"Natalya came here as a, she came here from Russia to be a bride. Benton — this

95

here's Benton Parch — they met online and he brought her over and married her. But then she met me, and, well —"

"He is *bad* man," Natalya interjected hastily. "Bad husband. I am here almost two years. I work hard, I keep house. At first I try to make Benton happy, but he . . ." Her eyes filled with shining tears, but she wiped them impatiently away. "Is never good enough."

"*He* did that to her," Chip said darkly, pointing at her lips.

"Wow," Stella said. Never, in the years she'd seen a variety of bruises and lacerations and swelling and all manner of injury delivered at the hands of a man, had she seen anything quite like the swelling and malformation that marred Natalya's otherwise appealing face. Her professional curiosity was piqued, and she leaned in for a better look. "How, though, is what I got to ask? I mean did he . . ."

"Wait, I don't mean he did that *himself*," Chip clarified. "He *paid* a guy to do it."

Even up close, Stella couldn't see signs of laceration or bruising, just the swelling and a shiny patchiness to the lips, kind of like the fake leather on her knockoff Dooney & Bourke handbag. "Guy musta used something with a rounded edge . . ."

"He use *Botox*," Natalya said. "Only not very good at it."

"Now honey," Chip murmured soothingly. "It's hardly noticeable."

Natalya beamed. "You see why I am fall in love with Chip —"

Their eyes met and their mad romantic attraction threatened to propel themselves into each other's arms again, so Stella held up a hand to keep their attention. "Your husband paid a guy to inject you? Not a doctor, I take it."

"He see picture in magazine, talk friend at work who his wife have Botox super cheap. Get phone number for practice doctor, we meet him when school is closed. Benton tell him what to do, he likes the big lips, *big* big, like model from Brazil."

"Do you know how many muscles and nerves there are around the mouth?" Chip demanded in a tone of outrage.

"This doctor, he only has done the eyebrow before, the wrinkle, but Benton tell him go ahead. When this happen Benton find him after school one night, tell him he turn him in and he will *never* be doctor."

"Oh, he was a medical *student*," Stella clarified. "So your husband threatened to tell the AMA or whatever."

"Which is how *this* happened," Chip

sighed, ignoring Stella's comment and gesturing at the partial corpse with the meat fork.

"You mean, Benton threatened to report this guy so he . . . what, whacked him? And left him for you here to take care of?"

"He want to make it look like I am killer. Shut up two birds with one rock. Benton is dead and now he think I am too scare to talk."

"How exactly did he kill him, anyway?"

Natalya shrugged. "I don't know. He is just dead."

"What, you mean there weren't any marks on him? No injuries or wounds?"

"Nothing," Chip agreed, "and since we stripped him down I had a chance to check him out, you know, all over."

"Well, couldn't he have died of, I don't know, a heart attack or stroke or something? I mean, if he came to your door, it might have been just really bad timing. Say he wanted to talk to you, but you guys are out, he's ringing the bell, he's frustrated, getting madder and madder, blood pressure going through the roof —"

"No, it wasn't like that," Chip said. "He didn't just fall in a heap or whatever. He was sort of folded up with a couple of Hefty bags laid on top to cover him up."

"Hefty bags . . . huh."

"Sloppy, right? He could've at least used a sheet or something. These medical students — I can't stand 'em," Chip interjected. "Most of them, they just go through life expecting other people to clean up their messes."

Stella's confusion was deepening. "Uh, you know a lot of medical students?"

"I *work* with them, Stella," Chip said in an aggrieved tone. "I guess I know what I'm talking about."

"Chip works in Boberg Clinic, at St. Olaf's Hospital. Is how we met." The look of consuming devotion was back on Natalya's face.

"Wait, you were there when Benton brought her in?" Stella asked. "For the, uh . . . unofficially sanctioned procedure?"

"No," Chip said with contempt. "He did that at his place. Stole the supplies he needed or bought 'em black market or something."

"We go to his house late at night," Natalya added. "Very late, no one there but us."

"Then how did you . . ."

"After Benton threaten him, I am still like this?" She touched her fingertip to her swollen mouth. "It was even worse then, and I

99

think, I will go by myself, I will ask what can be done. I think maybe can be fixed, I can be nice instead of mean, convince better. So I go very early in morning, one day when Benton is on business trip. I take his car and park outside clinic. I think I will see each person go inside until I see right one."

"I was getting off my shift, and I see this beautiful lady all alone in her car in the parking lot. It wasn't even light out yet. So I went to see if everything was all right."

"We have love at first sight," Natalya added helpfully.

"She was crying, so I took her to Dunkin Donuts."

"He buy me coffee and fat-free blueberry muffin, he ask me where am I from, he is so easy talking!"

"Okay, okay, I get the picture," Stella cut her off. She'd been subjected to these sorts of stories before — only she had a more cynical view than most, having seen how badly some relationships ended up after equally promising beginnings. "So you meet, you start dating —"

"No, no date, we have to sneak. Benton is very, ermmm . . . he is having terrible jealousy."

"But we found ways, like when he had to travel for work. After a month or so we knew we had to be together. So I went to Benton's office and told him I was going to marry her no matter what, but he —" Chip glared at the leaking mess as though the man wanted to start up the argument again. "That's when he threatened me. Said if he couldn't have her, no American man would, and he'd send her ass right back to Russia."

"Could he do that?" Stella asked dubiously.

Chip's face darkened with fury. "Stella, if you knew the half of it — why, the way the immigration law's written they might as well just stand at the border waitin' for Cupid to fly overhead and shoot him right down like a, like a damn *duck*. The American government — it's coldhearted as hell."

"Residency permit says I must reside in country for two years after marriage," Natalya said dolefully. "Two years anniversary is July 4, that is only six weeks away, but —"

"Bastard said unless I covered all his costs since the first day he went scrolling through the LovelyBrides site on the Internet and came across Natalya, he was going to report her before the anniversary. They can deport her then."

"That's where he got that number?" Stella asked. "The thirty thousand?"

101

"That's what he said. What with the lawyer he got to help them get the K-1 visa, and all the flights back and forth, and the wedding itself and all the —"

"No, no, I understand, it adds up." Stella's clients' tales of woe occasionally included visits to attorneys they didn't stand a chance of affording, attorneys whose hourly rate could feed their kids for a week or buy a set of tires. "What I don't understand is, why couldn't you just marry her right quick? She leaves him, gets a divorce, *bam,* next day she marries you. With no downtime, she wouldn't really have a chance to get illegal again, at least not for very long, would she?"

Chip's murderous scowl deepened. "Well, you'd think that, wouldn't you. Problem is, Benton had such a bug up his ass he wasn't gonna let that happen. He was going to see this one old golf pal of his, a judge down at the county seat, and withdraw his residency petition and have them come after Natalya before we could do a damn thing about it."

"I have friend, Yuliya, from home," Natalya said wistfully. "This happen to her. She and I join LovelyBrides at same time, she is meeting man from Oklahoma. In six month time passing, husband divorce her. Lawyer tell her, she can file petition to stay here while pursue permanent status, but —"

Natalya made a slicing motion across her neck — presumably to indicate deportation and not something worse.

"So your girlfriend's ex wanted cash?" Stella turned to Chip. "I assume from what you're saying that your, uh, financial position hasn't improved any?"

"I'm not gambling, if that's what you mean," Chip said, rooting in his pocket and producing a key chain. He flipped it over to expose a circular bronze medallion stamped with a telltale triangle design, which he proudly showed Stella. "Six months in recovery, I go to meetings."

"Well, that's, uh, marvelous," Stella said. "Seriously, Chip, big props to you on that. Still, I'm guessing it's been a little difficult to build up the old bank account with the, ah, entry-level employment . . ."

Chip nodded. "I had to work my way up. Got on at St. Olaf's doing janitorial, but I been there almost a year now and I got promoted twice, and now I work in the Boberg Clinic."

"What's that?"

"It's affiliated with the University of Wisconsin, like an extension program they run up here at the hospital. They got a bunch of specialty residencies they do up here. Like, if you're a med student who wants to go into plastic surgery, once you're done with your regular surgical residency, you can come up here and put in a couple of years at the Plastic and Reconstructive Clinic."

"That's where you work?"

"Yup. What my job is, is I clean and stock all the surgical labs, and one of them is where they do the cadaver practice. Which is how I got the *ear* and —" Chip stopped midsentence, holding up a hand for silence. "Did you hear that?"

Natalya sniffed the air like a bloodhound, her brow knit anxiously.

"I didn't hear nothing," Stella said. "What-all are you worried about?"

"I don't know, just jumpy, I guess," Chip said. "Thought I heard something out front, probably just a car going by. I wish I could just keep chattin' and all, Stella, but I really think I ought to wrap this up."

But Stella was already headed for the front door, gun in hand. *Todd* was out there. She'd locked the truck, sure, but the idea of a killer roaming around outside — even if it was only a pansy-assed medical student, as Chip said — didn't sit well with her.

She burst out of the house and the profanity died on her lips as she saw that the truck's passenger window had been shattered, the door standing open on a pile of glass that sparkled in the first golden rays of dawn.

CHAPTER EIGHT

"Shit, shit, shit."

Stella cradled her head in her arms on the kitchen table, beyond caring that only moments earlier Natalya had been giving it a final going-over with the Windex, removing any traces of the carving and packaging operation.

Chip had left a little while earlier with the neatly wrapped pieces of Benton Parch loaded in the trunk of his car, a beat-up Hyundai Sonata with rust pocking its lower panels. Chip's plan was to dispose of the dead man in a variety of Dumpsters all over town, and Stella had to admit she couldn't come up with any better ideas. Sure, she could have advised Chip to weight the packages down and toss them in silty farm ponds, or cut holes in drywall or pour concrete in basement floors, but the truth was that all that extra trouble, in Stella's experience, rarely bought you any more peace of mind than just using the Dumpster for its intended use — disposal of rubbish. The odds of the cops finding something you no longer wanted — say, a gun wiped of prints but a little too familiar to the fellow you'd been waving it at earlier in the day — once you'd wiped it clean and wrapped it in aluminum foil and bubble wrap and newspaper and packing tape and stuck it inside a Green Foods bag — were approximately zero. It just went to the dump, like every other crazy thing folks threw out every day.

After Chip left, Stella had made a tour of the neighborhood, armed and angry and desperate to find Todd, but turned up nothing but a few bleary folks staggering out their front doors for a jog or to pick up the paper.

She was disgusted with herself: She'd managed to lose Todd before they'd been in town for even an hour — and he wasn't just lost, he'd been stolen, possibly by a cold-blooded killer . . . although Stella was having trouble figuring out what an inept medical student who hoped to be a plastic surgeon could possibly want with a fourteen-year-old boy. Stella knew she had to call Sherilee, and soon, but she hadn't yet come up with the words to explain how she had lost the boy she'd sworn not to let out of her sight. Given the ear thing, it was unforgivable that she had left him alone at all — severing and slicing and murdering were all cues that great care should have been taken, and yet she'd been careless.

The sight of the body — well, that had been startling, of course. Stella had seen a number of dead bodies in the course of her career, not even counting Ollie. She'd even seen things that were at least as alarming as the sight of half a torso: A mummified woman with her desiccated skin stretched taut over her skeleton had been every bit as gruesome . . . and the unfresh corpse she'd encountered during her most recent case, dead long enough to be showing signs of petrification — if Stella had to choose, she would say that was worse. At least today's fella had been newly deceased — he didn't even have a foul smell yet.

The important thing, though — the only thing that mattered at the moment, especially since Chip was definitely still attached to both his ears and was not, as far as she could tell, missing any of his other parts — was Todd.

"Tell me one more time," she demanded, fixing Natalya with her most focused, get-down-to-business gaze. "Think real, real hard. Who would be in your neighborhood at this time of the morning?"

"Like I am telling, is only newspaper deliver car. Exercise people . . ."

"Tell me about the neighbors."

Natalya shrugged. "I do not know neighbors. I am come here only daytimes until few weeks ago. Never for night, only during day when Benton is at work."

A cheery trill sounded from the direction of the counter, and Natalya fetched a cell phone. She squinted at the display, and her face fell slightly.

"Hello?"

Stella heard a male voice speaking rapidly, but she couldn't make out the words.

"What? What? Who is this?" Natalya demanded, the color draining from her face. The voice on the phone escalated, and suddenly Natalya dropped the phone on the floor and bolted from the room. Instead of running for the door, she raced down the hall toward the back of the house.

"Natalya," Stella called after her, but the woman didn't even slow down. Stella followed her down the hall, but Natalya had a head start; she flung open one of the bedroom doors and started shrieking in Russian in the direction of the bed, where — Stella was startled to see — a figure lay with the covers over its head.

The doorbell rang.

Stella froze, practically paralyzed by the chaos all around her. "I better get that," she said. "Todd's out there —"

"Do not answer door," Natalya pleaded. "Now they are after Luka!"

Stella had no idea who Luka was, but she sprinted back to the front of the house, crouching low in the living room, even though the drapes were drawn tight and no one would be able to see in no matter how hard they peered. She went to the adjoining dining room and parted the drapes just far enough to peep through.

Cops.

There was a cop car parked behind BJ's truck. One uniformed officer was crouched next to the broken window, examining the pile of shattered glass. The other stood at the door, a rotund fellow with his hands clasped behind his back, rocking back on his heels.

Stella's mind raced. She should tell them about Todd, get them to call it in, get them on the job. The dead body was gone; Natalya had disinfected and wiped every square inch of the place; there was little risk of them finding anything amiss inside the house. She raced back to Natalya.

110

"It's the police, Natalya. I've got to let them in."

"You cannot tell them about Benton!" Natalya whispered. She was seated on the bed, patting the figure, which did not appear to have moved underneath the covers. "Please, Stella, do not say a word. Our lives depend on you. We will stay very quiet — do not let them find us here. Get rid of them, you have to."

"Who's that under the —"

"Go!" Natalya hissed, her voice thin with terror and choked-back tears. "If you care for Chip at all, you must not tell!"

More confused than ever, Stella went back to the door, where the knocking had resumed, louder now. Her thoughts raced as she tried to piece together the latest developments, the phone call, Natalya's panic, the mysterious figure on the bed. The sliced and disposed-of ex-husband. Whether she could believe Chip, who she really didn't know very well at all, or Natalya, who she had just met —

There was no time for that sort of conjecture just now. She pasted what she hoped was an innocently inquisitive look on her face and opened the door.

The cop on the steps narrowed his eyes at her as though she were not what he was

111

expecting. "Excuse me, ma'am." He held up a badge, which didn't look a whole lot different from the one Goat carried around. Same basic shield shape, same flip-out leather case. "I'm Officer Petal. Can we come in?"

"Hello," Stella said uncertainly. Should she just tell them about Todd? Convince them to marshal the resources of the entire department, start a full-scale investigation? Except if she did that, the odds of the police discovering wrongdoing in the house — any lingering evidence of the earlier carnage — went up exponentially.

What was worse, Stella knew all too well how these small-town law enforcement teams worked. Prosper was lucky to have the fierce and dedicated Sheriff Goat Jones, who was willing to do whatever it took to get things done, but most little municipalities had to make do with a lot less awesomeness and a lot more bureaucracy and incompetence. Stella didn't doubt that the Smythe PD would get the forces corralled and dispatched — eventually — but first, there would be a whole lot of hemming and hawing and calling up the road and checking in with nearby departments, notifying higher authorities, and calling in specialists. In the time it would take to mount a proper search, Stella could be hitting the streets and hunting down leads herself.

And in situations like this, Stella always bet on herself.

"Is there . . . I mean what are you . . . what's going on?" she hedged.

"Well, we had a call. Concerned neighbor, said he heard a scuffle going on here. Thought he heard a fight going on in the house but looks like what happened here was your truck was broken into. That your truck?"

He pointed at BJ's truck, as though to differentiate it from any number of other pickups and flatbeds and crew cabs lining the street, though the only other vehicle parked along the curb was a grimy old white Ford Probe that had been liberally patched with Bondo.

"Yes," Stella said, thinking fast. She wished she'd taken the time to clean up the glass, make it look like the window was merely rolled down. Except maybe this was better; a break-in might distract the cops from the report of trouble coming from inside the house. "Well, a friend's, anyway. I borrowed it. Oh, no. He is not going to be very happy to see that."

"Did you leave any valuables in sight, maybe on the seat? A purse?"

"No, I —" Stella hesitated, trying to get her rusty, middle-aged brain to catch up with the latest developments, and thinking of her purse, which was indeed inside the house, but which also contained the unregistered and filed-down SIG that she got for a song when an ex-client of hers decided, a few weeks after treating herself to it as a get-out-of-relationship gift, that she'd be even happier with a higher caliber. "Um, I mean, there was . . . sunglasses . . . and a, an iPod."

Officer Petal shook his head as though she were just the dumbest thing he'd come across in weeks. "Ma'am, you can't be leaving stuff out like that. Not in a neighborhood like this. So how about if we come in?"

"Yes, please," Stella said, stepping aside and holding the door open. There wasn't any way around it; refusing would only make her look suspicious. The other cop ambled up the walk and the pair came in and stood in the small living room, sniffing; the potpourri stench that had nearly knocked Stella over when she arrived had now been overtaken by strong notes of Windex and bleach.

"Hello, ma'am, I'm Officer Kruger. It smells . . . clean in here," the second cop said. "This is your home?"

"No, actually, I'm visiting. My nephew. My, uh, stepnephew, actually. I just came up from Missouri for a few days."

"Is he home, ma'am?"

"No, I'm afraid not," Stella said. "He, um, wasn't feeling well. He went out for some of that Theraflu." She had an inspiration. "He's been throwing up something awful. I would've gone to get it for him but I thought I'd stay back here and clean up. I'm telling you, that poor man couldn't quite make it to the commode."

She pointed at the kitchen floor and raised her eyebrow suggestively, as though the vinyl flooring bore traces of vomit rather than a dismembered body. The cops followed her gaze, and Petal, who was closer, stepped back in alarm.

"Is it that flu bug's been going around?"

"Oh, I think it must be," Stella said. "I'm just so afraid I might be catching it myself. I'm feeling a little queasy. They say it's very contagious."

"Well, look here, we can do this outside," he said. "That's where the break-in was, anyway. We'll take down some information, just need to see your ID, and we really ought to speak to your nephew."

"That's fine," Stella agreed, relieved, as

the cops backed toward the door. She got her wallet from the purse, as well as her reading glasses, shoving the little handgun farther down in the depths and pushing the purse to the back of the counter. As she followed them outside, the thin morning sun lighting the dingy neighborhood a soft gold, she saw Chip round the corner, behind the wheel of his beat-up little Hyundai.

For a moment their eyes locked, and Chip slowed and veered as though he were considering a U-turn and a hasty getaway. Stella could see the surprise and consternation in his expression even at twenty yards.

If he turned around now, he would draw the cops' attention, especially since they thought there had been a break-in. Stella waved at him and gave him what she hoped was a reassuring smile, and after a second Chip steered the Hyundai toward his driveway, concentrating fiercely as though he were navigating through close-spaced buoys. The garage door stuttered open, creaking on old tracks.

"Well now, there he is, poor thing," Stella said. "Oh, I don't want to worry him about this."

"Been a few break-ins in this neighborhood," Officer Kruger said. "Won't be a surprise to him, I don't expect."

116

Chip got out of the car and shuffled toward them with an ashen face, a look that certainly could have been the expression of a man who had just come from or was about to resume heaving his guts out.

"Oh, Chip, sugar, I was just telling these officers how *poorly* you're feeling, and how you had to go to the drugstore for something to settle your stomach, and how I wished there was someone else here with us who could go fetch the medicine for you but it's just us. Just the two of us, you and me, no one else here."

Chip regarded her as though she were speaking Sanskrit, and then his confusion slowly cleared. "Oh. Uh. Right."

"Sorry you're not feeling well, sir," Officer Petal said. "If it's all the same to you, I won't shake your hand. Don't need to be catching that bug of yours."

"No, no, that's fine."

"My truck got broke into," Stella said, continuing to enunciate very carefully, as though Chip were a dullard instead of merely out of sorts. "I'm going to fill out these forms the officers have and then I'll be in. Why don't you lie down, Chip, and see if you can catch a little more sleep? After that awful night you've had puking and all."

"I. Um. Okay. Er, thank you, officers,"

117

Chip added, causing Stella to reflect that somewhere between now and the last time she'd shared a holiday table with the young man, he'd acquired a modicum of manners.

CHAPTER NINE

"Just who the hell y'all got locked up in that back room?" Stella demanded as soon as the cops drove away. Chip had closed the door of the bedroom gently after checking on its occupants.

"That's Luka, Natalya's boy. Didn't we tell you about him?"

Stella bit her lip in an effort to keep from snapping at Chip, which in the long run would not be the least bit helpful — but the temptation was just too great. *"No.* You never mentioned, in all the time that I was watching you carve up your girlfriend's husband, that you had a whole other person here who could've come out of that room at any moment and scared the shit out of me, and me with a gun in my hand! *Honestly!"*

"Oh, no, Luka wouldn't've ever got up," Chip said, evidently taken aback by Stella's tone. "Seriously, Stella, that boy'll sleep through anything. Why, sometimes we go

119

on in there, he's got that, that shitty music the kids like blarin' out the speakers, and he's all curled up like a little pup on his bed, and he don't even budge when his mama tries to wake him up so she can get the covers on him. Well, you know how kids are."

"Wait — so let me get this straight. That's Natalya's son?"

"Yeah. Didn't I — ?" Chip smacked his forehead with the back of his hand. "Oh, man, I guess I wasn't thinkin' straight. You know how they're always sayin' don't operate power tools and shit like that when you're sleepy. Only it wasn't like that little job was gonna keep for morning, you know?"

"Natalya's. Son." Stella enunciated very carefully, snapping her fingers in front of Chip's face. "Talk. To. Me."

"Yeah. Yeah." Chip managed to look wounded.

"That's who's back in the spare bedroom?"

"Yeah. Name's Luka."

" 'Cause Natalya took a call on that phone that made her pretty upset, she went racing back there —"

"Oh, that's probably just his friends, up to something. You know how moms get, Luka

120

probably forgot to tell her they got caught breaking curfew or something. That's his phone on the counter, but she answers it sometimes."

"How old *is* he?"

"Seventeen."

Three years older than Todd. Which was interesting. Stella did the math in her head: If Natalya'd had her son at the tender age of twenty, she'd be thirty-seven, nine years older than Chip. "I'm not sayin' I know a whole lot about the mail-order bride business —"

"They don't call it that anymore, Stella, and I sure wouldn't be using that term around Natalya, if you want to stay on her good side."

"I don't care about her fucking good side!" Stella bellowed out her frustration and fear and, while she immediately regretted losing her temper in front of Chip, it did make her feel better, and she considered doing it some more. "I don't care what you call it, and right now I don't even much care who she married or didn't marry or wants to marry, I got a missing boy and a fearsome headache and no idea what to do next 'cept askin' these questions and tryin' to figure out what to do so if you don't mind, Chip, how about you cough up some answers instead of arguin' with me?"

Chip had the good grace to gulp and look both chagrined and worried. "Okay. Okay. Sorry."

"So what I was going to ask was, my impression was that gents generally prefer an unencumbered lady when they send for — er, get hooked up with — erm, uh —"

"Gain an introduction," Chip said helpfully. "That's what they call it, on LovelyBrides-dot-com."

"Yeah, that. I'm just surprised Benton was, you know, happy to get a kid thrown in on the deal when he married Natalya."

"Oh no, well, he wasn't, at first. He just wanted Natalya that much. Back when they were corresponding, she used her wiles and all, her beauty and charm and what have you, but I don't blame her, not one bit. She did it all for Luka, in fact, is the whole reason she married Benton. It wasn't any kind of love match for her, but she was willing to do it to make a better life for her son."

"So she talked Benton into marrying her and bringing her son over here, too?"

"Pretty much, even though it took a lot longer to get Luka here after Benton brought Natalya over. All the legal shit and delays and all. The whole time, though, she made a good-faith effort. That part's true,

Stella, she tried to be a good wife. But Benton was always yellin' at her, ordering her around, wouldn't take her anywhere nice, expected her to stay in his place all day like she was in some sort of prison. And jealous like nobody's business."

"So I imagine things got worse when the boy came over. What with him being a teenager and all."

Chip grimaced. "Yeah, and that's how Natalya ended up finding the strength to walk out on Benton. You know how it is with a mother, she'll just do anything for her kid."

Stella wondered where Chip had picked up that observation, since his own mother had spent most of his growing-up years in a prescription-drug haze, after which they barely ever saw each other until her death a few years ago. Was it wishful thinking? Was his attraction to this older woman based on some sort of twisted-around desire for maternal attention?

"So how are *you* dealing with having Luka around, anyway?"

"He's a nice kid, Stella — he really is."

Something in Chip's tone caught Stella's attention, like he was working hard to convince himself. "Uh-huh. That don't exactly sound like a ringin' endorsement."

"Well, I mean, sure, it's tough on him,

leaving everything he's ever known and coming here where everything's unfamiliar. I'm not saying he's not having a few, you know, adjustment issues, but who wouldn't? And Stella, when you consider what he's seen and endured in his life — sharin' a room with four other kids, all of 'em distant cousins or something, never enough to go around, hand-me-downs and ice on the inside of the windows —"

"Okay, got it, he's fuckin' Oliver Twist —"

"I mean, you're a mother, so you understand."

That shut Stella up, because it was at least a little bit true. What would she do, if Noelle faced hunger, and terrible medical care, and food lines, and those horrible kerchiefs Russian women wore — well, yes, she supposed she'd be willing to make all kind of sacrifices to give her daughter a better life.

"So when do I meet this kid?"

"They'll sleep until noon, I bet," Chip said. "I told Natalya to stay with Luka and get some rest. He's gonna start school in the summer session, but he's only been here a month, so for now he pretty much stays out late and sleeps all day."

"Natalya's okay with that, is she?"

"Aw, she's just happy he's making friends with the local kids."

"The stayin'-out-late kind don't much seem like the sort she might like him to consort with."

"Oh, but it's different in Russia, she was telling me, the kids, they hang out all night. It's no big deal there, and we're trying not to change too much at once for him, we're just going slow, a little at a time."

"Hmmmm." Stella had seen how vigorously and strenuously Sherilee had to object and interfere and threaten and punish to make Todd adhere to his curfew, and had in fact helped her enforce it on more than a few occasions. Chip's plan didn't sound very promising, but she didn't guess she needed to be giving parenting lessons to Chip, especially since it wasn't exactly resolved yet that he was going to need them. "So, seein' as they're not getting up anytime soon, what do you say we go see this crooked doc of yours? Find out if he knows anything about Todd?"

"Med student. He's not a doctor yet. That's a two-year specialty they got there. This guy was still in his first year."

Stella shook her head in disgust. "I wouldn't let anybody near my face with a knife or a giant needle, not unless they'd been trained up good. Not for any amount of money."

"Well, the money was kind of important. Benton was a world-class cheapskate, even after he hit the big time."

This was news to Stella. "What big time?"

"I didn't tell you? That's what makes this so damn ridiculous. Benton is rich."

"If he's so rich, why did he have to go shopping for girls overseas? In my experience a big wallet's all it takes to attract the interest of all kinds of ladies." In fact, Stella had had a few clients who wished they'd taken more time to consider just how enjoyable it was to have a platinum Visa if the price of it was marriage to a man who caused you all manner of suffering when you weren't shopping.

Still, for rich men, it seemed like there was always another gal waiting for the opportunity to drape herself on his arm, no matter how homely, crass, or otherwise unappealing he was. And though Stella figured she hadn't seen Parch at his absolute best the evening before, she'd say he was no worse than average looking.

"He wasn't rich when they got together. That's been pretty recent, ever since he sold the ManTees patent to the LockeCorp folks."

"Man-*what?*"

"ManTees. Support garments for gentlemen? He pretty much invented 'em. Well, him and a friend of his from work."

"I'm sorry, I'm not entirely following. Is this like those wraps for folks that got a hernia?"

"No, Stella, it's like, you know those Spanx they sell for ladies?"

Stella was intimately familiar with the Spanx product line, having relied on it to mold some of her bumpier parts into appealing shapes before all the Bowflex and jogging kicked in and accomplished that naturally. She was still on the curvy end of her recommended weight range, and occasionally a special garment called for a little extra support, which was why she owned a drawer full of midthigh shapers and slimming camis and bodysuits and shaping panties.

Still, she considered this sort of thing the domain of women. "So you're sayin' men put these on so they don't have to suck in their guts?"

"That's the idea. Benton had one on when we, uh, found him, in fact. Benton and his friend, they work for this company that makes specialty fabrics, and they figured out some sort of new kind of stretchy cloth in their free time, and then they had the idea to make it into these T-shirts and underwear and so forth. They had some sort of partnership, and they were putzing around trying to get some local jobber to start producing them. Then I guess they both kind of lost interest, is what Natalya told me, until one day they got contacted by a company who wanted to buy 'em out. So Benton sold the patent, and got a giant check for it. But did that loosen up his purse strings any? No ma'am," Chip said, shaking his head woefully.

"Well, cheap's not usually a good enough reason to get killed over," Stella said. "Come on, let's go see the bastard who you figure did it."

Fortified with a tankard of coffee, Stella and Chip set out to look for Todd. Stella hadn't slept in more than twenty-four hours, but her fears for Todd, combined with all that caffeine, had her feeling wide awake.

Their first stop was the clinic where Chip worked, so he could get the medical student's home address. Since regular classes didn't meet on Saturday, he thought he could get into the lab without running into anyone. Stella drove, and he gave directions through the sleepy town. They passed the same churches, strip malls, and humble neighborhoods that Stella had seen for the first time in the dead of night. Luckily the day was warm and it was no hardship to keep the windows down — or more accurately the *window,* singular, since the one on the passenger side no longer existed.

"This here's the hospital," Chip said, as they arrived in front of an imposing clot of buildings featuring a big square limestone main structure and any number of added-on bits in a variety of architectural styles, making the whole thing look like a LEGO play set designed by a drunk and hostile modernist.

Chip directed Stella around to the back. As she pulled into a parking space, Chip cleared his throat nervously. "Listen, Stella, how about you just wait for me in the truck."

"No thanks. I'm more of a hands-on type when I'm working."

"I get that, but — look, I got to prepare you a little. It's kind of hard on folks that haven't seen this sort of environment before."

"You told me you take care of the labs, right? Trust me, sugar, I'm not one to be put off by the sight of a mop or a bucket."

"Well see, Stella, ever since I got promoted I got some more . . . specialized type duties. I had to take a training course. They even sent me down to Madison for a couple of days, put us up in a Holiday Inn and all, had to learn all kinds of shit and pass the certification tests. What it is is, nowadays you got your infectious disease concerns, your fears about bacteria outbreaks, your resistant microbes, you can't have just a regular Class One custodian in there. Not to mention all the red tape with the disposal. You need a specialist."

"So let me get this straight, you're cleaning up after a bunch of med students and all the messes they make with their lab projects."

"Yeah . . . but Stella, they work on actual *cases*."

"So what do they do, get some volunteer in there, knock 'em out and everyone stands around the table in their white gowns and shit taking notes while the professor does a nip and a tuck?"

Chip pursed his lips. "Uh . . . yeah. Something like that. But it'd just be easier if you'd stay here."

"Look, just trust me, okay? I'm not going to faint on you or anything."

Chip sighed heavily as he led the way to a homely-looking concrete structure attached to the backside of the University Hospital like a barnacle. No-nonsense metal letters screwed into the sides of the building spelled out BOBERG CLINIC.

"They're doing a special weekend seminar today. The lab manager probably already has it set up. Only this isn't strictly kosher, me bringing you here, so if we see anyone, let me do the talking, okay?"

Chip took a heavy set of keys from his pocket and unlocked the door. Inside, the building was cool and chemically smelling, with an odor somewhere between a dentist office and the Ace garden center. A neat glassed-in announcement board featured want ads for house sitters, roommates, lost puppies, yoga classes, massage therapy. They passed a nook housing a row of glowing vending machines.

Chip paused in front of a wide set of doors, searching his large key ring for the right key. "Now like I said, Stella, you might want to, like, brace yourself a little here. You haven't seen —"

"Whyn't you let me worry about what I've seen and not seen, Chip," Stella said gently. "I've been around things you can't even imagine. Besides, I'm going to be fifty-one to— uh, soon."

Tomorrow. She was going to be fifty-one years old tomorrow, and rather than spending it at home with Noelle and her beauty

131

treatments, and a special lunch with Chrissy at the China Paradise followed by a gallon of pistachio ice cream, and possibly even a little further exploration into BJ's amorous intentions, she was going to be stuck up here in the middle of Wisconsin. Even if the door opened to reveal not just Todd but Benton's killer holding an I DID IT sign, there was no way she could turn around and make the drive all the way home today, not without some sleep.

So, best case scenario, she'd spend her birthday driving home with a pain-in-the-ass teenage copilot. No cake, no gifts, no birthday nooky — only a sore ass from sitting in the driver's seat, all swollen up from the road food and coffee.

Worst case . . . well, the worst case was so much worse. She'd tracked down a kidnapped child once before, when the mob had snatched up Chrissy's son, Tucker, and she'd had to go down to the shore of the Lake of the Ozarks and fight off a slew of Kansas City mobsters to get the little boy back. But in that case the abductors wanted the child for themselves, and he was an adorable flaxen-haired blue-eyed angel of a baby, too. Todd was none of those things — he was a foul-mouthed noxious-smelling slouch-spined big-footed clumsy oaf of a teenager who made about as good a first impression as a mutt who's been rolling in roadkill. She adored the boy as though he were her own, but that had been after several years of him growing on her. His kidnappers didn't have that advantage, and if they didn't much care for his sass mouth and defiant attitude, well, what then?

"It's just that most people don't realize —" Chip tried again, hanging on to the door and blocking the view of the room inside with his body.

"I *said* I'm fine," Stella said, a little more testily than necessary, and pushed past him.

And stopped dead in her tracks.

Inside the room were half a dozen long tables, about the size of the buffet tables on which they served Sunday doughnuts at Calvary United Methodist, but a little sturdier looking, with sinks at either end and cabinets below and stools tucked neatly underneath. On top of the tables' pristine white surfaces were aluminum trays like you might use to cook lasagna, lined up true and square, four to a table.

Nestled on top of the trays were human heads.

"Oh holy fucking mother of . . ." Stella stammered, feeling her stomach pitch and roll, bile burbling up and threatening to send her heaving into the aisles between the neat rows. "Those are . . . oh my God . . ."

"They're sterile," Chip said hastily, "and they came here voluntarily. These are all voluntary donors, Stella, and it's all very regulated."

"I, uhhh . . ." Stella swallowed hard, and then swallowed again, gripping Chip's arm tightly to ward off the dead faint that was threatening to overcome her. He wrapped an arm around her, clucking softly to himself; perhaps he had a right to be a little peeved at her, since she had refused to listen to his warnings.

The heads, which might well have been every bit as regulated as Chip said, ranged from an odd and not very lifelike shade of grayish-pale to various tints of unnatural brown — and they stared back at her with expressions that ranged from boredom to disappointment to, in one case, what appeared to be eager anticipation, as though the gentleman couldn't wait to experience the procedure for which he'd been brought here. Any spine bones or nerve endings or blood vessels or what have you were tucked discreetly out of the way. Their hair was uniformly short, buzzed military style, leading Stella to suspect that they'd received a postmortem trim in preparation for their next adventure, one in which efficiency was valued over fashion. After all, when one was studying the finer points of face renovation, it was probably pretty important not to have hair hanging in front of one's canvas, so to speak.

"What are they about to do to these, anyway?"

Chip went to the instructor desk in front and consulted a clipboard. "Blepharo-plasty," he said. "Eye lifts. 'Course, that's just to start. After that they'll be doing sub-periosteal lifts. Those go pretty deep, so that'll pretty much take care of this bunch."

"They do more than one . . . thing to them?"

"Oh yeah, you don't want to waste a chance like this. By the time they're done, these heads will have had the works. Which is fine since they go from here to incinera-tion."

Realization dawned on Stella. "These heads get incinerated?"

"Well, yeah, I mean it's sterile and you can't beat it for mass reduction, plus there's a shitload of regulation on infectious waste —"

"No, what I mean is, if you're the one who bags them up for transport to the cremato-rium or whatever . . . well, I suppose it woulda been easy as pie for you to grab you an ear offa one of them. What'd you do, wait until there was an ear that looked like yours, slice it off with a pocketknife?"

Chip had the good grace to blush. "It wasn't like that, Stella," he said. "They were learning otoplasty — that's ear pinning — and this one went kind of wrong. The kid went way too far with the cartilage scoring. That ear was barely attached by the time he was done. It wasn't any big deal for me to take it the rest of the way off."

"Weren't you worried that it wouldn't match?"

"An ear's an ear, Stella, especially when it's dried out some. Plus I pierced it and put my old earrings in, which wasn't any big deal because Natalya's been after me to get rid of them anyway. That's all Dad and Gracellen noticed, I bet, was my earrings, especially since the tissues were probably starting to break down something serious by the time the box got there."

"I'da known," Stella said, with conviction. "If it was my Noelle. I'd know her ear anywhere."

How many times had she touched her daughter's ear, traced its shell-like edges with a fingertip, counting the freckles, wiping away baby shampoo, cleaning gently with a Q-tip? Dabbing the lobes with rubbing alcohol after taking Noelle to get them pierced on her twelfth birthday? Stella had held Noelle's hand tightly in the little shop in the mall and squeezed her own eyes shut when the gal positioned the needle gun. She'd given Noelle her first pair of diamond earrings, tiny little sparklers for a high school graduation gift — she'd saved up the extra grocery money for over six months for those, and Noelle still wore them.

"You're a *mom,* though," Chip said. "I know Dad loves me and all, but he wasn't around much when I was a kid, and then when we started seeing each other more, it's not like he was staring in my ears much. Way it worked, Mom would have me all clean and my clothes washed and my stuff packed when Dad picked me up for a weekend, and then by the time I went back I was a mess, since I usually just wore whatever was on top of my suitcase the whole weekend. Heck, half the time Dad forgot to make me take a bath."

"Oh, Chip," Stella said, suddenly sorry she'd mentioned it. "That must have been hard."

Chip shrugged. "It got better when Dad married Gracellen, anyway," he said. "She kind of took over that part. She even used to take me shopping and all, helped me out with my school projects . . . came to my soccer games."

Stella made a mental note to appreciate her sister more the next time she saw her. She knew Gracellen loved Chip but had no idea she'd been so involved in his life — more so than Chess had been, it seemed. Her affection for the boy grew, thinking of all his tender feelings that had gone unnoticed and trampled.

Chip seemed to be thinking along the same lines, because he took a deep breath and swiped at his eyes. "Hey, let me get what I need and we can get out of here."

He went to the computer at the front of the class and poked around for a few minutes. Stella sat up front next to him in a chair she dragged around from behind the tables, and faced the screen so she wouldn't have to look at the staring heads, which were a sight she didn't reckon she'd be getting used to anytime soon.

While Chip muttered and tapped, she thought about what he'd been like as a little guy, the first time she'd met him. He'd been seven then, a wiry thing, with big dark eyes and long fringy lashes, his olive skin smooth and perfect, not yet afflicted with the teenage acne that would come later. His hair was long, with a little tail that came halfway down his back. When Gracellen had explained to Stella that his mother had a fondness for prescription drugs that took up all her free time and some of the time that was supposed to be used on parenting as well, his general state of neglect made a little more sense — the too-small sweater and too-short pants, the shaggy haircut.

Mostly, little Chip had been quiet at the Thanksgiving table — taking occasional bites of his food until after a while he appeared to simply run out of steam, after which he just sat and stared at his plate. Chess had tried to cajole him into talking, and Chester Senior, who even then was hard of hearing, had boomed questions at him across the table and then yelled at him to speak up. For her part, Gracellen had piled his plate high with the best slice of turkey, the homemade relish, potatoes with butter and gravy — anything she could think of to win his favor. Chip had been unreachable back then, though, a lonely, confused little boy who barely recognized the man who showed a sudden and unprecedented interest in being his father.

"Hah, got it," he muttered now, clicking the mouse a couple of times and then snapping off the computer. "It's only a couple miles from here. If we're lucky, he'll be home, getting ready for class. Only, if he really took your boy, I'm not sure how you're gonna get him to answer the door."

"You forget," Stella said grimly, taking a deep breath and heaving herself off the stool. "You're working with a pro now."

CHAPTER TEN

As they retraced their steps to the car, Stella noticed a few sleepy-looking folks wandering into the building, suggesting it must be close to class time. These future plastic surgeons sure weren't what Stella expected. Her experience with practitioners of the discipline was limited to the improbably hot and well-dressed guys on *Nip/Tuck,* but these students were dressed in jeans and T-shirts, athletic wear and sneakers. Some looked even younger than Noelle and Chrissy; others were a bit longer in the tooth. None of them gave Chip and Stella any notice as they wove their way through the halls.

Stella lowered her voice while she walked. "Look here," she said carefully. "You know some things about me now that Gracellen don't even know, and I'd kind of like to keep it that way."

"You mean like the fact that you carry a gun and all?"

"Well, sure, that, for a start. But there's a little more to it. I, uh . . . well, I have a friend in law enforcement. A good friend, really, and he's let me do the citizen's police academy kind of on a, what do you call it, like an unofficial basis."

"What, you mean you do ride-arounds and stuff?"

"Kind of," Stella hedged, "and, you know, target practice and some, well, martial arts training, self-defense, that kind of thing."

It was true that she'd taken up studying martial arts, though it didn't come naturally to her. The whole focus on serenity, the centering and breathing and focusing, wasn't really in line with the middle-aged irritability she carried around.

Still, she needed to get the point across to Chip that if they happened to stumble into any dangerous situations, she was probably a better bet than he was, and he needed to set aside any notions of gallantry he might be burdened with and get out of her way.

"Well, that's great, Auntie Stella," Chip said, distracted, as they reached the truck.

"What I'm trying to say is, seeing as we don't have a lot of time here and we need to get some information out of this guy as quickly and efficiently as we can, how about if you let me take the lead?"

Chip regarded her doubtfully. "I don't know, Stella. I mean it's cool and all that you're learning new things and staying in shape, but you *are,* like, Gracellen's age and, no offense, if things get weird in there, if he doesn't feel like talking, well, I'm not sure you really want to be in a situation where a big guy — I mean, Stella, he's six feet easy — if you want to be going up against that."

Stella took a breath and held it. She got herself underestimated every day, and it never failed to irritate her, but she tried to keep in mind that this was a simple case of Chip not having all the facts.

It would be easier to show him, though, than to try to convince him.

"Tell you what," she said, "how about I give it a shot when we get there. If it looks like I can't handle him, why, there you are to back me up. Deal?"

Chip hesitated, but in the end his basic good manners got the best of him. "Deal," he said, and Stella nodded with satisfaction and blew past the sleepy streets of Smythe for the third time in twelve hours.

"Let's go slow here, Chip," Stella suggested when they got to the wood-sided house, a holdover from the seventies when "Aspen

143

style" meant nailing cedar boards at an angle and wearing boots made out of yak. It and a couple dozen similar houses were tucked into a neighborhood thick with tall evergreens.

She parked behind a slick little black SUV that sat at a rakish angle in the drive leading up to the house. Bumper stickers plastered to the back declared FRIENDS DON'T LET FRIENDS EAT FARMED SALMON and EARTH DOES NOT BELONG TO US, WE BELONG TO EARTH.

"These med students," Stella asked, curious. "They get paid while they're still in the practicing stages?"

Chip shrugged. "I don't think so. Not much, anyway. Most of 'em live in dumps here and there, share apartments, rent rooms in houses, that sort of thing. I guess Doug is kind of the exception."

"Why don't you hang here a minute," Stella said. "Let me just check out the back."

"Check out the who?"

"You know, figure out what-all options this guy has for getting away in a hurry, if he has in mind to run out on us."

"This one of your citizen police academy things?" Chip asked with a roll of his eyes.

Stella gritted her teeth as she jogged

around the back. The house had a nice covered cedar patio that overlooked a wooded area, and she had to admit that the architecture, dated though it was, had a ski lodge sort of appeal. A bicycle hung from a complicated hook arrangement bolted to the overhang, and a wheeled device leaned against the wall, about twice as long as a skateboard and a bit wider, tapered at one end. She would have guessed it belonged to a neighborhood kid except that she'd seen enough of these types hanging around the state college at Harrisonville to know better: She'd lay odds that this was the latest thing in transporting oneself around campus, made with only the most sustainable, environment-friendliest, expensive materials and technology available on the market.

Why, the entire place looked like a page from a catalog Noelle got in the mail, where you could pay five times as much for a jacket made out of soda bottles as you could for the same thing at Walmart, except for a little logo on the front so everyone would know you didn't bust up a nest of endangered ducks or chop down any old-growth forests in the process. There wasn't a huge earth muffin crowd in Prosper yet, but in addition to the ones in Harrisonville, Stella had noticed a nest of them over in Coffey, and whenever business took Stella up to Independence, it seemed like the ground was thick with 'em.

It wasn't that Stella had anything against the eco-happy crowd. Hell, she dutifully sorted her recycling and bought the organic stuff if it was on sale and used eggshells and Ivory dish soap to keep the pests under control instead of the poison in the cans. She hoped as much as anyone to leave a tidy, healthy planet for any grandchildren she might one day have. Only, the way she saw it there were a number of holes in the logic spouted by some among the earth-saving crew. For instance, she thought as she peered in the back window of the house into the kitchen and noticed an expensive-looking canvas jacket slung over a chair and a couple of pairs of shoes — the kind made out of colorful woven straps and cork and who knows what else and cost more than an entire closet full of Naturalizer sandals — if they slowed down on the purchasing of rafts of hippie fashions and accessories and instead wore the perfectly good clothes they bought a few years ago, that would be a whole lot of manufacturing power that could be saved. Even when you made shirts out of hemp or alfalfa or old tires or what-ever, you had to figure there was a factory somewhere using up energy and belching out manufacturing by-products, and according to Stella's math that was still a check in the negative column even if every person who drew their paycheck at the factory planted a tree on their way home and composted their nail clippings and ate raw wheat berries for lunch.

And big toy skateboards for grown-ups? Stella shook her head with disgust.

Back in front of the house, Chip was drumming his fingers impatiently on the little hybrid SUV's hood. Stella tutted under her breath. Noelle had recently bought a hybrid, but only because she'd driven her prior car into the ground. Yuppie folks who protested rain-forest butchering and white flour but drove a brand-new car every few years — Stella wouldn't mind giving them a piece of her mind either.

"You know, Chip, down in Cuba they're still driving cars made before you were born."

Chip blinked, confused. "Uh . . ."

"Yeah, no one's bought a new car there in like forty years. They make parts out of melted beer cans and old radio components and stuff and they keep that fleet running — I saw a show about it on TV. You ever think about how much shit we could keep

147

out of the landfills if we just fixed it now and then and kept on using it?"

"How does . . ."

"Like for instance, the stove in my house used to be my mom's. It was built in 1959 and it works fine, but you go on over to the Home Depot and they got them four-thousand-dollar ranges all lined up and none of 'em with more than a year or two warranty. Then when they break they tell you it's gonna be cheaper to get a new one than fix the one you have. That make sense to you?"

"But what . . ."

"Never mind. Just thinking out loud. Hang on, give me a sec here."

Stella reached into the backseat and grabbed a couple of her smaller Tupperware containers, the contents clanking around inside. She tucked them into a mesh bag she'd lifted from the Green Foods up in Independence for that purpose — yet another brilliant idea from the eco-nuts, manufacture bags to haul groceries around in as though every household in America didn't already have half a dozen gym bags and sewing totes and advertising freebies lying around. Then she and Chip tromped up to the door, not bothering with stealth.

Within moments of her knocking, the

door opened and a bleary-eyed, shaggy-haired, handsome young man stood blinking in the sun, pulling a T-shirt over his bare chest. He was wearing what appeared to be ladies' drawstring pants in a shade somewhere between taupe and brown. Around his wrist he wore what looked like a friendship bracelet made by a Girl Scout who'd run out of ribbon and used her dad's boot laces and dental floss instead.

"Hey," he said, covering up a yawn. "Good morning. What can I do for you?"

"I was just wondering if we could have a few minutes of your time," Stella said. "I'm Dora Whitney and this is my associate, Caleb Gomez. We're speaking with people who have supported sustainability initiatives in the past, about a new threat to the fragile ecosystem of, uh, midsouthern Wisconsin."

"Um, sure . . ." Doug said, rooting around in the sagging pocket of his lady-pants and digging out an iPhone. He thumbed it and squinted at the display. "Yeah, I got a few minutes before I need to get motivated. Come on in, I just put on some coffee. It's Nicaraguan fair trade."

Stella winked at Chip, who looked like he was about to object, and followed Doug into the house, through a nicely furnished living room into the kitchen. The coffee smelled

149

wonderful, so it was a great disappointment to see that there was very little of it, slowly dripping through what looked like a science lab experiment beaker.

"It's French press," Doug said, getting three dainty cups down from a cabinet. Stella noted to herself that all her favorite men — her dad when he was alive, Goat, BJ, Jelloman — drank coffee out of big mugs and didn't stint. *Man* mugs, you might say.

"Nice dishwasher," she said.

"Oh yeah, it's a Miele. Crazy good, the lowest water usage you can get. So anyway, what have you guys got?"

"It's the green-bellied saw beetle," Stella said. "Practically extinct in this county. Let me just . . ."

She opened her Tupperware and removed a couple of items. "I can do a simple re-creation for you of the, um, effects on the, er, strata of sustainability. It's the best way to show it. I mean, so dramatic. Say that your floor — what is this, anyway?" she asked, noting the unusual grain of the polished floor.

"Oh, that's bamboo! Totally sustainable. I had the tile ripped out, it was like this seventies gold color? Really wrong, man."

"Uh-huh. Well, anyway, say that the floor

is, you know, the planetary mantle."

She ignored Chip, who was looking at her as though she were deranged, and knelt down on the floor.

"Here, come on down with me."

Doug obliged, evidently without a second thought. Hard to fault the boy for his enthusiasm or good nature.

"Now right here in the middle of the table leg, say that's the loam. That's where the green-eyed beetle nests, and —"

"Bellied," Doug said. "Didn't you say, green-*bellied* beetle?"

Stella blinked. "Yes. Yes! The thing is, that whole damn beetle is green. Everything, from the little feelers to the wings to the tail, all green. Part of our research is into its, uh, pigmentation. But anyway, so here it is nesting in its loam . . ." She waved her hands at chest level and then wrapped them around the brace attaching the leg to the tabletop. "And then the beetle rises up on the cottonwood shrub, to a branch. Here, put your hands on the branch there . . ."

To her amusement, Doug didn't hesitate but wrapped his hands — nice ones, strong and long-fingered and sprouting a bit of nice dark hair at the knuckles, which went a long way toward countering the emasculating effects of his unfortunate pants —

151

around the brace.

"Yeah, like that. And then comes the threat, the thing we are here to talk to you about today, the completely terrible . . ."

While she rambled, she opened the zip cuffs and then slipped them quickly onto Doug's wrists, looping them through the triangular space made by the brace. In a matter of seconds he was shackled to the table.

"There," Stella said cheerfully. "Now excuse me, if you don't mind — when I stand up these here knees of mine are liable to make a variety of unwholesome sounds, but that's just middle age for you. Which I guess you know all about, being a man of medicine and all."

She stood in stages, crackling and popping. A series of squats that she had added into her cardio regimen had given her some temporary soreness while her muscles registered their surprise and irritation over the novel moves.

"I don't get it, man," Doug said, as Stella sat down in the chair and snapped the top back on her Tupperware. In the other box she had a small handheld battery-powered prod and a nice set of Crown chisels, but she was hoping that she wouldn't need them today. Instead, she reached in the purse for her SIG and laid it on the table. No need to go waving it around just yet — she was guessing that just the *suggestion* of violence would be enough to put this tree hugger into a state of cooperation.

To her mild disappointment, he merely regarded her with wounded surprise.

"Aw, man, you're here to *rob* me? Not cool. Not cool at all."

"No, Doug, we're not here to rob you," Stella said. "You ain't really got anything I need. I mean, I'm sure you get a ton of use out of that six-burner stove of yours, cooking up your barley and dandelion greens and all, but I don't really have room for it. Plus I already got a friend with a skateboard, which I imagine he'd lend me anytime I want."

"You don't even recognize me, do you?" Chip asked, with an aggrieved note in his voice. "I'm the dude that takes care of the labs. I've seen you like, half a dozen times."

Stella turned to Chip impatiently. "You might want to stop there," she said. "Usually in these circumstances we try to limit what-all we tell the person we've just tied up about our*selves.*"

"And you," Chip said severely. "I think you've been holding out on me, Aunt Stella. I don't believe most ladies your age tote handcuffs around with them in the car. Does Gracellen know about this?"

Stella paused and fixed Chip with a baleful glare. "Let's get one thing straight here right now, Chip. Your stepmom sent me up here to help you, and that's what I aim to do. But I'm not about to have an ex-con gambler who I've known since you had braces and that unfortunate mullet passing judgment on *me*. Yes, there are . . . things . . . that I do that my sister knows nothing about, and if you want my help — and lemme tell you, from what I seen here the answer to that is a pretty clear 'yes ma'am' 'cause it don't appear you and Natalya got the juice to do much of anything 'cept fuck things up more than they already were — so anyway, if you want my help, you keep your opinions to yourself and you keep everything you see — every word I say, every move I make — in the vault. As in, secrets that *die* with you."

She had been getting more and more worked up while delivering this impassioned speech. Her face was warm, and little dots of sweat had popped out along her forehead. Heck, it was more effort to get Chip up to speed than it had been to subdue the eco-cowboy cowering on the floor.

"Here's what we're gonna do now," Stella

said to Doug, after taking a calming breath or two. "Chip and I are going to ask you some questions. You answer straight the first time, it stops there. You give me any shit, or give me cause to think you're lyin', I'm gonna make you regret it. And let me add just one more thing. You look at me, you see a nice middle-aged lady with a few pounds to lose, right?"

Doug gave her a goggle-eyed stare that took in her elastic-waist yoga pants, her comfy sandals with the gel soles, and her easy-care faux-wrap top with the decorative stitching around the neckline. He took a closer look at her face, which Stella knew was not at its finest, since she hadn't managed anything more than a quick splash with cold water in Chip and Natalya's bathroom, and a swipe of lip gloss.

He grunted in affirmation.

"Well, that's what I am, I guess — but there's a little more to me than that. I've got like a graduate degree in hurtin' people. I know all about pain and how to lay it on folks who deserve it, and I know how to do it so's it don't leave any evidence."

Doug's eyes widened with doubt, but he stayed scared looking.

"Great. So let's get started, okay? Chip, you just jump on in if you got something extra to say. And pour me a cup a that coffee, will ya?"

Stella took care of the basics first, more from curiosity than any particular bearing on the case. She learned that Doug was twenty-eight, that he'd grown up in Orange County and taken a year off after graduating from UCLA to backpack all over Nepal and Tibet and some other places she'd never even heard of, before entering medical school. He was single, and there were a couple of ladies he saw from time to time.

"They know about each other?" Stella asked.

"They — my schedule — I mean, everyone's just keeping it loose," Doug stammered. "I'm at the library around the clock anyway."

When you aren't riding that two-thousand-dollar bike around, Stella thought darkly.

"No time for a job, then."

Doug looked wounded. "The study of medicine *is* my job. Do you have any idea of the hours that we —"

"So besides your basic med student allowance, you might say money's tight. Got a steady check coming in from home?"

Doug reddened. "I don't see how that's any of your business. I mean, you come in my house, you pretend you're here for a good cause . . ."

His voice petered out as Stella rooted around in the container and took out a small pair of needle-nose pliers and tested the tips with a flick of a fingernail, holding them up to the light and squinting at them. "Oh, it does pay to buy the very best tools you can afford," she interrupted. "My dad taught me that."

There was a long silence while Stella waited for her performance to sink in. When Doug gulped and went a shade paler, Stella set the pliers on the table.

"Those are more of what you might call a novelty than anything else. Good for detail work, I guess, but I got a lot more serious equipment out in the truck. So let's try again. Money from home?"

"Yes," Doug said. "Like just about every other intern I know, I get a little bit of help from home."

"But I'm guessing it's not enough to cover your, uh, expenses. Am I right? What'd these renovations set you back, anyway? I mean, I've seen bamboo growing along the edge of the creek for free, but I wouldn't know how to cut it down and install it myself, I reckon that takes a specialist. And all these fancy appliances, and the toys on your back porch

— that's got to add up."

Doug frowned, his bottom lip trembling.

"Look, Doug, pal, I could take all day making you cough up the details, but I'm on a schedule here, so let's cut to the chase. You're broke, you're on the lookout for an opportunity to make some cash. Some of your friends are no doubt selling scrips on the side" — Stella had learned about that gig firsthand when she tangled with a murdering pill-vending crooked doc last fall — "but a nice young man like you, I don't see you going that route. 'Cause you're principled. I can see you care deeply about the world, about people, right? So when a fella comes along offering to pay you to do exactly what you're supposed to be learning anyway, hands you an opportunity to improve your handiwork on a live patient rather than just a head on a tray — why, that had to be an easy jump, right? I mean, who could blame you for taking a short view on the risks and returns. It's just a few shots here and there. And word of mouth, maybe you were banking on this lady telling her friends and soon you'd have a whole party circuit going like they do in the big city, ladies drinking chardonnay and writing checks while the handsome doctor lines them up for a little light work in the hostess's kitchen."

Doug's mouth had fallen open, and real fear had replaced his indignant expression.

"Only . . . when things go a little sideways, when a patient has an unfortunate reaction, the kind of thing you might have been able to prevent if you'd done everything the way the *real* doctors do it — when she ends up puffed up like a trout who had a stroke — sorry, Chip — that little sideline gets shut down fast. Am I right?'

Doug didn't respond, but Chip's face darkened with anger and he looked like he was about to jump in with comments and suggestions of his own. Stella rolled right over him — second opinions weren't help-ful in situations like this.

"And you suck it up and decide you'll have to go back to the bank of Mom and Dad, like you should've in the first place, only unbeknownst to you, the gentleman who retained your services is one very, very unsatisfied customer. Benton Parch, you remember him?"

"I — I never knew his name," Doug said. "It was a cash transaction."

"Cash — like, he was wanting his cash back, right? How much did you stick him for, anyway?"

"Look, I *told* him I'd get it for him, if he'd

just be reasonable, but he didn't want to wait, and he wanted me to pay extra. Like, *way* extra. Called it punitive damages. I mean, nobody's sorrier than me about what happened to, to the lady, but it might — I mean, it probably, in a few months that swelling's going to take care of itself and that texture's going to improve and I don't see where, I mean where am I going to get my hands on fifteen thousand dollars?"

"Where, indeed," Stella said drily, letting her gaze travel from the expensive appliances to the man's shoes, which she would bet cost more than all of hers put together.

"I *know,* right?"

"So he starts talking about going to the authorities. About *exposing* you. And then what's going to happen — you'll be tossed out of the program in a heartbeat, I imagine. Far as I know, doctors aren't supposed to start getting crooked until they've been in the business for a while."

Doug shook his head. "He never said — he only wanted his money. I said I'd try to get it, I *am* getting it, it's just . . . it's taking longer than I thought. I have to, uh, my dad, he's gonna come around, I just have to explain it in a way he can understand."

"Your dad won't give you the money, is that it?" Stella demanded. "He's tired of buying skateboards and gourmet coffee for his grown son, figures it's time you learn a lesson?"

"Look, if this, this guy *Parch* sent you, you tell him I'm good for it. End of the week, I know I can have the money wired by then. Or look, I can send along collateral. I got stuff — my watch, that's worth almost what I owe him. Hell, I'll give you the keys to my car."

"Nice try," Stella said. "You're a first-rate actor, Doug. Maybe you should consider that line of work, in fact, seein' as you're kind of a butterfingers in the operating room. Only you and I both know that Benton isn't waiting around to get his money back anymore. You took care of that, didn't you?"

"I don't know what you're talking about," Doug wailed.

"Luckily, I know just how to make sure," Stella said softly. "Chip, honey, I need you to go wait in the truck."

Chip needed a little convincing before he agreed to leave them alone, but once he did, it didn't take too long for Stella to get what she needed out of the young man on the floor. A few rounds with a basic C-clamp and a little horse hair crop led her to believe that he really *hadn't* done anything to

Benton, who he truly did intend to re-imburse.

Stella had become a sort of truth machine, more reliable than any lie detector or serum that she was aware of, and she'd refined her art to the point that she was a master of the light touch. She did only what was needed and no more, so that when she was finished with Doug he was a blubbering, babbling, pants-wetting shadow of his former self, but his injuries were nothing that a couple of days on the couch with a gallon of ice cream wouldn't fix.

Not only had he not taken Todd, however, he had never been to Chip's house, didn't even know where it was.

"I'm sorry this was a dead end," Stella said tightly, as she snipped his restraints and packed up her supplies. "Sorrier than you know. Now, you remember what I told you? Tell me all four things."

"I'll never discuss what happened here with anyone as long as I live," Doug snuffled, rubbing his wrists and wiping his nose on the shoulder of his T-shirt.

"That's good," Stella said. "What else?"

"No more practicing on people until I have my degree."

"And?"

"If I come upon any information about

Benton Parch or Todd Groffe, even if it seems unimportant to me, I will call you immediately and I won't discuss it with anyone else."

"Excellent! One more, Junior, and we can call it a day."

Doug hesitated, staring at the table and hanging his head.

"Come on, Doug," Stella cajoled gently, snapping the tops on her Tupperware and slipping her gun in her purse. "What's the last thing?"

"I'm gonna give away these pants and buy a pair of Dockers," he said miserably.

CHAPTER ELEVEN

Stella was backing out of the driveway when her phone rang. She stopped halfway into the street and got her phone out and squinted at the tiny numerals.

"It's a 715 area code," she muttered. "Who the hell is that?"

"Lemme see," Chip said, taking the phone from her. "Smythe is 715, but . . . nope, I don't recognize the number."

"Who'd be calling me from around here . . . tell you what, go ahead and answer for me, tell 'em I'm not here," Stella said. It was probably connected with the fake break-in, someone from the police department following up on the report, and Stella was feeling worn out from the interrogation and exhausted from a lack of sleep and dispirited enough about the state of affairs that she didn't feel up for a lot more creative lying at the moment.

"Hello?"

Stella could hear a voice, loud and unhappy from the sound of it, but couldn't make out any words. "Yeah, who? Oh? Oh!" Chip held the phone away from his ear in a state of great excitement. "It's Todd, Stella, it's your boy Todd!"

Stella screeched the truck to a halt, the sensitive brakes locking and throwing her and Chip against their shoulder restraints, and snatched the phone.

"Todd? Todd, is that you?" Her heart felt like it was going to clang out of her chest, and she gripped the steering wheel so hard that pains shot up into her wrist. *Please please please please please Big Guy,* Stella prayed, the prayer of someone who'd trade in every good moment she ever had for things to turn out right this one time.

"Stella, you got any idea how long I been hikin' and it turns out they sent me in the wrong *direction?*" Todd, to Stella's astonished relief, sounded irritable and frustrated but not the least bit maltreated or abused.

"Where are you?" she demanded shrilly.

Todd's voice took on a muffled tone as he spoke to someone away from the phone. "Where'd you say I am again exactly?"

"Is that them? Is that the people that took you? Put them on!" Stella yelled. "Todd! Todd! Listen to me, put them on!"

A car passing in the other direction tapped the horn and gave Stella a what-the-fuck sort of gesture. She was vaguely aware of the fact that the truck was taking up more than one lane of traffic, and at an improper angle to boot.

"Ma'am?" a polite, female, soft-spoken voice said.

"What have you done to the boy?" Stella bellowed, almost launching herself out of the seat with anxiety.

There was a pause, in which Stella could hear Todd grumbling in the background, and then the voice said, in somewhat aggrieved tones, "Ma'am, I just found your boy in my garage about fifteen minutes ago, getting himself a root beer from the refrigerator. Wess, that's my husband, he had the garage door up because he's got the lawn mower out. I was fixing to drive into town and, why, there he was, your young man."

"Wait," Stella said. The tension had taken up residence in her forehead, splitting pains of postadrenaline agony spiking down behind her eyeballs. Todd, it seemed, was safe, so there was nowhere for all that pent-up terror on his behalf to go. "Todd's fine, you're telling me he's not hurt, he's alone, there's no, like, other people, other kidnappers, with him?"

"Why no, ma'am, he didn't mention any kidnappers. He just said he got dropped off and he's been walking. Apparently he took a wrong turn because we're about eleven miles out of Smythe down Chokeberry Road."

Stella let a moment pass as she felt the blood rush to her face. "I, uh, am very, very sorry about the way I spoke a moment ago. It is not my habit — you see, I was just so very worried — look, can I come and get him?"

"Certainly," the lady said, with no hesitation at all, leading Stella to imagine that she might be eager to be shut of her newfound acquaintance.

Emily Allgaier was a proper lady, however, endowed with enough old-fashioned courtesy that she couldn't bring herself to let Todd go without offering everyone a glass of tea and a slice of blueberry buckle.

"That was delicious, Mrs. Allgaier," Todd called as he leaned out of the window of the truck, waving good-bye. "Thank you!"

"Nice manners," Stella said dryly, adding her own little wave and then accelerating to a good clip. Grateful as she was to the silver-haired Good Samaritan for delivering Todd back to her, the whole episode had left a hollow taste in her mouth, the result of terror and self-recrimination and an uncomfortably close brush with all the ways the situation could have gone terribly wrong. Todd was tired and cranky and dusty but otherwise unharmed, and while he swore he'd walked twenty miles since his captors released him on an unpopulated stretch of farm road earlier in the morning, Stella figured it was more like five. "Now you tell me everything."

She'd gotten only a few details out of him, after the initial crushing hug in Mrs. Allgaier's living room, when Stella had surprised herself by tearing up a little. Since she didn't think it was wise to disabuse Mrs. Allgaier of her misbegotten notion that this was nothing more than a case of a family getting its wires crossed, dramatically so perhaps, she'd gone along with the idea that she was merely collecting the boy from a sleepover that had ended in confusion.

"How about you thank me first?" Todd demanded, leaning across Chip, who was sandwiched between them in the front bench seat.

"Thank you for what?" Stella was trying to keep a lid on her temper, but she was a little short on patience now that she knew Todd was all right.

168

"For not letting that lady in on the fact of what you're up to, you'n Chip and all."

"And what exactly would that be?"

"Well, taking out Chip's bookie, of course, like you told me about at the Arco."

"You told him what?" Chip demanded. "Stella, I showed you my key chain, I'm six months clean!"

"Well yes, but I didn't know that yet," Stella said. "And Todd, I never said anything about *killing* anyone —"

"Killing, or beating the shit out of him, I guess that's up to you to figure out, whatever works," Todd said placidly. "Only I don't guess people like Mrs. Allgaier would really see it that way, even if they knew that he kidnapped me first. I mean, it's not like they treated me terrible or whatever, so you don't got to kill 'em on my account."

"Tell me exactly what happened," Stella insisted, figuring the boy's misinformation regarding the nature of the mission could be dealt with after she had the facts.

"Well, you probably know just about as much as I do. I was just sleeping in the truck, I didn't even know we'd stopped anywhere, and all of a sudden there's this big crash and I wasn't even all the way awake and someone picks me up and they're pushing me into a car."

"Oh, Todd. Oh, good Lord in heaven," Stella said, her pulse going haywire just imagining the scenario, even though the boy was safe back in the truck with her now. It made her trembly through and through to consider what might have happened, the terrible things that occur when innocent children are taken, and so she didn't; she pushed those thoughts back into the box marked TOO AWFUL in her mind, and resisted an urge to stop the truck just so she could hug him again.

"And first thing I thought was, this was probably one a them things you got mixed up in like what happened to Tucker."

"That ain't —" She wanted to say that would never happen, she would never allow it; but the memories of feeling helpless as they frantically searched for Chrissy's son were all too fresh. Besides, she knew she couldn't promise safety to anyone on God's green earth — all she could promise was to keep doing her damnedest. "I'm gonna do my utmost best to make sure nothing like that happens again," she promised, in a wobbly voice.

"Well, thing is, I know I fucked up with hiding in the back of the truck and all. But still, I was mad, you know? So I'm all kicking and yelling, even though they got some

170

sort of hood thing on me before I could see who they were and I kept getting the fabric in my mouth. I think there must've was two of 'em because they got me in their car pretty easy, in the backseat, and then they stuck me with a needle and knocked me out."

As scrawny as Todd was, Stella figured it wouldn't take but one large and reasonably muscular bad guy to pick the boy right up and stuff him anywhere he felt like, but on the other hand the boy was tough and scrappy as they came, even if he barely crossed the hundred-pound notch on the scale.

"You felt the needle?"

"Yeah . . ." Todd rubbed his upper arm, then pushed up his T-shirt sleeve. There was no mark on his skin that Stella could see. "I mean it wasn't super big or anything, more like a little pinch? Anyway, after that I woke up lying under this big old tree. And it was weird 'cause it felt like I'd been napping maybe five minutes? Except when they got me it was dark and when I woke up it wasn't. I think I was layin' right on a chigger nest 'cause I got them little buggers down . . . you know."

By way of illustration Todd scratched vigorously around his privates, while yawn-

171

ing hugely. Stella felt enormously relieved that there appeared to be no lasting psychic damage, no post-traumatic stress from the encounter. Todd's greatest discomfort seemed to be the little red mites — and Stella knew how they loved to go straight for the nethers.

"Don't be scratchin' like that in public," she said automatically. "So you couldn't say who it was got you? Man or woman, tall or short, nothing like that?"

"Nah . . . hey, you think they injected me with some sort of experimental mind control drug thing, like in that one movie where the old guy falls down the stairs in his wheelchair trying to prove the government was doing experiments on 'im?"

"What the . . . wait, are you talking about Mel Gibson? In *Conspiracy Theory*?"

"I don't know. The *old* guy."

"He's not old, Todd — Mel Gibson is only a few years older than me! I mean, that's Mad Max you're talking about!"

Todd shrugged. "I only watched it 'cause Mom fell asleep and it was free on the On Demand. But in the movie he had to live like in a storage locker or something because the government poisoned his mind and loaded him up with all these dangerous secrets. You think that's what they done to me?"

"I don't know — them folks they got running things down in Madison's pretty nefarious, for sure."

"They aren't that bad, they're just a bunch of damn liberals," Chip corrected her. "But back to the subject of who killed Benton, now we ruled out Doug, I'm starting to wonder if this whole thing was a case of crazy jealousy. I mean, look at Natalya, she's a knockout, men can't help themselves around her."

"Uh . . . wouldn't that make you the main suspect?"

"Not *me*, Stella, I didn't need to kill Benton, Natalya already loved me. I'm talking about some other schmuck, someone who maybe was crazy over her and she wouldn't even look his way."

"Do you have someone in mind there, Chip? 'Cause from what y'all've told me, she didn't have much opportunity to dazzle anyone besides the grocery checkers and the guys at the gas station, seein' as how Benton kept her so close to home."

"Well — there was the lawyer, he was helping them get Luka."

"Chip, lawyers don't generally try to steal their clients' wives. I mean, it would really cut into their word-of-mouth business, don't you think?"

"Well — what about Benton's friend from work? When Natalya first came over here, they socialized together. And he's a *single* guy. Don't you think that's a little bit . . . inappropriate?" Chip had reddened slightly, his voice going thin and agitated, and Stella realized that there certainly was a jealousy issue going on — *Chip's.*

If she had a nickel for every time she'd seen that sort of thing she could buy Todd a Corvette on his sixteenth birthday.

"Are you telling me you're jealous because Natalya — when she was married to another man and before she ever laid eyes on you — happened to be in the same room as another man? This is your girlfriend we're talking about, the one who makes big goo-goo eyes every time you're in the room? That one?"

"Uh . . ." Chip had the good grace to look embarrassed.

"Lemme give you a little relationship advice here, Chip, free of charge. Don't go making the same mistake with her that Benton did. How do you think he managed to turn Natalya against him? I mean, no lady likes to feel like she's chained to a man, like she can't go about her business without her husband freaking out because a stranger

174

said hello."

"Yeah . . ." His chin ducked lower.

"*Promise* me you're gonna work on that."

"I will. I know, I know. It's just that she's so *beautiful.* And a guy like me . . . I mean, what have I got to offer her?"

"Seriously? How about devotion, respect, doing your fair share of the chores, maybe takin' her out somewhere nice now and then? How about telling her she looks pretty and askin' her about her day and remembering her job is important, too? Oh, and maybe not burping at the dinner table, and hanging up your wet towels?"

"I'm — I can do all *that.*"

"Well, then you're about ninety-five percent of the way there. Oh! That reminds me," Stella said, because her list of "do's" had brought a familiar face to mind. "Todd, I got something I need you to do real quick. Text Mr. Brodersen and tell him . . . tell him we're all doing just fine, that I'm having a nice visit with my nephew and we're uh, we're working everything out."

Chip dug Stella's phone out of her purse and started poking at it. "Damn, Stella, he's called you like twenty times. Are you goin' out with him or is it just a hook-up type thing?"

Chip stared at her with sudden interest.

175

"Is that your boyfriend, Stella? Mom's never mentioned him. I didn't know you were . . . you know."

Stella rolled her eyes. "Dating? Yeah, now and then I get down to the Red Robin for the senior citizen plate with some old geezer's just got his Social Security check."

"No, no, I didn't mean that, only that it's just. Well, you know, you being a widow and all, I thought there was some sort of grace period or something."

"It's been four years, Chip!" Stella was secretly relieved. The family fiction that she and Gracellen seemed to have evolved between them was that Stella's accumulation of rage, acquired over thirty years of being mistreated and disrespected and smacked around, spurring Stella to deliver a deadly blow to her husband Ollie's head with a wrench, had been no more than a momentary leave-taking of her senses. Of course Gracie was relieved and overjoyed when Stella was released from custody and the case thrown out, but Stella figured it was just too hard for her sister to come to terms with the fact that she'd moved across the country and left Stella back in Missouri to be knocked around.

Stella, with her newish wealth of knowledge about domestic violence and its perpetrators and victims, could have reassured Gracie that there was nothing to be done until the day that Stella woke up ready to take care of business herself. Ready was ready, and one day early was still too early. That's why Stella waited for her clients to come to her, even in situations where she knew women were living with abuse. Sure, she occasionally made a stealth visit in the most urgent cases, like when Stew Walters nearly drowned on a solo fishing trip in the county supervisor's trout pond after he'd landed his wife, Gia, in the hospital with her third concussion in two years — but in general, you had to wait until a lady was ready before you began discussing ways you might straighten out her man.

It was funny. Stella could speak bold and plain with any woman who sat in her living room telling her tales of woe, and she could talk to Gracie for hours at a time about nothing at all, but there were still subjects that she and her sister couldn't touch.

Maybe she ought to do something about that.

"You know," she said, suddenly inspired, "when we get this mess figured out, maybe we should talk about getting your dad and stepmom out for a visit. How about this summer, we'll have us a weekend down at

177

the lake, you come down and bring Natalya — like a family reunion!"

"That'd be nice, I guess," Chip said dubiously. "I mean, Dad and I . . . you know, we're not close."

"That can be fixed," Stella said with conviction. She had been estranged from Noelle a while back, but they were closer than ever now. "Blood ties are — and even nonblood ties, what you got with your stepmom, for instance, or even me, and I know I haven't been the best about keeping up — well, what I'm trying to say is, family's family, and we ought to all work a little harder to stick together."

"Can I come? Down to the lake?" Todd asked sleepily.

"Well, yeah," Stella said, unable to stop herself from reaching over and giving his too-long hair a good ruffling. "You're a pain in the ass, but you're family, too."

CHAPTER TWELVE

Back at the Papadakis-Markovic home, the plastic flowers in the window boxes swayed gently in the breeze. Stella's stomach was growling, a reminder that she'd had nothing to eat but SweeTarts and a bag of Cheez-Its and a couple of Cliff Bars in the last however many hours, but otherwise she was feeling considerably more optimistic than she had earlier in the day. She desperately needed a nap, but if she didn't get something to eat first, her stomach was liable to keep her awake.

Natalya waited in the kitchen with a fresh pot of coffee, which she immediately set to pouring. Chip had called ahead to share the results of the last few hours of suspect visiting and teenager retrieving, and when Natalya saw Todd, she squealed with delight and folded him into one of her bone-crushing hugs. "Luka is in bathroom, will be out in moment. He will be so happy to have young friend for visit!"

Stella was mildly disappointed that there were no snacks on offer with the coffee as they all assembled around the kitchen table, which, only hours earlier, had been the scene of the dismembering.

"So we got Todd back, got your little problem more or less disposed of, your ear's not sliced off, and your girlfriend's no longer, uh . . . committed elsewhere — what do you say we call your folks and tell them to stop worrying, and then we can all get some lunch and Todd and I'll head back home?"

Natalya, who had been passing a little pink china milk jug, froze, a horrified expression on her face. "Stella, we need your help. There is matter of Topher Manetta. I am thinking while you are gone, is maybe Topher who kill, he is wondering now, where is body of Benton? If Topher wants poke this on Chip, he is expecting police to come find body."

Stella, who'd been plenty confused several times already on this trip, found herself sinking further into a surreal sense that she was several steps behind. "Uh, who's this Manetta?"

Chip interrupted hastily, darting a glance in Stella's direction. "Now Natalya, that's ridiculous. Just because a couple of guys drift apart don't mean there's any murderous feelings involved." Evidently he was taking Stella's minilesson on jealousy to heart. "It's like I always tell you, men and women process things differently."

"Chip is explain to me about Mars and Venus," Natalya confided to Stella. "Is theory that the man and the woman —"

"Oh, I've heard of that," Stella said, trying to keep her skepticism to herself. Years ago, she'd belonged to a ladies' reading circle at church. They'd read that dratted Mars and Venus book, as well as Dr. Laura's *Proper Care & Feeding of Marriage.* Stella was not the least bit impressed; she figured all those folks writing about relationships ought to have tried marrying Ollie for a while before they started dishing out advice. "But I still don't know who Manetta is."

"He was Benton's best friend."

"And business partner," Chip added. "The one we were talking about. With the ManTees."

"They have misunderstanding, this is while ago, they divide up company."

"You're saying that Manetta might have held a grudge against Parch? Friends going into business together, doesn't work out, something like that?" This was a new wrinkle, one that had gotten buried under the earlier firestorm of jealousy, and one that might bear looking into.

"Oh, yes," Natalya said. "I never trust that Topher. He is . . . what is word?" There followed a torrent of Russian.

Chip looked at Stella and shrugged. "Can't help you there. I'm thinking of taking Russian classes, so if we have kids we can raise 'em up bilingual, but half the time I don't have a clue what she's saying."

"He is man you can not be trusted," Natalya said with exasperation. "Man with scheming."

Chip shrugged, as he opened one little yellow packet after another and dumped sweetener into his coffee. Stella had a memory of him at the age of eleven, pouring sugar into his iced tea — the boy had had a terrible sweet tooth. "Natalya, Stella's awful busy. It was nice of her to try to figure out who killed Parch, but now she's got Todd back, she probably needs to get back to her own life. You know she's got her store to run, the sewing machines and such."

Despite herself, Stella felt torn. Chip and Natalya, as efficiently and dispassionately as they'd conducted the body disposal, did not seem like they would hold up well under vigorous questioning, should the police

182

come knocking. And the only way to ensure that they didn't end up taking the fall for the man's death was to find out who *had* killed Parch. All of which was arguably not her concern, except . . .

Well, there was that little speech she'd just given about family. Chip wasn't the most impressive specimen of humanity she'd ever come across, but he mattered to Gracellen, and that meant he mattered to Stella, too. As for Natalya — well, it seemed plain that Chip was determined to marry her right into the family as well, after all the legalities — which would be considerable, given the twin challenges of her dicey citizenship situation plus the fact she would be unable to physically produce the man she wished to be estranged from — were sorted out. Then Natalya would be family too, if a particularly confusing stripe of family — a stepniece-in-law, or some such.

The long and short of it was that Stella had just got done reminding Todd that family was family, and even if he had wandered into the other room and was playing video games and not listening, Stella made it a point not to lie to the kid, whenever possible.

Besides, she *was* already all the way up here. Sure, tomorrow was her birthday, and she would miss spending it with Noelle and Chrissy and Tucker and Sherilee and a variety of other friends and well-wishers. On the other hand, the backflips her heart did every time a new text or call came in from BJ — and *not* from Sheriff Goat Jones — had convinced her that she was in a seriously confused state over her romantic life, and a few more days away from home was probably a better treatment for that particular complaint than the type of obsessing one usually got into when one was mere miles from the source of the confusion.

So all in all, pursuing this thing just a little further might not be the worst idea ever. Providing, of course, she didn't faint from hunger. "Maybe we could, you know, talk through the problem, brainstorm a little," she said. "Over *lunch*."

Unfortunately, Natalya didn't seem to be picking up on her need for sustenance. Also, the milk jug held skim milk, which to Stella's way of thinking was an insult to a perfectly good cup of coffee. "Stella, you can maybe visit Topher, tell him back himself off? Or maybe you threat him good? With maybe some hurt him for prove we are serious?"

"Hang on there a minute, sister," Stella said. "Just a little while ago we were thinking this was all the doing of your, uh, cosmetic surgeon. We've barely got Doug checked off the list and you want to go full-bore on to the next suspect? I think we might want to have a bite to eat first, do a little further considering and thinking."

Natalya didn't look entirely convinced, but a clattering down the hall got her attention and she jumped up, clasping her hands.

"Oh, there he is! My little Luka!"

The boy who lumbered into the room was hardly little — he was a gangly six feet, with overlong arms and legs and bony elbows. He was in the middle of a yawn, but when he closed his mouth and gave everyone a halfhearted grimace, the sort teens reserve for the presence of visitors, Stella had a revelation.

The boy, with his longish brown hair and expressive eyes and generous features, was the spitting, if slightly taller, image of Todd. Whoever had snatched Todd thought they were getting Luka.

"Oh well now, that explains it," she said, standing and shaking hands with the young man. "Very pleased to meet you, Luka."

"It's, ah, Luke, actually," he mumbled in surprisingly good English, his voice squeaking just a little. "It's nice to meet you, too."

"This is Mrs. Hardesty, Chip's aunt.

Stella, this is my son, Luke, he is make me call him by American name. But at home he is Luka. I make egg, yes? And nice ham."

"I don't want anything, Mom."

Stella couldn't help resenting that the boy was turning down the snack she had been hoping for, and she was considering asking if she might have it instead when Natalya called into the living room. "Todd, Todd! Come here please."

Todd shuffled in from the guest room; clearly he'd been napping, as his hair stuck straight up on one side. When he saw Luke, his posture underwent an instant but subtle realignment wherein his swagger got swaggerier and his slouch slouchier. "Yerm," he mumbled.

"Say hello," Natalya and Stella said in perfect unison, and then they stared at each other openmouthed for a brief second and burst into laughter.

"And stand up straight," Stella added.

"And put shirt in pants."

The boys rolled their eyes as though controlled by the same invisible hand, and Stella figured that Todd's day, at any rate, had just gotten a little brighter.

There was a diner within walking distance where they made omelets with four eggs and

186

a buttery sheen. Bacon sizzled in the deep fryer and toast given a quick spin on the grill rounded out a meal that, Stella had to admit, had been worth waiting for. For her part, Natalya nibbled the underdone curly edges of her bacon and left the rest, and ignored her toast entirely, but she drank at least a gallon of coffee. With the boys at a neighboring table, shoveling in great stacks of pancakes and multiple cups of hot chocolate, conversation was kept to bland topics that did not include any crimes considered or actually committed — though the boys ignored the adults entirely, checking their phones and texting furiously, occasionally exchanging a few words or showing each other the tiny screens.

That reminded Stella that she'd switched her own ringer off, and she took her phone out of her purse and squinted at the screen.

BJ had evidently given up after the handful of texts and gone back to old-fashioned calling. There were six missed calls, four from BJ, one from Chrissy, and one from her friend Dotty Edwards.

"I wonder if you'll excuse me a moment," she said, getting up from the table and sucking in her stomach, which was pleasantly full of brunch. "I've got a couple of calls I need to return."

Outside, she stood under the diner's striped awning, enjoying the sun. First she tried Chrissy at the shop.

"You are not going to believe what-all I've seen in the last couple of days," she said without preamble when Chrissy answered.

"Well, it better be good, because I been pickin' up after them paper piecers and I'm just about clear outta patience."

"Oh . . . it's Saturday, isn't it."

"Damn right it is," Chrissy said moodily. "That bein' the day you swore up and down you wouldn't make me run that damn class by myself."

"I'm, uh, sorry," Stella said. From noon to two on Saturdays, the Paper Piecing Posse took over the shop to work on their latest quilt projects. The technique, which Chrissy had mastered with the alacrity and skill with which she tackled anything related to computers or sewing machines, involved tiny paper patterns that got stitched into fabric designs and pulled out with tweezers afterward. The problem was that a few of the ladies, mature ladies with imprecise eyesight, liked to have Chrissy go after all the tiniest shreds of paper that got stuck in seams — and these were the same ladies who tended to miss all the bits of paper and fabric and thread that ended up on the

188

floor, so that late afternoon usually meant a vacuuming marathon with the special attachments to get into every little nook and cranny in the shop.

Chrissy harrumphed. "I'll take them needleturn gals any day. Or even those fussy-ass hand-quilters."

Chrissy, whose own quilting projects tended toward the artsy and abstract end of the spectrum, actually had far more patience with her more traditional students than she let on. Pride kept her grumpy, and Stella was willing to play along — especially when it was so easy and so amusing to get the girl's ire up.

"Well, poor you — imagine that, a plague of women wantin' to stitch, and in a *sewing* shop, no less. It's practically criminal."

"Just sayin', I hope that trip up north ain't turnin' into some sorta pleasure cruise while I'm back here slaving away."

"Uh, Chrissy — what exactly would I be cruising *on?*"

"Well, they got a great lake or something up there, don't they?" Chrissy was a quick study at virtually everything she undertook, but there were vast areas where she had neither experience nor interest, many of them centering on subjects most people studied in high school, a time in Chrissy's life that had been spent on pursuits like boys and sunning and drinking rum coolers. Geography was one of the subjects to which she'd yet to turn her attention.

"Well, yeah, like the entire north and east edges. But you don't exactly — Chrissy, it's like hundreds of miles long. Big as a state, like maybe West Virginia, or maybe Vermont plus Massachusetts, practically."

"It *is?*" The girl's astonishment seemed genuine.

"Yeah. Look, we got to get out there one of these days, show you a little of the world."

"Uh-huh. So how are you?"

Stella gave her assistant a quick run-down, including the loss and subsequent return of Todd, the gruesome discovery of half a body on her nephew's kitchen table, and the leads she'd tracked down so far.

"So you got *two* hormonal teenage boys, a bloody murder, illegal doctorin', a business feud, a illegal immigrant situation, all of it circlin' around a relative you don't hardly even know, and tomorrow's your birthday. Well, ain't you managed to step into just a fine mess."

"Well — yeah, I mean, I don't know how much of that's actually relevant . . ."

There was a longish pause while Stella could practically hear Chrissy calculating and thinking. "And you feel like you got to stay up there and figure it all out just 'cause it's blood. Well, family, anyway."

"Mmm."

"Even though you might be better off lettin' things lie than stirrin' them up."

Stella sighed. "Chip seems to really like her, Chrissy. If we get the cops on it, she'll be deported. And she seems . . . well, she seems nice. Plus there's her son to think about. I mean, Chrissy, he's just a *boy.*"

"Uh-huh. Well . . . it may interest you to know that we had a unexpected visitor over here to the shop this morning."

"Yeah?"

"I was totin' up a couple of yards of that Hobbs Thermore batting for Janice Sheeter and I look out the window and there's the sheriff's cruiser pullin' up in the parking lot."

Stella's heart did a little skip at the news. "Sheriff Jones?"

"No, Sheriff Rosco P. Coltrane from Hazzard County. Who do you think, Stella? He comes in and I'm acting all innocent, I tell him good morning, and don't you know he wanders around for a good ten minutes looking at every damn one of them Horn sewing cabinets. Why, he went up to that one Airlift Embroidery model and got down on the floor and looked up into the joints. I thought he was gonna ask could he test it out."

"And you didn't ask to help him, Chrissy?" Stella kicked herself for not being there for his visit. "Didn't ask him was there something you could do for him?"

"Oh, I asked him all right, but he just seemed determined to wander around for a while getting his courage up."

"Courage up for what?"

"To ask where *you* were, of course. Said he'd been by the house and wasn't anyone there."

"He went by my house?"

"Yeah, 'cause he thought it was your birthday. Said he remembered it was in May and had in his head it was today. So he went by your house and Stella, what do you suppose the odds were he had a big bouquet a flowers out in the cruiser and a box a chocolates and a plan to give you exactly what you been needin'?"

"Chrissy!" As crude as the girl's speculation was, Stella had been wondering the same thing, and the instant zippy ramp-up of her hormones was plenty of proof that, despite her earlier suspicions to the contrary, she was still a woman of red-blooded wants and needs.

"Well, I'm just sayin'. Seemed to me like he's planning to set up camp starin' at your house until you get back. How's it gonna look when you come drivin' up in your boy-toy's monster truck?"

"What did you tell him, anyway?"

"Only that you went up to visit relatives. I mean, c'mon, Stella, I'm good at this shit. I left it all open-ended, let him think what he wants, right?"

Stella was silent for a minute, thinking things through. "Tomorrow's Sunday. What're you gonna do with your day off?"

"Well, I was gonna bake you that caramel cake you like so well, and see did you and Noelle want to go bowling, but since you hightailed it out of town, I might have to go on a date."

"When are you going to tell me who this man is?"

"Not yet, Stella, don't get all excited. Got to see does this one stick or not."

"Sugar, I can't believe you said that. They all want to stick. You're the one who un-sticks 'em before they can catch their breath." Chrissy's romantic life featured a constant stream of men who couldn't be-lieve their good fortune, dating such a pretty, sexy, fun-loving kind of woman, right up until the moment she gently disentangled them and sent them on their way.

"Well, now, this time I'm not so sure."

Stella hung up wondering if it was starting to get a little chilly down in the underworld, because the day Chrissy got settled on a man would be the day hell froze clear over.

CHAPTER THIRTEEN

The walk home was even pokier and dawdlier than the walk to the restaurant, because after the boys took off to explore whatever delights awaited in the sleepy streets of downtown Smythe, there was no particular reason to hurry. Stella was no longer hungry, and that freed up her brain to explore the various possibilities of the case.

When they got to the house, however, an old white Saab was parked in the driveway. Sitting on the porch, in the plastic chair next to a plastic table with a vase full of plastic tulips — all Natalya's doing, no doubt — was a middle-aged woman with long silver hair held back by a leather clip. Her eyes were closed and she nodded faintly. She held her right forearm with her left hand, her fingers flying over her smooth and freckled skin to the beat that Stella belatedly realized was coming from the earbuds hidden under the masses of untamed hair.

Only when they were a couple of feet away did the woman's eyes fly open. She jumped up, knocking the chair over backward; she grabbed on to the table for support but it was no more substantial than the chair, and the vase toppled to the ground and the tulips went flying. "Oh," she said, yanking the earbuds from her ears and trying to untangle the cord that wound around her arm and into the folds of a long crinkly embroidered skirt.

"Well, hello, Alana," Natalya called with little enthusiasm.

"Friend of yours?" Stella asked.

"This woman, she is Benton sister."

"God damn," Chip muttered.

The woman was tugging at the cord, which had somehow gotten tangled in the folds of her skirt and trailed down to her knotted leather sandals. She gave the cord a hard yank and it came flying up and snapped against her face.

"Ow, *ow!*" she exclaimed, covering one eye with her hand.

"Are you all right?" Stella asked, but the woman waved her away with her free hand and jumped around for a moment, causing Stella to wonder if she was about to lose an eyeball. Finally she calmed down and took the hand away from her face, blinking and grimacing.

"Hello, Natalya," she said in a thin, reedy voice. "I'm sorry, I would have called, but . . ."

"Benton is hardly ever allowing me mobile phone," Natalya said coldly. "It is wonder you are finding me here."

"It took some doing," Alana said. "May I come in?"

"Is business you have with me that can be done on porch." Natalya's tone grew frostier still as her accent deepened.

"This isn't good," Chip muttered to Stella.

"Just hush a minute," Stella replied, digging her nails into the soft skin on the inside of his arm. In Stella's experience, a great many situations — especially those with uncertain outcomes — were best handled by giving as little as possible away.

"Hi there," Stella said, stepping forward with a big smile on her face. "I'm sorry, but I don't think we've met. My name is Stella Hardesty."

"I'm Alana Parch-Javetz," the woman said, hesitating before offering her limp fingertips for Stella to shake. "I'm Benton's sister. Are you a friend of Natalya, or of . . . I'm sorry, I don't remember your name."

"My ass, you don't," Chip muttered, but then he, too, forced a pleasant expression and spoke up. "Chester Papadakis. So nice to see you again."

"Well, I suppose you are coming in if you have discussion," Natalya said. "Is terribly uncivilized talking on porch."

She swept past Alana as though she were royalty on parade and unlocked her front door, not bothering to look over her shoulder to make sure the rest of them followed. Alana, in the lead, stumbled over the threshold and nearly fell, catching herself only by grabbing the back of the sofa inside the living room, her pale storklike legs akimbo. Stella tried to find a resemblance between the ungainly woman and the part of Benton Parch with which she was acquainted but came up short.

"I'll come right to the point," Alana said, once she had regained her footing. "As you know, Benton and I talk every Sunday."

"Even if is not convenient," Natalya said, her face darkening with fury. "I am marry your brother almost two year. Every Sunday I am putting dinner on table at six o'clock like Benton say is right time to eat, and every Sunday you are calling at few minutes after six. He ask you to not be calling at time for dinner and you are calling every week."

Alana's pinched expression grew even more irate. "I don't know what you're talking about. Once my brother married you, the only way I could even talk to him was to call on the phone —"

"I am inviting you every week!" Natalya shrieked.

"Yes, if I want to clog my arteries with all that — that fat-laden diet you insist on cooking. Bad enough you're poisoning Benton, but —"

"Poisoning? Poisoning! I am making food of Russia! I am taking care of husband!"

"He gained thirty-five pounds the year after he married her," Alana said to Stella. "She'll be the death of him."

Stella exchanged a quick glance with Chip, whose own complexion was taking on a grayish pallor. "Can I get anyone a cup of —"

"What is it you are wanting?" Natalya demanded, arms folded over her chest. Though Natalya was six inches shorter than Alana, and hardly a robust woman, Stella would have bet on her in a matchup. She found her affection for the woman growing as she glowered at the uninvited guest.

Alana dug around in her purse, a floppy

arrangement of knotted jute and wooden beads, eventually coming up with a tattered envelope. She drew out a sheaf of stapled papers and a needlepointed glasses case, sliding a pair of half-moon specs onto her long, narrow nose, so that she looked a bit like a witch with her long unruly hair and sour expression.

"As I started to say, I speak to Benton every Sunday, but for the last two Sundays I haven't been able to reach him. I know you've been shacking up over here —"

"Hey!" Chip protested.

"— since the middle of April, and I'd be just as happy as you, I'm sure, to declare our association well and truly done with, but unfortunately you are still legally married to my brother and I've run out of ideas to find him, short of hiring a private detective."

There was a long silence, and then Stella decided to chime in. "Isn't that funny," she said carefully. "How Natalya's been looking for Benton, too."

"What do *you* want from him?" Alana demanded.

"As your attorney I advise you not to answer that," Stella said quickly. "Ms. Parch . . . what was it?"

"Parch-Javetz," the woman sniffed. "Hyphenated since marriage."

"Uh-huh. Anyway, Ms. Parch — that is to say, Ms. *Natalya* Parch, just to avoid confusion — has retained me to oversee her interests as she pursues a divorce from Mr. Parch."

Natalya stared at her, wide-eyed with surprise. "I . . . That's . . . yes," she finally stammered.

"Perhaps your interests are not so far apart after all," Stella suggested. "May I ask what brings you here today?"

"Well, I'm not going to sit here and pretend I was ever happy my brother married her," Alana said, refusing to look at Natalya. "She's never made him happy. She's made him miserable since the day he plucked that tramp off the boat."

"I am giving him best years of my life!" Natalya spat in outrage.

"Not to mention the fact she dragged that bastard child of hers into my brother's home. The two of them only ever wanted his money."

Natalya made a sound in her throat — half human, half animal — and lunged for Alana. Luckily Chip had a tight hold on her hand, which he'd been clutching in a proprietary fashion, and was able to reel her back in before she could inflict any damage.

201

"I am not wanting Benton money!" Natalya shrieked, and Stella had the eerie realization that with the arrival of Benton's sister, Natalya had more or less forgotten that he was not only dead but disposed of at least partially by her hand.

Stella knew well that the hurts from a failed marriage ran deep. Sometimes it took more than a simple slaying to bring closure — that was a lesson Stella had learned firsthand, when Ollie's death was only the start of the long and painful process of figuring out exactly who she was without him.

"Benton is bringing Luka here fair square," Natalya wailed. "I tell Benton I am paying him back, I will take job, I will work waitress or cleaner of house. But Benton is not letting me work."

"Two things I have to say to you," Alana said, drawing herself up to her full height, which only further accentuated her skinny and awkward frame, her stalklike neck, and her bony elbows. "First of all, you never told Benton you had a child while he was courting you. You waited until you were engaged and he couldn't do a damn thing about it. Secondly, how long was your bas— was your kid here before you ran out on my brother? A week? Two? You only stayed married to him until you got what you wanted all along, which was to bring your son to this country so you could both live off the generosity of the American government, never working a day in your life. You're leeches, is what you are. Parasites. Well, you're not the only one who can hire a lawyer, do you know that?"

A sickly feeling started to uncoil inside Stella as she realized that Alana might be the sort of runaway train she wished she'd known about before it came speeding into the station.

"I am not fearing lawyers," Natalya snapped, but a quick look at Chip's ashen face confirmed for Stella that of the three of them, Natalya was alone in that view. "You cannot make Benton to divorce me."

"*Divorce?* Oh, honey, that's gonna be the least of your worries by the time I'm through with you," Alana said, stuffing the envelope back into her purse as she strode to the front door. "There's a phrase we have here in America, I don't know what it translates to in your language, but maybe get out your little pocket translator and look it up: Eat my shorts."

"She is trying beat deadline," Natalya said worriedly after they sat down at the kitchen table with a pitcher of iced tea. "She is wanting to send me and Luka back to Russia."

"I don't think so," Stella mused. She was thinking about the envelope Alana had produced from her purse. For some reason the woman had put it away, but clearly she'd come here with an ulterior motive. "I'd say she's got something else on her mind. You know . . . I'm not a lawyer, obviously, but I'd be willing to try to look into this a little further . . . What do you think?"

Natalya waved her hand distractedly. "What I think is, whatever you can do to keep that terrible woman away from me and my Luka is big help."

"Do you have her address? Phone numbers, place of employment — anything at all about her personal life?"

"Yes, I can get this. I am sending card to Alana and her husband, Jeffers, every Christmas. Also I make for them *kutya*. Alana is Benton's only living relative. I am trying make friends, but . . ." There followed a quick-fire blast of Russian that Stella could not follow but whose tone implied that her efforts had failed.

"She didn't return the love," Stella guessed.

"No, she is capital-*B* Bitch."

"Natalya!" Chip gasped.

"I am sorry, is no other word." Natalya went to a drawer in the kitchen and got a vinyl-bound address book and a sheet of notebook paper and began copying an address in a beautiful script.

"There's one more thing I need, while you're at it. Please give me everything you have on that Topher Manetta."

"I thought we are deciding is bad idea?"

"Well, we're no closer to knowing who killed your husband than we were when I got here. I know we're all hoping this just sort of blows over, but I think that little incident with your sister-in-law is a good reminder that folks don't tend to go quiet-like into the hereafter. They got all kinds of attachments and entanglements with life here on this planet that can make for trouble when they're gone. Now you tell me that this Topher's on good friendly terms with Benton and that's great, only some-times things ain't exactly like what they seem, 'specially when you throw a few male egos into the mix. So I need to check him out, just the same as I'd check out anyone else."

"All right." Natalya sighed and flipped through the pages of her address book and continued writing.

For a few moments everything was pleasantly tranquil. Natalya's pencil scratched on the notebook paper, and Chip hummed quietly as he rooted through the fridge for a snack, and it was almost possible to imagine that the last twenty-four hours had not occurred at all and Stella could choose among a variety of pleasant activities, like calling Noelle to see what time she could come over with her portable manicure kit, or Chrissy to see if she felt like barbecuing steaks or chops — or even Goat, to flirtatiously remind him of the true date of her birthday and perhaps suggest a kiss for luck.

Stella had let herself go quite a ways down the wouldn't-it-be-nice-path, had in fact arrived at the you-deserve-it-honey cul-de-sac, when a blast of the doorbell broke up her pleasant fantasy.

"That's an awful *strident* bell you got," she groused.

"It's a rental," Chip shrugged, as he got up to answer.

"Maybe get set to make yourself scarce," Stella suggested, but Natalya was miles ahead of her, racing down the hallway to hide in their bedroom.

Chip turned to give her a brief thumbs-up. Then he opened the door.

BJ Brodersen stood on the other side.

CHAPTER FOURTEEN

"Aw, I'm sorry," Stella said for the fifth time. "I can't even believe my poor manners. Why, I wouldn't blame you for never speaking to me again."

"But I don't care about the truck, Stella," was BJ's rejoinder. This, too, had been trotted out several times without resolution. "All's I care about is your safety. I'm just glad I've got the tracker on the GPS, so I knew where you was at."

Stella exchanged a glance with Chip, grimacing briefly while her face was turned away from BJ. It was one thing to have a man concerned about her — kind of nice, actually, in a chivalrous sort of way — but damned inconvenient in this particular instance, when she had been just about to take the gentleman's truck on an errand of interrogation.

"What-all have you got in the back, anyway?" BJ asked, as though reading her mind.

"You helped me load it all in there . . ."

"Yes, but . . . I didn't want to pry, only I got to wondering, in between worrying about you being dead in a ditch or lost or held up by robbers."

"That's just so awful nice." Stella beamed and helped herself to a cookie, her fifth. It was almost impossible to resist a nerve-steadying snack while she was working overtime on dealing with BJ's unexpected arrival and keeping her story straight. Natalya had emerged from the bedroom to say hello, upended a package of Pepperidge Farm Geneva cookies on a china plate and brewed a quick pot of coffee, and then tactfully disappeared, claiming that she needed to lie down.

Chip, for his part, had been employing an increasingly dramatic set of gestures to indicate his willingness to join Natalya and give Stella and BJ privacy, maneuvering himself behind BJ's chair while pretending to fetch milk for the coffee or fill a glass from the sink. It was sweet, the way he was trying to create privacy in the name of romance, Stella thought — and the timing was reasonably good since the only truly immediate problem, locating Todd, had been taken care of, though the boys had managed to slip out while the adults were occupied and were wandering the streets of town, a notion that worried Stella enough that as soon as she dealt with BJ, she meant to go out and retrieve them.

BJ was looking good in his pale green golf shirt and what appeared to be a fresh haircut, sticking pretty much straight up in a way that complemented his broad and ruddy face. He smelled nice, some cologne that he might have been just a tad too generous with.

"It was unforgivable of me to take such a valuable . . . piece of machinery out of state without keeping you apprised of my where-abouts," Stella continued. Then she gri-maced — her nerves were making her all wordy and silly sounding, and it really was ludicrous, BJ worrying about a fender bender after the actual events of the last couple of days. "I'm especially sorry you had to drive the Subaru up here."

The car in question, an ancient Subaru Impreza, belonged to BJ's helper at the bar, Jorge, who was a much smaller man and hence didn't mind driving a car whose driver's seat practically lined up with the windshield, to hear BJ tell it. He'd been un-able to sit down for the first few minutes of his visit while he worked all the kinks and cricks out of his back and neck, twisting and popping this way and that.

Stella had tried not to stare, but when BJ lifted his arms above his head to stretch, she couldn't help but get an eyeful of that broad torso tapering down to those neat pressed slacks. BJ had a bit of a spare tire on him, but Stella found herself thinking that it would be kind of nice to cuddle up against a substantial man like that . . . and she had even considered that if things got going in a vigorous fashion, it would be good to know she wouldn't accidentally asphyxiate the man, which was something she might worry about with a skinny partner.

BJ twisted to the side, and Stella could see that the man had a nice profile, the kind of butt you could get a good grip on, and a broad neck with a hint of a tan already, though it was barely lawn-mowing season.

He twisted the other way and she just about convinced herself that she might as well take him for a spin and *then* do all the soul-examining and heartfelt getting-to-know-each-other part of the romance.

Now, though, with him sitting across the table from her, much of his appealing physique concealed beneath the table, Stella found that she was able to see things a little more clearly, and there were lots of things wrong with the scenario. For one thing, if they went to bed right now, or at least as soon as she located the boys, Stella would be asleep within moments, her exhaustion reaching a critical level. Even if she got a nap in, it wasn't like they could go on a proper date here in Smythe, and they couldn't really even have a romantic drive home to Missouri, since two cars had now made the trip north as well as a pesky teen who needed to be delivered home.

"You know, I'm worried about the boys," Stella said.

"Oh, don't fret, Stella, Luka stays out all the time. Natalya likes him to come home for dinner so she can see for herself he's eating good, but then he's off again with his friends."

Stella considered pointing out that neither Chip nor Natalya had a good grasp of the dangers lurking on the streets of even the tiniest rural midwestern towns these days, but that was a conversation she probably needed to have with them in private, when she had their full attention. She figured that Chip, who had been raised on the neglect plan by his pill-popping mom and absent father, meant no harm and probably didn't know any better. As for Natalya, the woman was clearly devoted to her son, but she seemed to be truly naive about what went on in America. Besides, it seemed prudent to assume that Luka's would-be kidnappers might still be in the mood to kidnap him.

"All the same, I'm thinking maybe BJ and I will go for a walk and see if we can find them."

"Oh." Chip blinked, and then his smile broadened. "Ohhhh. Sure. I get you."

Stella rolled her eyes at the lack of subtlety, but she carefully noted down the places Chip suggested she look: a sandwich shop that was apparently quite the hangout for local teens, and the little veterans' memorial park near the town hall.

As they strolled outside, afternoon shadows lengthening along the streets, BJ slipped his hand around Stella's. He stared straight ahead, his hand warm and very slightly damp, and Stella was charmed that he was nervous.

"I got to tell you, Stella, I was so worried about you I called over to the sheriff's office. Thought I ought to check did they have any reports from the Highway Department, or whatnot."

"You did? You didn't speak to . . . Goat, did you?"

BJ gave her a funny little sideways glance, his mouth set in a sort of grimace. "Nah, I talked to Irene and she checked with Ian. Goat was out somewhere, I guess."

"Oh." Stella tried to look like she didn't much care, but the damage was done. Ian Sloat, one of Prosper's two deputies, was sure to say something to Goat — if Irene, the departmental assistant, didn't beat him to it. All of them were aware, one way or another, of the ongoing whatever-it-was between Goat and Stella, which was a funny thing because Stella herself couldn't decide what it was half the time.

"Listen here, Stella," BJ said earnestly, and Stella knew what was coming. Damn, but the man had an uncanny way of going straight to what ever was on her mind — especially things she was trying to keep concealed from him. "I'm just, ah, wondering. Are you seeing the sheriff? I mean like is he your boyfriend?"

"No," Stella said quickly — probably too quickly, judging by the relief that washed over BJ's face. "We're friends, good friends. But there ain't any, not anything really going on between us."

"Oh! 'Cause I thought . . . I mean, I seen you with him here and there, and folks say . . . well, you know how folks talk, but I guess I should know as much as anyone most of it's just a bunch of horse manure. I mean, you wouldn't believe some a the rumors I heard about . . . uh, some people."

"Is that right." Stella knew the rumors he was referring to were about her, and she could only imagine, given that much of BJ's time was spent across a narrow wooden bar from drunk folks who felt like revealing their deepest secrets and wildest conjecture — and at times that conjecture probably touched on her exploits. Stella had chased down more than a couple of ne'er-do-wells at BJ's, though she was always careful to conduct her business far away from the establishment — aside from that one time when she'd hid out in a lawn chair on the other side of the electric cattle fence on the side of the parking lot that butted up against Neils Persson's buckwheat field late one Thursday evening, waiting for Cray Tollifer to lurch drunkenly out to his wife's Pontiac, the same one he'd been driving since she was laid up with a broken wrist that made it difficult to drive.

"And a'course I wouldn't want to get in the way of that," BJ continued, though he did seem to grab on to her hand a little tighter and the clamminess was entirely gone, making the experience that much more pleasant. "But I have been thinking, Stella, I'd sure like to get to . . . ah . . ."

His voice trailed off and his pace slowed a bit as they approached the park, a little triangular affair in what was once probably the center of town but, now that strip malls had siphoned much of the business a few blocks away, lay shadowed and abandoned on the back side of the imposing limestone town hall. It looked like the local garden club hadn't visited in a while, either; the lowest branches of a ring of untrimmed fir trees bowed down close to the ground, shielding much of the center of the park from view. Only by peeking between the boughs did Stella glimpse the marble obelisk rising in the center of a number of benches.

It was the occupants of these benches that had given BJ pause. Four heads bent over an object that was blocked from their line of vision, but the hunching of shoulders and general furtive air did suggest that something illicit was going on.

"That sure does look like that Groffe boy," BJ added. Stella murmured her agreement. Since Noelle had taken on the supervising of the boy's grooming — Noelle being in the beauty business and viewing Todd as a sort of brother she never had — it was hard to miss his hair, which had a sort of punky two-tone look and reached down around his shoulders. There was also the matter of his shoes, giant boatlike sneakers, which looked like they belonged on someone twice his size, and which were visible under the bench, along with three other pairs of similarly outsized and unlaced shoes.

Next to him, the tallest of the four boys looked like a sure bet for Luka, and Stella was pretty sure she remembered that blue shirt.

Positive enough ID for her.

"Um, BJ, I wonder, would you mind waiting here for a moment?" Stella asked, gently disentangling her hand from his. "Here" was a cracked segment of sidewalk beneath a lilac bush, so it had the advantage of being pleasantly fragranced, and Stella hoped she wouldn't be long — hoped, in fact, that she was wrong entirely about what she thought she was seeing.

"Sure, Stella," BJ said doubtfully. It would take too much time — and be a bad idea for lots of other reasons — for Stella to explain that she had become awfully good at sneaking up on people, and that that was a task best done solo, so she set off on her own, sticking to the inside edge of the sidewalk that was shaded by overhangs and awnings, until she was situated behind one of the fir trees and had a clear view of what was going on.

Her heart sank to see Luka holding up a little plastic bag. While Stella couldn't make out the contents, she did note that one of the other boys was smoothing out a stack of crumpled bills. As she watched, Luka palmed it smoothly, and the boy stuffed the bag into the pocket of his jeans.

No time to waste. Stella sprang out of her hiding spot with the focused release of energy that she'd been practicing on the heavy bag during the warrior burst drill. In half a dozen nimble steps she was ideally positioned to deliver a groin kick to the buyer. Before any of the others had time to react, the boy was doubled over, clutching himself and moaning.

"Awww, no, man," Todd exclaimed. "Shit, Stella — really?"

"Yes, really," Stella said, puffing from exertion while she grabbed the downed boy's hands behind his back.

"What the hell?" Luka demanded, as the fourth boy squeaked with surprise and fear and took off at a sprint.

"Don't bother running," Todd said gloomily. "She'll find you. I know she don't look like much, but trust me on this, man."

"Look, Mrs. Hardesty, I don't know what you think you saw," Luka said, talking fast, "but me and Todd and these guys, we were, uh, just talking about these codes? For Final Fantasy?"

"Can it, I'm in no mood," Stella snapped and gave the boy's arms a firm upward yank. He howled as Stella dug in his pocket and pulled out the ziplock bag.

Pills.

"Oh, good lord," Stella sighed. "Todd, I don't got my specs — read me what they say."

"Those are for allergies," Luka said quickly. "He ran out and —"

"I said shut the fuck up," Stella snapped.

Todd took the little bag and squinted at it. "Wyeth," he read in a resigned tone. "Got a big *A* on the other side."

"No fucking way. Ativan?" she demanded. "Tranks? Do you have any idea what those can do to you, young man?"

The boy shook his head vigorously.

"I want the rest," Stella said, holding out her hand. *"Now."*

Luka hesitated, then started digging around in his own jeans.

"Now listen here," she said to the boy while she waited. "I'm DEA. Special division. It ain't just me, either, there's a whole bunch of us old ladies have got dispatched up here. So every time you're tempted to buy yourself a quick little high, you think

218

about the lady you seen in line at the grocery or next to your family in church or helping on the playground at your little brother's school, and you remember that could be one of us."

The boy nodded vigorously.

"This Russian shit they're importing, it's all fake," Stella continued. "You can't ever know for sure what it's gonna do to you. Sad case last week, boy about your age, over in a little town to the north of here — thought he was getting Concerta and ended up with his balls shriveled up about as big as a couple of grapes. Doctors sayin' the damage is permanent, too — they ain't ever gonna *un*shrink. You want that to happen to you?"

The boy shook his head so hard it was a wonder it didn't fall off his neck, and after a final "ow"-inducing squeeze Stella released him. He took off down the street, never once looking back.

Then Stella regarded the two remaining boys with narrowed eyes. "I'm gonna get up now, and sit my ass down on the bench, 'cause crouching down like this is hell on my back. I can count on you two to stay put, can't I?"

"Yeah, whatever," Todd said glumly.

"I was right, wasn't I?" Stella asked, addressing Luka. "You're getting it from back home?"

"Yes," Luka sighed.

Stella knew a little bit about the prescription drug market, having learned more than she cared to a while back when a good friend of hers had gotten himself hooked and subsequently unhooked from painkillers only to find himself accused of having killed someone while he was out-of-his-mind high.

"You got a friend sending it to you? What's it cost, anyway, them two pills you just charged that boy thirty bucks for?"

"About . . . forty cents," Luka said, "but you got to think about all the overhead, the postage —"

"Leaving you about what, a fifty thousand percent profit or something, right? Which I can understand would make this little business of yours pretty irresistible and all. But here's something you don't know. There's folks who got here before you, the ones who gave the people in this town their first taste of diazepam or Rohypnol or hydrocodone, convinced them they liked it enough to spend their hard-earned money — or allowance, as the case may be — on the shit. Laid the foundation, so to speak. Primed the pump. And how do you think they're gonna feel about you coming along after they've put in all that work and just start milking the cash cow? Hmm?"

Luka was staring at her as though a horn had sprouted in the middle of her forehead. "I thought you were, like, Chip's grandmother or something."

"*Grandmother?* What the hell, I'm fifty years old" — for a few more hours, anyway — "and Chip can't be more than thirty, so how the fuck would I be his *grandmother?*"

"Okay, aunt. Whatever."

Stella took a moment to let her irritation simmer down. She'd expected Luka to be a bit more easily intimidated, but he stared at her with wide and curious brown eyes and no trace of fear. "Look here, do you not understand what I'm telling you? When I say you're horning in on someone else's territory, I'm not exactly talking about a vacuum cleaner salesman. These are big-time dealers, gangbangers, who've come up from the city looking to expand their reach into these little hick towns. Just because it's a small town don't mean they operate any different."

"I'm not scared," Luka said. Todd was watching the conversation between them, head bobbing like a fan at a tennis match, not saying a word. "I appreciate what you're trying to do here, Mrs. Hardesty, but they've already come around and told me to stop, but this is America, yes? They can drive by and kill me in any city, anytime. In America you have to accept violence as part of the society. Like taxes."

"Is that what they teach you over there? Along with very nice English, I got to give you that, but do you really — wait a minute." Realization flooded through Stella like an ice-water bath. "When they snatched Todd. That was them, wasn't it? Your gang-bangers?"

"How should I know, I wasn't there," Luka said with maddening calm. "I was asleep. Besides, I sleep with a knife."

He slid a wicked-looking curved-blade hunting knife from a holster hidden under his jeans, his moves so unflinching and steady that any doubts Stella had about his bravery were put to rest. "Let me explain something to you. In Russia, I was selling DVDs since I was nine. We knew this guy, he'd get bootleg copies of new-release American films. The sound was shitty, it was just some guy taking film in a movie theater, you could see people's heads, but we sold them for two dollars. Alexi, he let us keep seventy-five cents. That's enough to feed a family over there, and lots of nights it did."

Despite herself, Stella was fascinated. It took a little work, but eventually she got the rest of the story out of him. After everything went digital, and the market for DVDs dried up, he switched to selling knockoff prescription drugs.

"Wow . . ." Stella said when he finished.

"Look, don't think you got a right to judge us. Mom's not asking for a free ride."

"And you like Chip?"

"He's all right."

Stella figured that was the closest thing to an endorsement she was going to get. "Okay, let's go. You two are coming with me."

Stella didn't expect them to be happy about it, but when Luka stayed where he was, slouching back against the bench with his arms folded across his chest, Todd hesitated, too.

"Oh, hell. Seriously?"

"Stella, he's fine, don't make him —"

Stella's arm shot out nearly as fast as it had the first time, and she grabbed the fine downy hairs at the nape of Todd's neck, twisted them around her pointer finger, and gave them a good yank. Todd squawked like a stuck pig, and Stella kept up the pressure, dragging him up from the bench.

"Just defy me one more time, I'm asking

you, Todd Groffe, because I cannot wait to tell your mom I been covering for your ass all this way up here and through all your shenanigans by mistake, and that you was evading the sheriff so's you could vandalize your dad's property in a cold and premeditated fashion. Because Kemper Boys' Academy? They got a bunk just waiting for you, bucko, and unlike what your pal Luka here's evidently used to, seventy-five cents won't buy you a whole lot there except a package of stale Cheez-Its."

Todd was trying to wrench himself free of Stella's grip, mewling while tears of pain streamed down his face, but the more he fought her the tighter his hair coiled around her finger.

"As for *you*," she told Luka, "I'm sure you're a nice young man, and you've been through a heck of a lot, and I salute your mama for her patience and dedication. Only, you're not *my* kid. So I don't got to try it the hard way first. I can go straight to the tough love without a second thought. Now, I'm taking Todd with me. You're gonna come home and stay there, and you're not coming out again until we get a few things worked out."

Stella was relieved when both boys shuffled after her when she started walking away. She wasn't sure about Luka, who was as cynical as any grown man she'd ever met — but then again he was still a kid in many ways, with the faint speckling of acne along his hairline, the wad of gum in his cheek, the baggy jeans that hung low on his narrow ass. He stayed close as he shuffled along behind Todd, and Stella felt herself soften a little.

"I realize you're some sort of teenage thug where you're from," Stella said. "Maybe you *are* that tough, I don't know. But here's what I do know. Your mom is important to someone who is important to me. And he has asked me to help. And I'm going to do so, whether you like it or not, and whether you like my ways or not. I'm not really DEA —"

"Well, no shit, Stella, I think he knows that," Todd interrupted.

"— but I am a little more capable of defending myself and the people I care about than the average middle-aged lady. Do you get what I'm saying?"

Luka regarded her skeptically. "I guess, but I think you're overreacting here. It's just a —"

Stella felt her reserves of patience quickly emptying. "What it *is* is, it's not your place to judge. You are still a minor. In this

225

country, that means that grown-up people are still in charge of you. Specifically your mom. Do you have any idea — I mean, you of all people should understand the sacrifices she's gone through for you. To make a better life for you. Do you realize, if you play your cards right" — and if Benton's dead body went undiscovered, and Chip and Natalya remained unaccused of murder, and the INS viewed any future applications for permanent residency favorably, and Natalya obtained a divorce from a man who the rest of the world considered merely disappeared, not dead — all significant challenges, Stella had to admit — "then you have a chance at growing up in this country, going to college here, getting a job in a field of your choosing that is *not* against the law. I mean . . . Luka, you got a shot at the American *dream* here."

Stella was getting herself so worked up that beads of perspiration popped out along her forehead. She was as patriotic as the next person, but the idea of kids forced to sell drugs on the cold and forbidding streets of an indifferent and hostile nation was enough to make her practically tearful. "Don't you see," she finished hoarsely, "if you don't fuck things up, you could *be* somebody."

BJ was still standing where Stella had parked him, rocking back and forth on his heels, his hands in the pockets of his slacks, looking somewhere halfway between bored and confused and concerned.

"Hey, Mr. Brodersen," Todd mumbled, giving him a half-hearted handshake.

Luka did a little better, standing up straight and using a firm grip. "Hi. I'm Luke."

"These fellas have managed to get themselves into a whole lot of needless trouble," Stella said.

"Well, that's what guys do at their age," BJ said, grinning. "I could tell you stories, put the fear in my poor mom eight ways to Sunday. Came out of it all a lot wiser, though, I'll tell you that much."

"BJ," Stella admonished, "this ain't on the scale of lifting a can a Skoal from the filling station or shootin' at mailboxes. This is the kind of serious that could land 'em in jail or beat to shit. I know neither one of 'em has a lick of sense, and I almost wish there was some way we could knock 'em out and keep 'em on ice until their powers of reasoning were a little more finely developed but, well, you men don't seem to pick up much common sense until well into middle age so I guess that's out."

"We can just go back to Luke's and hang out," Todd suggested hopefully.

"Ha!"

"Or we could go to a movie or something —"

"No chance. I've got — appointments, and Mr. Papadakis and Mrs. Markovic don't need to be babysitters." More to the point, Stella figured she couldn't trust Chip and Natalya to keep them in one place.

It was a real problem. It would be easy to whisk Todd away and decide that Luka-Luke was Natalya's problem, and leave it at that. Except that Natalya's problems were Chip's problems, and according to the way Stella had chosen to view her family obligations, that made them hers as well.

So the gangly, handsome-in-a-scruffy-and-vacant-eyed-way, hoodlum boy in front of her was her problem as well.

Stella'd been circling the problem in her mind, but from the start she knew deep down how it was all going to go down. She just hadn't wanted to admit it to herself yet. Now it looked like she was out of options.

"Come on," she told the little group. "I'm going to buy us a pizza and we're all going to have a talk."

CHAPTER FIFTEEN

Once they were settled in at Smythe's one and only sit-down pizza joint, a large combo on order for the boys and a small one for her and BJ, Stella excused herself to make a couple of calls.

One, in particular, she was dreading . . . but in a heart-flutter weak-kneed sort of way, because it was straight to the personal cell number of the cornerstone of the Prosper, Missouri, law enforcement team.

"Sheriff Jones speaking."

"Hi, Goat, it's Stella."

"Stella! I was just gonna call you, matter of fact."

"Is that right?"

"Yeah, Irene told me your birthday's tomorrow."

Stella grinned to herself. So her little scheme had worked. She had a complicated give-and-take relationship with Irene Dorsey, the sheriff's departmental assistant, that recently had stretched to accommodate a college-age nephew of Irene's who Stella was keeping tabs on. He was a reasonably good boy, but Stella occasionally paid a visit to remind him of his priorities and suggest modifications to his work habits, using only the mildest of her persuasive techniques. In return for helping to ensure that the first of Irene's relatives ever to go to college actually finished, Irene was on the hook for a variety of little favors here and there.

Like dropping hints about upcoming birthdays, for instance.

"Oh, that, I'd practically forgotten," Stella lied.

"I was thinking, I know you're probably already busy, but I'd love to take you out to dinner to celebrate, I mean if not tomorrow, then soon. Maybe drive over to Casey, try that new steakhouse they got."

Stella raised her eyebrows. She knew exactly the place Goat was talking about, because she'd recently overheard a few ladies down at the post office sharing the opinion that charging more than forty dollars for a piece of meat was a crime, even if that meat had grown up in a field of daisies taking butter baths and wearing wreaths of clover around its horns.

The restaurant was bound to be fancy-schmancy, an opportunity to wear her silky mauve boatneck blouse, over the neckline of which her black lace bra could be counted on to occasionally peek in a coquettish fashion. Maybe get Noelle to do her nails in OPI Shangri-la-la Lilac and wear heels that would bring her lips a few inches closer to Goat's in case there was any lingering to be done in restaurant doors or such.

"I'd love to," she said, "only it's going to have to wait a few days, if that's all right."

"That's fine, I can move things around — you name the night, I'm yours."

His words gave Stella a delicious little thrill as she imagined all the ways that Goat might, indeed, be hers — and then she forced herself to put the possibility out of her mind for now, until she got more immediate matters settled.

"I was actually calling because I have . . . well, sort of a professional favor to ask."

There was a pause, long enough presumably for both of them to remember just how successful such favors had been in the past, which was to say not very much at all, when you took into account the degree of violent tendencies and gray-area delving and line crossing that had gone on. Goat had saved Stella's ass once or twice, and she'd extended the unofficial reach of the law on a number of occasions with her off-the-record contributions, but none of these were the sort of thing one could talk about in public and, in fact, none of them were especially pleasant memories for Stella. Nor, apparently, for Goat.

"Is that right." His tone was perceptibly chillier.

"Yes. Remember my sister, Gracellen?"

"I seem to remember you mentioning a sister . . . yes."

"And how she's got a stepson, Chip, who's taken up residence in the middle of Wisconsin?"

"Now, that I don't recall."

"Huh. I guess I must not have mentioned him. Nice young man, hardworking . . . anyway, his girlfriend's son, he's seventeen, well, he got himself into a bit of a scrap up here with the local, uh, well, I guess you'd call them a bad element. Mighta been some drugs involved, bad judgment, that sort of thing."

"Mmmm." Goat's tone was guarded, noncommittal, and Stella steeled herself to put on the hard sell in the push.

"So I was just wondering if you might be willing to, you know, reach out a little on the boy's behalf, make sure he doesn't get swallowed up in something over his head his first time out of the gate."

"What are we talking about here, Stella, you want me to talk to him, give him some direction? Or what, has he already been picked up, you want me to put a good word in for him with the sheriff up there?"

"Uh. Well. Those are great ideas, but see — I'm kind of up here with him."

"You're in Wis*con*sin? But Irene said she saw Camellia Edwards jogging around Nickel Pond last Saturday and she said you two were training this week."

"Oh, that was the plan. But then I got a call from Gracellen, and . . ." Stella coughed delicately, hoping Goat might be satisfied with only a vague suggestion of the business that had taken her north, so that she wouldn't be tempted to unveil any hints of the true reason for her trip.

"You went up to deal with a mess he made?" Now there was true alarm in Goat's voice. "You ain't, uh, been trying to *convince* anyone of anything up there, have you, Stella?"

Stella figured that the word "convince" was the sheriff's euphemism for all the brands of trouble that he would never actually utter aloud, which he was dimly aware of Stella's participation in, and which he probably had been working very hard to put out of his mind and which might even now be wearing down his determination to spend a romantic evening with her. Nevertheless, she pressed ahead.

"No, I just came up here to check on him. See, the thing is, what I think Luke needs most is a change of scenery, a chance to get away from this bad element." At least for a day or two until Stella could figure out the rest of the family's troubles.

"Wait, wait, wait, Stella, if you think you're gonna drag that boy back here and let him loose on the streets of Prosper and turn him into *my* problem —"

"That's not *exactly* what I was hoping for," Stella said carefully, trying to sound as reasonable and sweet as possible. "I actually need to finish up, ah, a little thing I got up here, and what I was hoping was that I could send him to you in the care of a — a friend who's with me, and then you could just watch him until I get home. You know, put him to work in the office, have him wash the cars or something — you could maybe even put him in the Dumpster overnight. Kind of a 'scared straight' scenario."

Stella instinctively pulled the phone a few inches away from her ear just before Goat's outraged bellow.

"Are you out of your mind? I am not going to use the county facilities to store some kid who's worn out his welcome in his own hometown. It's, it's *fraud* for one thing and wrongful imprisonment and probably a half a dozen other kinds of illegal."

"No problem, no problem," Stella said hastily. She didn't really think that Goat would agree to house Luke in Prosper's single temporary holding cell, which had been built on the site of the old Dumpster enclosure behind the Hardee's restaurant that had been turned into the Prosper Municipal Annex a number of years ago. However, she had learned that sometimes it paid to ask for more than you planned on settling for and bargaining your way down. "I totally understand. But I forgot to mention this boy is a skilled laborer. He learned, uh, all kinds of trades in his native country, and I'm thinking you could take him out to your place with you in the evenings, you know, after you get him to clear the parking lot or whatever down at your office. And maybe he could bunk with you, and you could tell him all about, you know, the American system of justice and how you got interested in a law career and what all. Be a chance to make a difference for, uh, the next generation."

Stella realized that she had, without even

realized it, crossed her fingers for luck and squeezed so hard she was about to break a bone. She exhaled slowly, trying to calm herself and waiting for what was sure to be an explosive response.

Goat surprised her, though. Very quietly, after a moment passed, he spoke again. "Stella Hardesty, from the moment I met you, I have known there was something special about you. I thought maybe the jumpy feeling I get when I'm around you was related to some sort of, I don't know, attraction or something between us, but now I'm suspecting it's just a reaction to the fact that you have got the biggest set of solid-steel balls on the planet."

Before Stella could entirely process his comment, and before she could even remember to move the phone away from her ears, he hollered, "*No one* else in this entire county would have the nerve to offer out my own home as some sorta, I don't know, halfway house for hoodlums imported from a whole other state, a state which, I shouldn't ought to have to tell you, has got itself a way more generous social services budget than Missouri, which is probably equipped to handle him through its own legal and social channels, but oh, *no,* that ain't good enough for *you,* Stella, cause you ain't ever satisfied to let the law do what the law's supposed to do, you got to jump on in there and stomp all over it and make a mockery of the system and do everything your own way and plus turn a man's well-deserved quiet evening into a carnival road-show. Plus I ain't even been to the grocery."

"Does that mean . . . yes?" Stella asked timidly.

"Have I ever, ever, been known to say no to you?"

If anything, the sheriff sounded even angrier than he had a moment earlier. Which made the next part all that much more tricky.

"That's fantastic, Goat, I'm really, really grateful and I just know this is the right thing to do and you're gonna look back on it and be ever so glad you decided to offer this young man a hand up. There's just one more, uh, little bit of information I need to share with you."

She took a deep breath, sure she could feel the flames licking at her face through the phone.

"I'll be sending him down with BJ Brodersen."

"Remember, no cash," Stella admonished BJ for at least the third time.

"I know, I know," BJ said wearily. He was being as good a sport as could possibly be expected, Stella figured, given the list of demands she'd given him. "Don't let 'em have the keys, watch them if they go for potty breaks and make sure they come straight back, no set-down restaurants, and take Luke straight to the sheriff."

"You'll probably want to get Todd home right quick, too," Stella said. "I told Sherilee to expect you around midnight, but knowing her, she'll be pacing her living room until then. And, uh, maybe don't tell her about Luke and the sheriff and all."

BJ nodded gloomily as Stella fretted over the nature and magnitude of the lies she'd been telling. Natalya, when confronted with the plan, had few objections after Stella assured her that the sheriff was not only a close personal friend but had volunteered to take on her son as part of an ongoing effort by the Sawyer County Sheriff's Department to mentor at-risk teens. She'd told Noelle that she was helping Chip sort out a minor legal matter and that she was sure she'd be back by Monday to celebrate her birthday a little late. That might be putting an unrealistic deadline on her project, but Stella wasn't sure she could stand to spend a whole lot more time in Smythe, since the longer she dallied there, the further her personal, not to mention romantic, life seemed to be unraveling.

"BJ, look, I don't even know how to thank you for coming all this way, and taking the boys back, and loaning me the truck and now Jorge's car, too. I swear I'll take good care of it and —"

"I keep telling you, Stella, I don't *care* about any damn vehicles. I just wish you'd turn yourself around and come on home. I don't like the idea of you up here with all these shady types."

Stella had saved what was possibly her best lie for BJ. She felt it worked because, like all good lies, it had a fair amount of truth to it. She told him that Chip was into local loan sharks for far more than he could come up with quickly, and that they were set to iron out a long-term payment plan that Chip, with his newfound fondness for Gamblers Anonymous and his steady income, combined with the encouragement and tough love of a good woman, was sure to be able to satisfy — but that had to be delayed until tomorrow, when said financiers were due to return from a multiday collections route along the western shore of Lake Michigan.

"But I'd love to take you out to dinner

next weekend to show my gratitude," Stella added, figuring that just because Goat was probably now too mad at her for a date, perhaps she shouldn't be deprived of every opportunity for a little birthday romance.

"Really?" BJ said, brightening. He cupped her elbow with one hand and led her around to the side of the truck that was shielded from the house.

Despite the fact that she hadn't slept in more than thirty hours, Stella felt her pulse speed up a little, particularly when BJ parked her against the passenger door and came well within her personal space, his face only inches away.

Inside the house, Natalya was helping Luke pack an overnight bag, and Chip was putting together some snacks for Todd, who claimed to be starving despite having eaten a mountain of pancakes and sausage only a few hours earlier. The knowledge that they would all come bursting out the front door at any moment only added to the thrill of being practically lip-locked right in front of anyone who cared to drive by.

"Really," Stella purred. "I can't imagine anything I'd rather do. Maybe we can run over to Quail Valley to Bambino's."

"I could drive," BJ murmured, leaning in a little closer.

Then Stella, who'd had the foresight to nibble on a handful of Tic Tacs as the adults were finalizing the plans for the boys and the transportation, took charge and kissed BJ Brodersen first, before he'd worked up all the courage necessary to do the honors himself. She kissed him squarely and decisively and suggestively and even a little startlingly, if his momentary paralysis were any indication, but then he quickly recovered and got into it, but good.

"BJ," Stella said when they finally came up for air, emboldened by his reaction, "I'm afraid I may have messed up the settings on the driver's seat. Seein' as I'm considerably more *petite* than you."

"I reckon I'll manage," he said huskily and pulled himself away from her with what appeared to be a practically unbearable degree of difficulty just as the boys came jostling noisily down the front walk, Chip and Natalya behind them.

Stella dashed around the truck, fixing an innocent look on her face and smashing Todd into a bear hug. "Not one word," she hissed in his ear.

" 'Bout you makin' out with Mr. B again or about I know you got a gun and *condoms* in your purse that you left on the counter?" he whispered back.

Stella shifted her hug a little so that she could reach the tender skin just above his waistband on his side and dug in for a vicious pinch, twisting before releasing him as he started to howl.

"I'll miss you, *too,* sugar," she said. "All my love to your mom."

Then she offered her hand to Luke, who shook it for the second time in one day, though it seemed to her that this time he did it with just a little more respect.

Chapter Sixteen

After a couple hours' nap on the living room couch, Stella took a quick shower and changed into the nicest outfit she'd brought, and enjoyed the supper Natalya served, which consisted of a surprisingly tasty bowl of soup made of thick noodles swimming in pickle juice. She chased it down with more of the coffee that seemed to be brewing around the clock, then helped Natalya clean up while Chip got ready for work.

He emerged from the bedroom showered and shaved and dressed in a neat blue uniform with his name stitched over the pocket. He was planning to attend a Gamblers Anonymous meeting before heading for the clinic, where he would presumably tidy up the detritus of all those practice surgeries. Stella worked hard not to think about the specimens she'd seen earlier in the day — and the condition they must now be in, having received a variety of maxillofacial modifications.

Chip had been chatty during dinner, but now he was subdued, despite the tired smile he produced for Natalya as she straightened his collar and tweaked a few wayward strands of his gelled hair. Stella knew Chip had to be at least as worried as she was. She mentally ticked off the list of outstanding problems: drug kingpins intending to wreak vengeance on Luka; a dead husband who inconveniently did not leave a clear path for Chip to marry Natalya before perishing; the threat of a murder being pinned on them despite their relative innocence.

But as she watched Chip checking his appearance in the hall mirror, accepting the neatly packed brown-bag lunch Natalya handed him before kissing her good-bye, Stella realized that her nephew was dealing with one other problem that had escaped her attention: how to support a family — an unorthodox one, perhaps — on a limited income and under the everyday pressures of an indifferent world. He was facing the challenge of being a responsible family man, the kind of man Stella had never suspected would ever emerge from Chip's reckless, selfish past.

So moving did Stella find that revelation that after Chip left, she stepped into the dirt-packed backyard for a moment of privacy and called her sister.

"Chip's a nice young man," she said without preamble.

"Oh, Stella, we've been celebratin' ever since you called to tell us he ain't killed. We got Papa over here settin' under that big fishtail palm out back, and Chester's gonna grill up some veggie burgers now the doc's got 'em both on them low sodium diets."

"Did you talk to Chip?"

"Oh yes, but he was just in an awful hurry, wantin' to get to his meeting and work and all. I think he might be hopin' for another promotion."

"No, I mean yesterday. Did you guys get it all talked through? The whole thing with the ear and all of that?"

"Yes . . ." There was a pause, and Stella could picture Gracie twisting a lock of hair around her finger like she always did when she was thinking hard. "He apologized a whole bunch of times. He said he knew it was a bad idea and he was just an idiot for tryin' it but now you and him are figuring out what to do. I got to say, when he told me how hard he was working at that Gamblers Anonymous they got, why, I was just prouder of that boy than I've ever been. But Stella . . . I don't think he feels like he can talk to his daddy about that yet. Like going to those meetings makes him weak somehow, like he can't fix things on his own."

"And let me guess, *you* didn't tell Chess either."

"Well . . . it's just, the two of 'em's men now, y'know? I mean sometimes . . . I just wonder if it's too late for them to have a regular-type father-son relationship. Too much water under the bridge, maybe."

"Gracellen Carol Papadakis," Stella said, "I'm surprised at you. Aren't you the woman who got herself hooked up with a two-year-old stepson when you weren't but a little bitty girl yourself, plucked out of that restaurant you worked in and hauled off to California?"

"Well, yeah, but . . ."

"And did you ever figure on becoming a mother to that child back then?"

"Well, I'm not his *mother,* Stella, for one thing —"

"You're the closest thing to a mom he's got now, Gracie, and I don't mean no disrespect to Iola's memory when I say it. But this is a funny world, sometimes a cruel world, and the strong folks have to step in and pick up where the weak ones leave off."

She waited for her words to sink in, sending waves of listen-up-honey energy over the phone lines. Suddenly it felt very important for Gracie to believe her, to understand how important she and Chess were to the young man stumbling around Wisconsin trying to carve out a life for himself.

And just as suddenly, a little plan popped into Stella's mind, causing her to catch her breath. A plan that might just work out for everyone, if they all did their part.

"I guess . . ." Gracie said slowly. "But if you'd seen those two, last time Chip was home — why, they couldn't even set in the same room together to watch the game on TV without one of 'em had to start snipin' at the other."

"Pfft," Stella said dismissively. "That ain't nothing a little hard work won't fix. Listen, I been estranged from a child before, and I know there was a whole lot of thoughtless things said, and pride held on to and hurt feelings and button pushing, but the minute the two of us decided to try our hardest, why, it's been put to rights."

"Well, but you did get shot up a bunch, too," Gracie pointed out. "That probably softened Noelle up some."

"What are you sayin', you want me to come out there and shoot Chess in the ass to get this rolling? 'Cause I will." Too late Stella clamped her lips shut — her hot temper was not the answer. "Look here, sugar, what-all did Chip tell you about Natalya?"

"Well, a'course, we know he's serious about her, else why else was he trying to get all that money from us to buy her an engagement ring . . ."

Stella raised her eyebrows. Not the worst lie in the world — not particularly creative, but then again Chip was just a beginner when it came to strategic thinking.

"You got to let that go," she suggested. "He never would have done it if he knew you didn't have the extra cash to throw around."

"Yeah, we talked about that, too. I told him his daddy and I are sorry we kept it from him, that we were just tryin' to keep him from worrying. I didn't have the heart to tell him about Bill and the embezzling and all, or how his daddy can't sleep at night worrying about how's he gonna find him a new warehouse manager."

"Well, now you got him all clued in and such, why don't you maybe think about if there's some way Chip could help?"

"Chip . . . help?" Gracie sounded genuinely puzzled and considerably doubtful.

"Yeah . . . you know, like maybe he could join the company."

"Oh, I don't know about that, Stella," Gracie said quickly. "Papa's still sayin' that Chess almost run it into the ground, and I got half a mind to agree with him. I mean he made up for it later, but in those early days before he met me, Chess didn't do no favors for Must-Be-Nuts."

"Yeah, but Chess didn't have the benefit of all that growin' up that Chip's got," Stella said gently. "You took care of that, I 'spect, and now Chip's got him a good woman and a boy to be responsible for and —"

"A what?"

Gracie's voice was genuinely puzzled, and Stella came to a screeching halt. Was it possible — had Chip really elected not to discuss Luke with Gracie? Here she was singing the praises of the little family, of Chip's maturity and work ethic, and she hadn't even gotten around to talking up Natalya's motherly and wifely prowess. But if Gracie and Chester Senior and Chess didn't even know bout the boy, how could they start preparing a room in their hearts for him?

"Well . . . Natalya has a son. Who will be Chip's once they're married."

"She's got her a little boy?"

"Uh . . . yes. That's what I'm tellin' you."

"Oh, Stella, here we just damn go again,"

her sister sighed, as though the weight of the entire world had just landed square on her shoulders. "I do love my husband, but if I knew back then what I know now, if God saw fit to give me a little peek at the path ahead of us, I don't know that I would have taken it on. It's very hard to become the brand-new parent of a little boy. I mean there's so many complications. What's happened to the father? Was Natalya married before?"

Stella couldn't quite figure how to answer that one — without invoking specters of Russian thugs and dead American entrepreneurs, which surely would not help her build her case. "He's . . . out of the picture," she finally settled on.

"Well, there you go. The boy's like to be a real handful, with no man in his life. Type of boy who's gonna get lured into the drugs and the skater crowd and all that bad element when he's older."

Ouch. "Oh, now, it's not as bad as all that," Stella implored. "Come on, Gracie, where's your compassion?"

Then she reached all the way back into their past and pulled out the wild card she'd been saving, the dirty punch that Gracie would never expect her to pull.

"What about Sprinkles?"

There was a silence, and Stella could practically sense Gracie pulling away from the phone.

"That was different," she whispered hoarsely.

But they both knew it wasn't.

After hanging up with Gracie, Stella called her favorite secret weapon.

"What'd you do after you got that paper piecing class cleaned up?"

"Aw, you know, the usual," Chrissy said. Stella could hear Tucker in the background, shrieking over the noise of the television. "Invited the first lady over for a cocktail, had us a side-by-side massage."

"You have time to look up what I asked you?"

"Yeah, sure, Stella, didn't take but half an hour. Tucker'n me even had time to get to the park so he could show all the other little guys how it's done."

"Oh lordy." Tucker, now that he was three and a half, had proven to have an alarming talent for climbing — not just the things he was supposed to climb on, like the play structure, but also things that were meant to be left alone, like the honeysuckle vine growing up along little brick building that housed the restrooms. On a recent visit to

251

the park, Tucker had scrambled up to the roof and then refused to come down, hollering at all the other little kids to come up and join him. While the other mothers dragged their children away, scowling at Chrissy, she scrambled up after Tucker and talked Lardner-style sense into him, accompanied with a swat on the fanny, before they both came down from the roof and enjoyed a chase around the park.

Tucker was going to be the sort of boy who was a natural leader, fearless and energetic. Boys would continue to flock to him, and mothers would continue to cringe. Unlike Chip, who'd been a sort of specter, a shy and invisible boy, slipping in and out of the crowd unnoticed. Stella felt a tug of sorrow for Gracie's stepson and resolved not to give up on him.

"So what did you find for me?"

"Well, they weren't pullin' your leg on that ManTees thing — dudes really are buying those things up and wearing 'em around under their button-downs. Supposed to take three inches off the waistline." She made a clucking sound, clearly unimpressed by the idea. "I got to tell you, Stella, the guys I been with? They come in all shapes and sizes and I guess I don't much mind any of 'em. Only, if I was diggin' down in a guy's drawers and come up against all that — all that *shiny* stretch fabric that wouldn't budge, gettin' between me and the good stuff, I think I'd be tempted to trade the guy in for a more *confident* model."

"But *women* wear them — have been for decades. Probably forever."

"You don't see *me* wearin' any of that shit."

Stella had to admit that was true — Chrissy, who was endowed with a curvy, generous figure, never wore anything but a bra and a pair of lacy panties — and Stella was pretty sure that occasionally she even went without the latter. "Yeah, but you're young still."

"I ain't never puttin' those things on. What I got isn't meant for any kinda *flesh* prison."

"Talk to me about that when you're fifty," Stella suggested, but she had a suspicion that Chrissy might be telling the truth. What was more, she wondered if the girl had a point. If she could get back all the hours she'd spent fretting over how she looked in a particular garment — if she could get back the few precious moments when she would have been enjoying Goat Jones's roving hands if her Spanx hadn't rendered her ass completely numb — then she might be willing to toss the entire collection in the trash and just go back to her naughty-enough Maidenform hipsters.

"Anyway, here's the interesting thing. This Manetta of yours and that Parch guy, they applied for a patent way back in 2006. Then they reserved themselves a domain name and even put up a little lame-ass content before letting it lapse in oh-nine."

"Uh . . . what? In English?"

There was a heavy sigh. "What I'm telling you is that they had a Web site for a while, but it was all 'coming soon' this and 'under construction' that — it looked to me like they never even went into production with any of it, though there was a picture of a coupla middle-aged guys that I'm pretty sure were Manetta and Parch, with their guts sucked in, wearing visors. I mean Stella, *shoot* me if I ever date a dude who wears a visor."

"What's wrong with a visor?" Stella demanded, thinking of the cute floral-print one Dotty Edwards bought her off QVC a while back, that she sometimes wore jogging if the sun was especially strong.

"Well, I mean, I guess for somebody out there . . . never mind. Anyway they *might* have been wearing these ManTees things under their shirts, I couldn't tell from the picture. So after oh-nine I couldn't find any evidence of anything much going on, and then bam! Back in January, all of a sudden guess what happens?"

"Uh, what?" Stella wasn't fond of Chrissy's guessing games, but she knew better than to rush the gal.

"The sale of the ManTees patent to Locke-Corp goes through to the tune of ninety thousand dollars."

Now *that* got her attention. "Ninety thousand . . . ? But I thought you said they weren't actually making the shirts yet."

"No, but see, they had registered the patent on them. Those two, Parch and Manetta, whatever they were doing over at Courtland Mills, they were working with some sort of team developing high-tech materials, which is I guess how they came across this one fabric they use. This super-stretch type stuff you insist on putting on your ass all the time, that sort of thing. I mean there's a lot of technical language in there, 'thermoregulating' this and 'melt-fusible' that. There's drawings and all."

"Wouldn't Courtland Mills have something to say about that? I mean, if it was developed on the job?"

"Yeah, but I don't think these two had much of a social life, Stella. Bet you anything they worked on this on the weekend in one of their garages or something. If they did all the work off-site, they'd own the rights to whatever they invented."

"Were there photos?"

"No, you don't need photos to get a patent. They must have hired somebody to make a couple of samples, or talked their sister or mom or whatever into doing it for them, which is I guess what they were wearing on their Web site."

"So . . . what exactly did that company buy from them? A coupla homemade shirts and a recipe for making this kind of special fabric? 'Cause seriously, Chrissy, I got a whole basement full of old sewing projects I'd be glad to sell if folks are going to be handing out hundred-thousand-dollar checks, and I know you can buy high-tech fabric up in Kansas City. Probably get it online, too."

"Yeah, but see Stella, you ain't looking at it right. What LockeCorp got for their money wasn't the actual product. It was — well, it was two things, really. First of all they got a kind of promise that Parch and Manetta weren't gonna march down to the copyright office and start suing them all over the place. And second, they got a guarantee that they weren't gonna go into competition against 'em."

"They paid ninety thousand dollars just to not get sued?" Stella clucked. "Okay, I guess I heard crazier things in my day. So then LockeCorp . . ."

"Parent company of LockeBrands Inc., third-largest maker of men's undergarments after Hanes and Jockey."

"So now they get to start selling Man-Tees?"

"Yup. And depending how fast they get them to market they could beat out the competition, be a real player in the men's shaper garment space — this could be huge for them."

"Huh. So, who was that check made out to, anyway?"

"Ha, now you're thinking. You'll be interested to know that it was made out exclusively to one Benton Keith Parch. Manetta was named as a partner on the Web site, but not on the patent."

Stella whistled and noted down the particulars. The rest of the conversation — address and phone details for Manetta and for Alana Javetz-Parch, as well as a confusing stream of patent numbers and citations and examiner names — was merely tedious, now that she had a legitimate suspect to pursue.

CHAPTER SEVENTEEN

The Impreza was hardly the smooth ride to which she'd become accustomed in the past few days, five feet off the ground in the driver's seat of BJ's truck, but it got her where she needed to go — the residence of one Christopher "Topher" Eugene Manetta. His address turned out to be part of a spiffy ring of deluxe condominiums that wound around a pond decorated with little footbridges and statuary, all of which were lit up with fancy landscape lighting. A young couple played tennis, the court as bright as daylight from the spotlights focused on it. Elsewhere people strolled along the walking paths and sat out at café tables on back patios, drinking and talking.

Singles heaven, was what the place appeared to be, with its parking lot full of shiny new cars, its recreational facilities hopping. Stella found Topher's building and parked in the guest spot, nearly opening her door into a young woman who was jogging by with earbuds in her ears.

According to Chrissy's research, Topher was forty-eight, which struck her as a little old for all this vigorous singles-set fun, but what did she know? Moments after she knocked on his ground-floor door, it was answered by a medium-tall man with short dark brown hair surrounding a perfectly round bald patch. He wore shiny athletic shorts that he might have been better advised to buy one size larger, and he was drenched in sweat, right down to the pristine white terrycloth sweatbands he wore around his wrists.

The thing that confirmed for Stella that she'd found her man, however, was what he was wearing on top. A sleeveless gray tank top printed with the words MISSOURI DEPT. OF CORRECTIONS was draped over a second tank, which was white, shiny — and very tight.

If Stella had a type, Topher would be far at the other end of the spectrum, but she was still glad she'd taken the time to fine-tune her appearance on the way to the door, tugging down her top, wiggling her jeans a little more snugly up around her ass, and slicking on an emergency coat of lip gloss. "Mr. Manetta?" she asked politely, holding her purse handle primly with both hands and smiling. "Am I interrupting?"

Topher reached for a little white towel draped over the back of a nearby chair and began vigorously mopping at his face, all the while staring and blinking at her. Aware of the way his gaze traveled up and down, Stella put one foot in front of the other, toe pointed slightly away, the way she'd been taught to pose years ago by her mother. The slight thrust of the hip, Pat Collier explained, lined all of a lady's endowments up as nicely as possible.

Her mother's wisdom was not lost on Topher, evidently. He gave his right hand a wipe-down with the towel and pulled a tiny bottle of hand sanitizer from his pocket and squirted a little goo on his hands and rubbed vigorously. Finally, he was ready, and he extended his hand and Stella shook it, trying to ignore the heat and general softness of his flesh.

"Have we had the pleasure, Ms. . . ."

"Hardesty. Stella Hardesty."

"Did we meet at the ski club mixer?"

"No, I —"

He held up one finger to shush her. "Darnell Burke's poker party?"

"No . . ."

"All right." Topher bowed at the waist and

rolled his hand in an elaborate display of chivalry. "I give up."

"Well, I'm . . . here on business relating to Benton Parch, I suppose you might say."

The change in Topher was immediate and startling. His pleasant smile vanished into a scowl. His eyes, a bland shade of blue and slightly smaller than average, narrowed even more. His posture, which had been breath-takingly erect, shifted slightly, his shoulders slumping and his knees turning in.

"What exactly is this *about?*"

"Well, really, I just wanted to come and ask you a few questions." Stella's plan, which she'd concocted on the way over, anticipated an unpleasant reaction to the mention of Parch, so she swung smoothly into her next step. "I'm from the Wisconsin Department of Intellectual Property. I've been trying to reach you by telephone, but I must have the wrong contact information, and I'm in town on another matter so I thought I would try swinging by for a quick visit. I hope that's all right. What with the budget cuts, our caseload is just through the roof, and I'm working evenings to catch up. We were doing a standard case review of patents filed in the final quarter of last year, and we came across a discrepancy in one on which you were named as a subagent."

"What . . . what sort of discrepancy?"

Stella took a sheaf of forms from her purse. If Topher got too close, he would see that they were copies of purchase orders for a variety of industrial cleaning agents that Stella had downloaded from Chip's university account, so she licked her lips as though she had a little tiny bit of something stuck in the corner and smiled encouragingly to distract him. "Oh, no worries, I think it's all to the good. We were contacted by an attorney retained by LockeCorp, who discovered this in the course of their postsale legal review. You see, they're, uh . . . there are funds involved that they are attempting pay out to the patent holder at the state level. In addition to the principal sale there are state fees and liens, and we have determined an amount is owed to the seller of the patent."

"You'd have to talk to Benton Parch about that. I'm no longer involved with the company."

"Well, we've been trying, but I was unable to reach Mr. Parch at any of the numbers we have for him."

Stella watched Manetta carefully but detected no change in his expression, which she would describe as a glum shade of disconcerted. "Yeah, well, we're not really in personal contact. You could probably reach him through his employer."

"Is that right?" Here was the hard part, where Stella tried to sneak in a personal question on top of what was already a fairly lightweight ruse. You never knew how things would go at this juncture — sometimes people got carried away with the conversation and didn't seem to notice you'd gone from chatting to prying and gave up all sorts of stuff; the sharper folks would generally shut down like clams when the pearl diver comes calling, and you'd have to work your way back through earning trust again from the start. "That's a shame. I know it's not my place to say anything, but . . . well, this patent caught my attention. My ex-husband, I was always on him to take care of himself. I don't know what it is with some guys, they hit forty and just let themselves go, you know? So when I saw LockeCorp plans to manufacture the ManTees . . . well, I just think if he'd of had a couple of those we might still be married."

Stella unleashed a giggle, letting her own gaze roam lasciviously all over Manetta's compressed and stuffed girth. She had to admit that Chrissy had a point; while the flesh in the middle region of Manetta seemed to be quite smooth and uniform under his gym shirt, the bit of ManTee that

263

she could see peeking out the top cut into him cruelly and shone with an eerily smooth patina, the skin underneath it robbed of all of its natural texture and packed in like so many pickled herrings in a tin. Looking at the shirt, Stella did not find her fingertips twitching with an urge to explore further, as she would, say, if Goat Jones showed up in gym shorts or for that matter in a garbage sack with holes cut out for his arms and head.

There wasn't one damn sexy thing about the thing, and Stella felt sad for all the fellows who, seeing the ManTee models on TV, surrounded by happy hot girl models, would rush out and buy the things hoping to be elevated in the eyes of their ladies. Damn the callous media and its obsession with physical perfection — and damn the human race for its vanity and thirst for self-delusion.

On the other hand, here she was in a Slimplicity Shaping Panty and Bra-llelujah Demi-Lift Bra, which she'd donned especially to have a seductive effect on Manetta. It appeared to be working, too, since he couldn't take his eyes off her nicely rounded cleavage and smooth, curvy ass. While the parts were all hers, the particular way they were arranged came courtesy of Spanx.

"Wow, I just hate hearing that," he said, speaking mostly to her breasts. "Men don't understand, the ladies do so much to put their best self forward, and what do guys think, that they don't have to make an effort?" Manetta shook his head as though the thought left him dumbfounded beyond belief. "I mean, look at you. You must work out, right?"

"Yes I do," Stella said, touching her fingers to her hair so that the swoopy part tipped forward over her eye in a sexy fashion. Encouraging man-lust was not the main reason she kept up her running routine and the near-nightly Bowflex sessions and the occasional martial arts bout, but it was certainly a nice by-product.

"And look how nice you've fixed your hair, your makeup, your outfit . . . your whole package, really. Um, I hope I'm not being too forward if I ask if you are over forty . . ."

"Why, yes I am, in fact," Stella said, trying to keep her earsplitting grin under control. "A *bit* over forty, anyway."

"I know it's a rude question to ask, and I hope you'll forgive me," Manetta said, "but it just goes along with my theory. A *lady* hits forty and she evaluates herself and makes whatever modifications to her routine are called for. A man who won't do the same, he just makes the rest of us look bad. Brings down the reputation of the entire gender. I myself am forty-two, and I'm in better shape than I've ever been in my life. I think earlier I was tempted to just coast, but now I understand that romance is a two-way street."

Stella was still feeling swelled up enough with modest pride that she decided to let him slide on the six years he'd shaved off his age. "That it is."

"I'm still, you know, hoping to find the right lady. I mean, a really special lady," Manetta said, slipping off his wristbands and dropping them on the hall table. "And when I do, I know we'll both make an effort for each other. I mean, that's what Man-Tees was supposed to be about — respect. Know what I'm saying?"

"Um, I think —"

"Hey, would you like a cup of coffee? A soda? I'd offer you a glass of wine but I know you're on duty and all."

Stella wouldn't have minded a little wine, or — even better — a little shot of Johnnie, which she hadn't had since leaving Missouri, but it wouldn't do to lose focus now.

"I'd love a soda, thank you. A *diet* soda, of course."

They laughed in unison as Manetta led the way into his condo, which Stella had to admit was tricked out nicely. As he busied himself pouring the soda over ice, she took in the soft green walls, the sofas loaded down with decorative cushions, the candles laid out on little gold plates.

"I like the way you've done this room," she said, though the truth was she preferred what Noelle called "eclectic clutter," which was just a nice way of saying a lifetime's worth of treasures and junk, arranged on whatever surface happened to be handy.

"Thanks. I read in a magazine, women like green. They find it soothing."

Stella was starting to think Manetta took his woman-prowling a little too far, if he based all of his decisions on the collective tastes of the fairer sex.

He brought her glass and toasted it with his own. Stella thought the cologne smell was stronger now and wondered if he'd spritzed himself on the sly while he was in the kitchen.

"Want to see the rest?" he asked, as she took a sip.

"Um . . ."

"Of my *place*." Before she could respond, he'd motioned for her to follow him down the hall.

"I use the extra bedroom for my gym."

"Nice," Stella said, peering in to see a treadmill and a rack of free weights in front of a wall entirely covered with a mirror. Next to them, copies of *Men's Health* and *GQ* were arranged on a little table.

"And this is my bedroom . . ."

The bedroom was painted a mauve-ish purple, with gold-leafed curtain rods holding bouffant sheer panels twisted and knotted this way and that.

"Wow."

"Yeah. Those curtains are silk, and that painting has genuine brushwork added to the print. The bedding's all down, and I have a little fridge in here with water bottles and wine."

"Huh . . . so you don't have to get up and go to the kitchen, is that it?"

"Exactly!" Manetta beamed at her, and for a moment she was afraid he was going to ask her if she wanted to take a romp on the spot, but to her relief he led her back out to the living room, and they sat on the sofa, Stella putting as much distance between herself and Manetta as she could.

Even if he wasn't a murder suspect, she doubted she would ever find him attractive. He was afflicted with a taint of desperation that was as unmistakable and off-putting as body odor.

"This might surprise you," he was saying, "but I didn't always have a lot of success with women. Nowadays, sure, I'm out three, four nights a week. Ski club, spinning class, Latin dance, you name it, I'm into it — and I'm having more fun than ever." Something about the grim set of Manetta's jaw made Stella wonder if he was telling the truth. "But there was a time when I couldn't get a woman to look at me. I mean, I'm a scientist — a geek, you might say. Well, other people said it, anyway."

He laughed, but there was little humor in it. Stella thought she saw a glimpse of the lonely, awkward man he'd been. Well, more than a glimpse, really — more like a full-on life-sized slightly older version, just with a makeover and a support garment.

"I can't even believe that," she lied.

"Yeah, I know, but it's true. Me and Benton, know how we met?"

"You worked together, right? That's what our records show . . ."

"Yeah, but more specifically — it was my first week on the job, and Benton had been off at some conference. I'd moved into my cubicle and I was trying to get to know the ropes, and there was this one secretary — really cute, a tight little redhead with big . . .

a big personality. She was being really friendly, showing me around, all that. She was *flirting* with me, saying we should have drinks, making all these suggestive jokes, and I was — well, I couldn't believe my luck, I was falling for it. Hell, I told myself it was because I'd landed this great job — I was successful, I had as much of a chance as the next guy, know what I'm saying?"

"Sure," Stella said.

"Then Benton gets back from his trip and sees what's going on and asks me to have a cup of coffee, and that's when he tells me. This woman, she's *playing* with me. She does it to all the new guys. Her and her friends, they get guys all riled up, convinced they're gonna get lucky. And then they wait until everyone goes out to happy hour, when they've had a few drinks — lead them on and then drop them flat. Cut 'em off at the balls, right in front of everyone. They think it's fucking hilarious."

The mask had slipped, Manetta's light tone giving way to the fury that was simmering underneath. His mouth twitched at the corner and he squeezed his hands into fists.

"That's terrible," Stella said.

"Yeah. Tell me about it. Benton said we had to stick together, that he wouldn't let that happen to me. He told me to just be polite but keep my distance, and that's what I did. After a while we started going out after work sometimes, places where the girls aren't as snobby. Or as attractive, but that was before I really started taking care of myself, so I couldn't be as picky."

"So let me get this straight," Stella said. "You were okay with hitting on plain, ugly girls because they were the only ones who'd have you?"

"Well, like I said, I hadn't done my personal *work* yet. Now, a fine-looking woman like you, you've never had to deal with that, I imagine, so maybe you can't understand what it's like. But Benton did. He was just like me. Average-looking guy, not much experience with the women. So we stuck together. We were each other's wing man. And when we came up with the idea for ManTees, we were the very first to wear them. We were the first success stories."

"You mean they really helped you?"

"Well, yeah. We started talking to women. We started getting dates. Like . . . on our own."

Stella didn't figure they'd taken each other along when one of them snagged an unsuspecting woman, but she let it go. "How'd it happen that only Benton's name ended up

271

on the patent?"

"That was no big deal. He said he'd take care of it, I said fine. Benton is more of a detail guy, I'm big picture."

"But when Benton sold to LockeCorp —"

"That wasn't anything more than a paperwork hassle. I mean, we had to pay the wiring fees and so on to split the funds into both our accounts —"

"What do you men, both your accounts?"

"Don't you have that in your paperwork?" Manetta gestured at her sheaf of papers. "We had to sign like a hundred different forms. It was kind of a hassle to figure out for taxes, but it worked out, and we both got half. I mean, within a few bucks one way or another."

There went his entire motivation. "So you're saying you benefited equally from the sale of the patent."

"Yeah. Which I guess means I need to make sure he gets half of whatever you-all have from the state."

Stella recovered from her disappointment. "Oh, oh yeah, sure, I'll make sure he does. Uh, if I can find him."

"Look, Stella," Manetta said, reaching over and squeezing her shoulder. "You can see I'm set up nice here. The money from ManTees let me do a few things. Got new furniture, clothes, some speakers would blow your mind. Sure, I've got all the bells and whistles. But some things don't change, you know? What's between a woman and a man, for instance . . . especially if they respect each other enough to always put their best self forward . . . well, I can just tell that you and I are cut from the same cloth. And if you'd ever like to explore that further, I know a place we can go where the waiters still wear ties and treat you with respect. Have you got a card on you?"

"Uh . . . well, I just moved offices and I'm having some new ones printed up."

"Okay, well, I'm easy to find. I'm Man-TeeMan on Facebook. Friend me, okay?"

Stella promised to do so, and endured a linger-y suggestive handshake before she made her escape, wondering what it was about a man who tried too hard — they were even easier to resist than the ones who didn't try at all.

CHAPTER EIGHTEEN

Stella could barely keep her eyes open on the way home. She was exhausted, and tomorrow when she woke up she'd be a whole extra year older and she wasn't sure how she was planning to feel about that, and she wasn't any closer to figuring out who'd left a dead guy in her nephew's kitchen than she was when she arrived in Wisconsin, and all she wanted right now was a tumbler of Johnnie and a good long night's sleep, though she'd settle for just the sleep. Now that they'd gotten the boys shipped off toward safety — or at least temporary storage, in Luke's case — she figured she could just hit the hay and deal with everything else in the morning.

When she got to the house, however, Natalya had the place lit up like blazes. Every lamp, every overhead light was turned on, and she was sitting on the living room couch with a tangled pile of yarn in her lap. She had the news blaring on the television. A plate bearing a few neat slices of cheese sat nearby, untouched, along with a neatly folded napkin and a glass of milk.

Stella, who'd used the key Chip gave her to get into the house, cleared her throat when she saw that Natalya was crying, great glistening tears sliding down her cheeks, streaking them with mascara. She was staring in the general direction of the television, but her eyes were unfocused.

"Uh . . . honey?" Stella said after a moment, not knowing what else to do. She was plenty accustomed to crying ladies and had entertained any number of them in her living room, usually while trying to pry and suss and untangle and coax their stories from them, stories of beatings and cruel words and slaps and punches and falls down stairs and teeth knocked loose. Natalya, as far as she knew, had been the victim only of general oafishness and jealousy on the part of her husband, but emotions were bound to be running high with all the murdering and so forth, plus discovering one's son was a drug dealer probably didn't do much for one's spirits.

"Natalya?" Stella said a little louder, making a move to put a comforting hand on the woman's shoulder. Instead, Natalya leapt from her chair with a shriek, tugging off the glasses that had been perched on the end of her nose and nearly knocking over the milk, and then both of them went for the yarn, which had fallen under the couch, and there was general confusion as the mess was cleared and the television turned down and tissues fetched and tears wiped away.

Then, not knowing what else to do, Stella guided Natalya back to the sofa and suggested she have a sip of her milk. Ordinarily Stella was quick with a hug in tearful situations, but Natalya's high-strung jumpiness made her cautious. Not to mention her own nerves, which were wound up tight from exhaustion.

"Look here, Natalya, you got anything stronger than milk around here? And also you got any more of them snacks?"

Natalya waved weakly in the direction of the kitchen. "You are helping yourself."

Stella took her at her word. She found a few dusty bottles in the cabinet above the fridge: the dregs of a bottle of peppermint schnapps, a few inches of gin, and a bottle of Scotch that still had a red plastic bow attached to the top. She squinted at the label: LAPHROAIG, it read. SINGLE ISLAY MALT SCOTCH WHISKY.

It was a dilemma of the sort she didn't

run into every day. "Y'all aren't drinkers, are you?" she called into the living room.

"No, is ruin of many men of my family. I tell Chip we are totalers."

"Huh. *Tee*totalers, I expect you mean. Well, see here, I'm wondering if I can do you a favor and take some of this off your hands."

Another limp wave was all the encouragement Stella needed, and she opened the Laphroaig. Not her brand, but she figured she could make an exception this once. She poured a healthy couple of inches into a juice glass and held it up to the light, then took a cautious sniff.

Damn. She wrinkled her nose at the scent, which was redolent with notes of tar and WD-40 and paint thinner and practically singed the hairs on the inside of her nose. You had to wonder what they were thinking over there on the British Isles. Stella had no idea whether corn could be made to grow along the soggy moors of Scotland, or whatever they called their fields over there, but surely they could have called up the folks in Kentucky and asked for a few pointers. After all these centuries, Stella couldn't imagine it hadn't occurred to them to stop roasting their whisky over patches of sod they dug up from the ground, which apparently burned like a pile of Goodyears and imparted its nasty taint to every ounce along the way.

Still, it probably beat gin all to hell, and Stella was not about to dig into the schnapps, seeing as she'd gotten drunk as a skunk on the stuff one memorable evening during her senior year in high school and couldn't even sniff it without wanting to run to the bathroom to throw up.

She took a deep breath and a healthy bolt of the whisky and shuddered as it went down.

And felt a little better, after she got her breath back.

"Okay," she said, wiping her mouth on a paper napkin. She settled into a love seat near Natalya. "What gives?"

"Promise me you will not tell Chip about glasses."

Stella blinked. Not what she was expecting. "Uh . . . what?"

"About reading glasses. He must not know."

"Fill me in here, sister — you're shacking up with the guy, you left your *husband* for him and all, and you're afraid he'll see you in your *specs?*"

"Is not just any glasses, you are not understanding. Is uh . . . how are you saying." She took the glasses and handed them to Stella, who examined them closely, peering through the lenses.

"These are cheaters," she said in surprise. "Magnifiers." They weren't as strong as Stella's — she'd made her way steadily through the numbers at the drugstore and was now a solid +2 — but they were, nonetheless, the sort of spectacles one didn't generally need until one reached middle age. "Just how old are you, anyway?"

"I tell Benton I am thirty-six," Natalya said miserably. "Chip, I am telling I am thirty-four."

"And . . ."

"And I am forty-four years."

At that, the leaking started up again, but this time Stella was a little too dumbfounded to react immediately. "Damn," she finally said.

Natalya nodded. "My grandmother is having very good skin, still very little wrinkle on face. I am thinking I can trick Chip, but soon my eyes are beginning to get bad. What if he finds out? Handsome man like Chip, he is twenty-eight, he can have any lady is attracting to him!"

Natalya's fears were so real, her trepidation so consuming, that Stella didn't have the heart to point out that Chip was perhaps not *every* woman's ideal, with his doughy middle and prominent Adam's apple and rounded shoulders and awkward posture. "But he loves you, Natalya. I mean, look at everything he's done for you. Giving you a home, taking Luke under his wing . . ."

Slicing up bodies and extorting money from his family, she considered adding, but thought better of it.

"He loves the woman I am pretending him. But men get very angry about age lie. When Benton is finding out, he is calling me terrible name."

"Wait. Benton knew . . ."

"Only when Luke is coming to America few months ago, when papers are coming with numbers on them. Benton is signing papers and finds out."

A cold unease started in Stella's gut and eddied out in growing circles. Benton found out Natalya's true age. Benton, perhaps, threatened to tell her new lover when he discovered the pair carrying on. How far would Natalya go to keep that secret?

"Surely you haven't been, you know, losing sleep over this," she said. "I mean, with everything else the two of you have to worry about . . ."

Natalya shook her head vigorously. "Oh no, I am very worry, trying hard to trick

Chip. I am exercise two hours with TV when he is going to work. I am putting on the makeup and doing diet." She patted her flat stomach miserably, and Stella remembered how little Natalya had consumed since her arrival.

Oh, vanity — it was the undoing of many an otherwise smart and competent woman. Stella saw the starved and skeletal gals they had on the talk shows, the frail actresses stumbling hollow-eyed and pale through their roles, the singers whose ribs stuck out of their hoochie outfits as they strutted around in the music videos. Not to mention all the plastic surgery —

"Wait a minute," she said. "The Botox — that wasn't Benton's idea at all, was it?"

Natalya's mouth wobbled and fresh tears welled. "No, you are wrong. Is Benton who is saying I am looking too old with the wrinkles."

"Well — I mean, other than the thing with your lips, you're very . . . smooth." Stella was not reassured by Natalya's claim. If she'd been desperate enough to stay in this country — having traded on her looks, using a currency of lies — it suddenly seemed more than a little likely that Natalya might have taken drastic steps . . . especially now that Stella knew she kept secrets from Chip.

For a long time the two women sat in silence, each lost in her own thoughts. Fatigue and the steadily draining whisky — which Stella had to admit lost its burning punch after the first few sips and became, in its own way, almost pleasant — were conspiring to make her pass out. Chip wouldn't be home until the wee hours, BJ was about to deliver the boys into safety, and there was nothing further she could do for now.

"Look here," she said, figuring she had all the next day to decide if Natalya was a killer or not, "I think I need to head to bed."

Natalya sniffed. "Before you are going, can I ask question, Stella?"

"Uh, sure."

"You are knowing how to knit?"

Stella blinked. She did indeed know how to knit — she'd learned from her mother at the age of seven, and had knitted a couple dozen sweaters and scarves and mittens and hats before being bit by the quilting bug and putting her needles away. Since her widowhood, and reinvention as a purveyor of justice, Stella'd had no time for any of the needle arts, but she was pretty sure she could still kick crochet or cross-stich or needlepoint or, yes, knitting ass all over town.

"What have you got?"

There followed a sleepily pleasant half hour of sorting through the mess Natalya had made of eight skeins of Lion Wool-Ease Chunky yarn and a pattern printed from their Web site for a pair of cable-knit sweater vests, one large in Indigo for Luke, and one medium in Redwood for Chip. Natalya explained that she hoped to finish them by Christmas, which Stella figured was a reasonable goal if she could teach her how to cast on properly and straighten out her gauge.

She tried to harden herself against the woman sitting next to her with yarn looped around her wrists, who was almost definitely a cold-blooded killer, but in the end the pleasant clicking of the needles and tug of the yarn was impossible to resist, and they got a few nearly perfect rows of k2p2 ribbing done before Stella staggered to bed and slept like a baby until the ringing of her cell phone catapulted her out of a pleasant dream in which she was wrapped in a baby-soft sweater that the sheriff was slowly unraveling.

CHAPTER NINETEEN

Stella grabbed the phone off the bedside table and was immediately deafened by the cacophonous racket of half a dozen voices doing an off-key approximation of "Happy Birthday."

By the time it was finished, she was nearly vertical and, despite her irritation at being woken up, and her even greater irritation that she was another year older, grinning.

"Who the hell you got there with you?"

"Just me and Tucker, and Mom and Dad and Danyelle and the twins. Y'all run along now," Stella heard Chrissy say away from the phone. "That's all you're needed for. Now git."

"Well, I suppose that was kind of nice. Thank you, Chrissy."

"That's just the start. Soon's you get back here where you belong, we'll celebrate for real."

"I'm trying. Believe me, I'm trying."

"Really? 'Cause it sounds to me like you're laying about in bed at nine thirty in the morning, when most decent folk are up and *productive,* like maybe running *businesses* for their lazy-ass *bosses* who are out of town on boondoggles."

"Ain't you just a little bit cranky."

"Well, I didn't get in last night until practically two and it was too late to bring Tucker home from my folks', which meant I had to help Mom fix breakfast for the kids 'cause Danyelle's fightin' with Ed again, and then I got an e-mail saying I won't get the Glue Baste-It I ordered until a week from Tuesday, which is exactly one fuckin' week later than I need it for the appliqué class, not to mention I just found out Hoff man discontinued that tractor print what I promised Harriet Fofana for the backing on her husband's birthday quilt and I'm tryin' to find it on eBay but it's got bid up to eighteen bucks a yard."

Stella, even in her semibleary state, knew right away that Chrissy had rolled out the last few details merely as an obfuscation of the first. "Got in late, huh," she said. "That mystery man a yours again?"

"What makes you say that? Maybe I went over to Tiffany's to play cards. Or worked on the quilt I'm makin' for Mom and Dad's anniversary. Or, or, went to a movie or —"

"Until two in the morning? Yeah, uh-huh. You was at Tiffany's, who I know for a fact just had her a new baby two months ago. Prob'ly readin' verses from the Good Book and drinking chamomile tea, too, right?"

There was a pause, and then a dramatic sigh. "Stella, here's the thing, I know you think of me as a big party girl and all, but I'm kind of maybe a little into this one. And I'll tell you 'bout him, soon's I know is he gonna stay around for a while."

Stella couldn't help noticing the unfamiliar uncertainty in the girl's voice. Whoever she was making time with, he'd gotten much more of a reaction out of her than any of her recent string of lovers, who she usually went through with good cheer and a healthy appetite for variety.

"Chrissy, I doubt there's a man alive who'd willingly leave your love trap," Stella remarked and then took the high road before she could change her mind. "But I guess if you want to keep it to yourself, why, I ain't got any business tryin' to beat it out of you."

"Mmm. Well, I got a little surprise for you. I went looking around to see what-all financial info I could find on Benton Parch, like you suggested. I found a few big with-

286

drawals out of his checking account for the dates you asked about, back when he was bringing Natalya over to the States and then when her son came over, and also a couple other withdrawals I'm thinking were probably for the wedding, all that shit. It all added up to over thirty thousand, so if that's what he wants to charge your nephew, I don't know, might be about right."

"It ain't like he's trading hogs," Stella said hotly. "This is a woman we're talking about, not somethin' to be bought and sold, a fugitive from a — a cruel life, on her way to enjoying the freedoms of a United States citizen . . ."

"Uh huh. Save the Stars and Stripes, Stella, I'm with you on this one. Family of yours is family of mine and all that. Just giving you background. Anyway, your guy Benton is pulling down fifty-three thousand a year at Courtland Mills, a little more than Manetta, but then he's one pay grade higher. I went back four years on his taxes, nothing special there. Kept up on his mortgage, paid regular on his Shell card, blah blah blah."

"This is what you called to tell me?" Stella yawned, stretching luxuriously. "It ain't exactly breaking news."

"No, what I called to tell you, other than

happy goddamn birthday, was that if you were thinking Benton was gonna buy an island or a Lamborghini or something after selling off the ManTees patent, you can think again. LockeCorp paid out exactly ninety-one thousand four hundred and eighty dollars, and I got records of a wire transfer of half of it into Manetta's account within a week. Parch put a chunk of his half into savings, prob'ly so he'd have it for taxes, and it's been sitting there pretty much ever since. Except for . . ."

Stella, who was quite familiar with Chrissy's dramatic pauses, knew she would get no further until she played her part. "What, what, whatever could it be? Why, I'm all aquiver with anticipation, Christina Jaynelle — please tell me your amazing news before I expire from curiosity!"

That got her a disgusted snort. "You just got to take the fun outta every damn thing, don't you? Okay, fine, I'll just tell you and then I'll go earn us both a living since you're too busy to work at anything that actually *pays.* A month or so after he got all that cash stashed away, Parch went and spent a big chunk of it. First was a charge for eleven thousand dollars at Hawthorn Jewelers, 444 Broadway right there in Smythe."

"No kidding?"

"The other was an insurance policy. Half a million bucks in the event of his death."

"And don't tell me — Natalya's the beneficiary," Stella said with a sinking heart.

"Nope. In the event of his death, all of his dough goes to one Alana Parch-Javetz."

If Natalya had spent the night planning and scheming to kill Stella because she was too close to the truth of Parch's demise, she hid it well. Stella found her standing at the stove, humming and stirring something in a pan, something that smelled heavenly and buttery and set Stella's mouth to watering.

Her reading spectacles were nowhere in sight. The sweater sleeve, however, was laid out carefully on the table, and Natalya had knitted several more reasonably neat and error-free inches.

"Look what I am doing after you are sleeping, Stella!" she said proudly. "Now I must hide it again. I put away before Chip is coming home."

Stella clucked her admiration and helped Natalya stow the project in a big cardboard box labeled KIRKLAND KITCHEN TRASH BAGS. Then she enjoyed a plate of eggs scrambled with chives and dill and some of Natalya's strong coffee. True to form, Natalya nibbled on some toast and ate one forkful of eggs. Stella noted that even if she pulled off the younger-woman ruse, she was likely to starve to death in the process.

"I need to go see someone," she said, after rinsing her plate off in the sink. "How late will Chip sleep?"

Now that she wasn't quite as convinced that Natalya had killed her husband, since another suspect was currently deflecting suspicion, she felt warmly toward the couple. She even considered telling Natalya it was her birthday but decided that should wait until she was sure there wasn't going to be a big awkward scene if it turned out the woman was a murderer.

"Oh, he will be up before too long. Today he is helping me washing the windows. We are spring cleaning!"

"Okeydoke, then."

As Stella drove through town and back onto the highway toward Madison, she made a few calls.

Potter's Auto would have the Jeep ready by Friday. That was the easy one.

Stella took a deep breath and dialed Goat.

"I don't know what kind of crazy I musta been to agree to this," he growled by way of a greeting.

"Well, hello to you, too, Sheriff," Stella said, trying to keep the Goat-wobble — a strange vocal effect that occurred only when she was talking to him, a circumstance that seemed to rob the air of oxygen — out of her voice. "It's my birthday."

There was a pause, and Stella crossed her fingers tightly, then hastily uncrossed them when her loosened grip on the steering wheel caused the little car to drift toward the median.

"Huh." Into that one syllable were layered so many emotions and hesitations and tempered enthusiasms that Stella couldn't gauge where she currently stood in Goat's esteem.

"I'm . . ." For a moment she thought of lying, of choosing a number on the junior end of fifty, but that wasn't her style. "Fifty-one."

"That's a nice number," Goat said brusquely, and suddenly it was. "Maybe that oughtta be celebrated, in some way, by us. When you get back. Like we were saying the other day."

"I guess that would be okay." Stella ground her nails hard into her leg, to keep her cheerful from showing — she had a feeling it might be evident even across the phone lines.

"Speaking of which." So much for the sweet. Goat's voice went all business, the

291

way it did every time Stella managed to bring trouble over to the sheriff's office. "Dale Savage came by this morning looking to get a permit for the shop."

" 'Bout time." Tornadoes had swept through Prosper the year before, tearing off the five-foot-tall paint can that had been perched on top of Savage Paint & Wallpaper ever since Stella had been a little girl, reducing it to a pile of crushed fiberglass and plaster, and also gouging the siding and wrecking much of the trim. Stella wouldn't go so far as to call it an eyesore, but she was happy that Dale was getting ready to spruce up the place.

"He'd got most of the t's crossed and i's dotted — Irene seen to that — but there were one or two points that were a little sticky. What with the building codes and all."

"Oh — that's too bad." That was exactly what Stella hated about the law, right there — a focus on the picky details getting in the way of the greater good.

"But we found our way around it," Goat continued, as though Stella hadn't said anything. "Seein' as I sent Luke over there to help 'im out for a few days. He's gonna get to the shop when Dale does, at eight, and work on through until he goes home at six. Fact, he's got himself invited to dinner at the Savages' long as he minds his p's and q's, and then Ernice can bring him back when she comes into town at nine to get little Bud from choir practice."

"Is that right?" Stella had to give him credit — Goat had had Luke all of a few hours and already managed to get him hired out and fed. Which led her to believe that Luke had been mighty careful to be on his best behavior. If even a sliver of his sly bad-boy side had been on display, Goat would have had him chilling in the waiting area under Irene's watchful eye, or washing down the department vehicles, or even mucking stalls out at Landers Stables.

The paint-shop job was a cushy one, and Stella suspected Goat saw something worthy in the boy, something redeemable and worth the effort and a measure of trust. The thought made her smile.

" 'Course Dale's only payin' him four bucks an hour," Goat said.

"Four bucks sounds about right," Stella concurred, wondering what he'd been pulling down in the playgrounds and school restrooms in Smythe. Whatever he'd been earning, it didn't much measure up to what she had started to have in mind for him. A plan was taking shape — a shadowy, uncertain, more-hope-than-reason type of plan, but so far so good. "You have any trouble with him, I'll take full responsibility."

That got her a snort of derision. "Stella, you're already into me for more favors and promises and IOU's than I can count, I don't know if I'd even notice one more or less."

"What's that supposed to mean?"

"Don't you be playin' the shy lass with me, Dusty. You know damn well — oh, hell. Just get your business done and get your ass back here where you belong, hear?"

"Why, yes, sir," Stella murmured after she'd hung up, after it was too late for Goat to hear, because she wasn't sure if she was quite ready for him to know how it stirred her up when he did that growly thing and pushed her around a little.

Stella had been pushed plenty in her life — Ollie'd not only pushed, he'd slapped and punched and belittled and reviled and insulted her practically every day of their three decades together — and she was not about to stand for one more hand raised against her, one more ill-considered outburst meant to shame her, one more joke of which she was the butt. That said, there was something almost magical about being manhandled, when you knew that man was guided by decency and a genuine fondness for the female gender and an all-around respect for the ladies he dated. When there was no fear involved, a remarkable door opened up, one that led to teasing and breathless risk-taking and dipping toes into trust, and wickedness for the sheer joy of the heart-stopping thrill . . . a smorgasbord of delights Stella had never imagined in her married days.

Stella checked the speedometer and saw that she'd been going faster and faster. She took her foot off the gas and coasted, grinning, thinking about how happy she'd be to see Wisconsin in her rearview mirror as she headed for home.

But first there was work to do.

CHAPTER TWENTY

She found Benton's sister's house with little trouble. The directions Chrissy'd given her were more than adequate, but she could have picked the house out on the cul-de-sac even without them, just thinking about the gawky long-jawed gray-haired woman she'd encountered on Chip's porch the day before.

The neighborhood, which was several miles from the outer limits of the student-and-professor chaos of the campus fringes, seemed to feature two styles of tract home: a shrimpy little asymmetrical one-story box, and a slightly more spacious trilevel with a lumpy stuck-on porch. Most of these had been landscaped and painted and primped in such a way as to convey a proper embarrassment at their humble roots, with swaths of faux stone trim or composite railing or at the very least Martha Stewart–inspired paint palettes suggesting that the owners, while chagrined at the homely bones of their abodes, had taken pains to rise above them.

But there, lodged like storm-drain flotsam between two much higher-reaching neighbors, was the home that had not aspired to much at all, unless you counted unfettered overtaking on the part of the invasive native grasses that had beaten back the sod, or the splintery original paint job that seemed ashamed of its own sun-faded mauve and blushed a rain-stained deep cherry. A fluttery row of tinkly chimes, hammered from aluminum leavings and sawed-off bamboo, kept up a dispirited cacophony in the background. Stella studied the front door — a dingy alabaster slab decorated with a frowsy plastic wreath — and willed it to open, to regurgitate its neglectful owner, preferably in a chatty and confessional mood.

No dice. Stella finally sighed and shut off the ignition. She gathered her purse and emergency kit, a bare-bones sampler of various restraining and intimidating tools packed into a Clinique gift-with-purchase vinyl cosmetic tote emblazoned with pastel strawberry vines, and got out of the car.

Stella glanced around for onlookers and potential witnesses — not something she wanted to encourage — and came up satisfyingly empty. That was why Stella didn't expect much as she got out of the car and approached the house. Alana had not given off any housewife vibe that Stella could identify. She probably spent her weekends canvassing for the local green party, or collecting obsolete electronic parts to turn in for recycling fees.

Stella pressed the doorbell while in the middle of her professional once-over. Rent or own, that was not immediately clear; the peeling paint and cracked concrete certainly didn't speak to an attentive interest, but the neat rows of fresh-planted rudbeckia and Indian paintbrush, the tole-painted mailbox, the pot of geraniums — all of these said "owner" to her.

Before she had time to decide, the door burst open and Alana popped out, wielding a watering can.

"Wait a second." She squinted, then patted around on top of her head until she was able to disentangle a pair of glasses that Stella hadn't noticed perched in all that unruly gray hair, and slipped them on.

Stella had heard the phrase "her face fell" but never actually seen a convincing example of it until that moment. Alana, who appeared to be somewhere around Stella's age, had fairly nice firm skin for someone who didn't spend a nickel on upkeep, but when she realized who had come to visit, it flattened and drooped. "Oh. It's *you.*"

Stella stuck out a hand. "Stella Hardesty, in case you don't remember the name. Natalya's attorney. Just following up on a few things. May I come in?"

Alana cast about her front yard, apparently finding no excuses there. She set down the watering can and sighed. "Well, I need to get to rehearsal before too long, but I guess I have a few minutes. I got coffee made, but it's probably cold by now."

"I'd love some."

Stella, who'd enjoyed about eleven cups of Natalya's never-ending brew, needed more coffee like she needed a bandeau bikini top, but she figured on taking advantage of the situation to check out Alana's place. She tiptoed discreetly into the dinette area, which afforded her a view of the entire first floor. The house was built in that soaring-ceiling fashion builders insisted on where all the heating and cooling kilowatts one purchased hovered high above where they couldn't do any good, and in a small-footprint dwelling like this one, one got the feeling the house had been set on its end, long ways.

The house smelled strongly of herbs. At

least Stella supposed they were herbs, since there was a top note of cinnamon or something like it — maybe tea. Or just layers of dirt: Alana was an indifferent house keeper, and though she had the blinds shut against nearly all sunlight and hence it was hard to see, Stella was pretty sure she could write her name in the dust that covered every exposed surface. Alana appeared to have a fondness for scarves, or perhaps shawls, or maybe just long lengths of silky fabric, which were draped over tables and looped over the drapes. An enormous set of speakers dominated the living area, along with what Stella, after a moment of confusion, figured out was a music stand. On a bench pulled up next to a chair was a violin case.

"Oh, you play violin?" Stella asked politely as Alana brought her a fussy flowery mug that was, indeed, cold to the touch, and sat down across from her with a glass of water.

Alana sniffed. "That's a viola. And I don't just 'play,' it's my vocation. I'm fourth chair in the Madison Symphony Orchestra."

"Really?" Stella was impressed. She'd been to the Kansas City Philharmonic once, years ago when she was in high school, on a field trip led by the ambitious student teacher who'd taken over the Prosper High Girls' Chorus that year. They'd gotten first-row seats, which was thrilling until Miss Klein explained that they were cheap on account of the fact that you got a heavy dose of violin and not much else. Stella, however, had been enchanted by the young concert-mistress, a woman who never once glanced at her music but gazed, enraptured, at the conductor and swayed as if guided by invisible strings and, at one point, played a solo that had her fingers dancing up the delicate throat of the instrument and impossibly close to the frenzied bow as a melody unwound itself in startling, brilliant crescendo. The entire concert hall had fallen silent as the young woman finished with a fling of her bow and a toss of her hair and then went limp, apparently drained by all that pouring of her soul into the music, and a second later the rest of the orchestra came back and picked up the thread, to the thunderous applause of the audience.

Stella generally preferred fiddle to violin, and never deliberately put on the classical station, but she had never forgotten that day or that performance. Somehow, though, she doubted the glum and musty Alana Parch-Javetz stirred the same kind of passion in her listeners as that long-ago violinist had.

"Now, playing in the symphony — is there a lot of money in that? I mean is it like

301

sports where the top guys get the millions and the rest of the folks sitting on the bench have to scramble? And is a viola like, I don't know, a lineman or something, where you got your violins being the quarterbacks?"

Alana fixed her with a frosty glare. "We're all compensated roughly the same."

Stella nodded. "That a good living? I mean, nice place like this — that's got to set you back."

"Nearly all of us give private lessons and perform commercially. I'm booked most of the time."

"Really? 'Cause I got this friend, he's always wanted to learn to play the fiddle, he just can't get over that one riff they do in 'Devil Went Down to Georgia' — you think you could teach him that?" Stella was deliberately baiting Alana, but it was actually true — her friend Jelloman Nunn always said that when he got his daughter through med school at Mizzou, he was going to take some time for his hobbies, and fiddle ranked right up there with tending to the best homegrown in the county under a bank of grow lights in the basement.

"I think not." Alana wrinkled her nose as though Stella had asked if she'd teach her how to swing her tits so the tassels spun in opposite directions.

"Well, yeah, anyway. I guess I should get down to business here."

"That's probably a good idea. What exactly is it that Natalya's paying you to do? As I understand it, the law is fairly clear."

Stella, whose acquaintance with immigration law spanned exactly what she'd been able to pick up in a half hour on Chip's computer with Natalya hovering anxiously behind her offering fragments of interpretation, felt it was probably best not to focus on specifics. "Well, yes, there are always legal guidelines — but it's the exceptions that hold our interest. My colleagues and I have been able to do some terrific things for our clients. I mean I can't go into any detail, given the attorney-client privilege and all, but I think Natalya's going to really enjoy becoming a full-fledged citizen. To be honest, though, I wanted to talk more about *you* on this visit."

"Me? I can't imagine why."

"Really? You and Benton, being so close, and now this sudden . . . rift in your relationship — well, it adds to our concerns. We had hoped you would be able to help us locate him. As you can imagine, Natalya is as anxious to find him as you, since he will need to be signing some of the documents that my, uh, paralegal is preparing." Stella made a mental note to tell Chrissy she'd been promoted again, in title at least. Though knowing the gal's skill with the Internet, she could probably download her own paralegal license and get it recognized all over the state of Missouri.

"What sort of documents are those? Benton already told Natalya he'll contest any divorce she tries to bring against him, and since you're a lawyer and all, I guess you know what that means in the state of Wisconsin."

Stella, who had spent many a long afternoon fantasizing about divorce back before she took decisive and unplanned action and became a widow, had never gotten as far as consulting an attorney or even looking up the laws. Without a college education or training or experience, she'd always believed that she would never be able to support herself. There was also the other little problem — that Ollie always told her he'd kill her if she ever tried to leave him.

So she was a little bit out of her element, but luckily Alana was warming to her subject. Her narrow face flushed with anger, and she took a break to chew at her nails, which Stella noticed for the first time were bitten past the quick. That, along with the calluses from all that viola playing, gave her hands an odd and creepy look.

"I don't do divorce law," Stella said. "And it's been a long time since I took the bar. And I, uh, used to live in Kentucky, so I'm not as familiar —"

"Well, I'm sure you know if one person contests it, the other one has to prove adultery or abandonment or separation, or else it comes down to intolerability." She blinked and spoke the next words in a rush, as though she'd memorized them: " 'The respondent has behaved in such a way that continuing the marriage would be intolerable.' The most subjective law on the books, to my way of thinking. It comes down to how sympathetic a judge is to your story."

"You sound like you've been down this path before," Stella guessed. There had been no evidence of a Mr. Javetz, who she assumed was the other part of Alana's clunky last name; the draped scarves and dusty potpourri smell seemed feminine to Stella.

"Enough to know."

"Sorry to hear that."

"I'm not. At least about the getting rid of him part. My ex was a bastard, even if it cost me a fortune in legal fees to make a judge see just how intolerable he could be. All I'm sorry about is that he's never in one place long enough for my attorney to find him and make him send his maintenance checks."

Aha. Here it was, the motivation Stella had suspected was there all along. "So . . . money is tight for you?"

"A musician's salary, even augmented by teaching, is not enough to support a mortgage," Alana said stiffly. "I would never have bought this place if I'd known Jeffers was going to take up with a flautist."

"A . . . what?"

"Flute player." Alana's flush grew deeper. "Evidently you aren't a fan of the symphony. If you were, you would already know the story, since Jeffers used to be the conductor of the Madison Symphony. Very well known, studied under Pierre Boulez — he even guest conducted in St. Louis . . ." For a moment her voice grew wistful, and the lines in her face softened. *Damn,* Stella realized — *she still loves her ex.* Then Alana's expression turned bitter again. "Jeffers is all about the latest hot ticket. I am mortified to say that when we met he was married to an oboist with little talent. Of course he told me they'd never truly loved each other — which is probably what he told the horrid little tramp he ran off with last fall."

"The . . . flautist."

"Yes."

Stella considered a moment, and examined Alana carefully, squinting, trying to see evidence of the "latest hot ticket" buried beneath the severe steel gray bangs, the deep-etched brackets around her mouth. It wasn't that Alana was middle-aged — it was that her body language pretty much screamed "not one bit of fun to be found here — move along, all zesty souls."

Still, Stella had learned surprising lessons in the outskirts of the counseling profession in which she practiced — the heart is a perplexing hunter, for damn sure. Maybe there was a day when this Jeffers Javetz, conductor of symphonies, looked upon Alana and thought to himself, "There, my man, is a tasty morsel." It was only too bad for Alana that on a subsequent day he looked elsewhere, the curse of the man with a roving eye.

It was almost enough to spark Stella's compassion.

Except Stella was here on a job. On behalf of Natalya and Chip. *They didn't do it,* Stella reminded herself — at least, Chip didn't, she was pretty sure . . . so she needed to find out who did, and Alana was her current best guess.

"So here you are, trying to hang on to

your marriage, in danger of losing your home . . . and then your brother goes and stumbles into some good fortune, the fruits of all his hard inventin' work — and you're thinking, why, that ought to be carefully . . . protected. You took the responsible step and, and, uh, you did a little proactive estate planning, which was —"

"Stella." When Alana finally got around to interrupting her, Stella was truly floundering and was almost grateful. "What are you talking about?"

"The, uh, the insurance policy."

"*What* insurance policy?"

Stella weighed her options. "Look here, Alana," she finally said, settling on a straightforward approach. She was a devoted fan of honesty, not so much due to any particular ethical leanings but because it made things a hell of a lot easier to remember, which was important when one was postmenopausal. "I know about the policy. In the event of your brother's death, you stand to collect a tidy sum. I mean it might not be much by, you know, *Real Housewives* standards or what ever, but for a couple of gals like you and me, it could make a real difference. What's half a mil after taxes in your bracket, anyway?"

Alana pursed up her lips and glowered,

but she didn't deny. "You're coming after me for *that?* No wonder you're taking on clients who can't afford to pay you, Ms. Hardesty — if that's what you think constitutes a case. There's no law against insuring someone even if I did it, but you've got your facts all wrong. Benton did that — he bought that policy and came around here to give me a copy. I didn't even want it. I tried to give it back. But he was just so . . . so *worked up* over her. Making me promise to take care of her if anything ever happened to him. He was worried that if he died before her residency was finalized, she'd never get the money."

Stella thought about Natalya, younger than her years, all that glossy brown hair cascading around her shoulders, her soft come-hither voice, her eager ministrations, her constant dieting . . . she may have been a bit of a cream puff, but she was a fluff y and fresh cream puff. How much would that hurt, Stella wondered — the brother you adored, who always turned to you for help, for assistance navigating the troubling waters of this life, and then he goes and falls for a pretty little thing and forgets all about you.

"I did ask Benton for money," Alana continued. "That much is true. I need it, since Jeffers hasn't sent a payment in six months. Benton told me when I first started up with him — he said Jeffers was no good. He said —"

Alana broke off midsentence. Her face, angular and spare at best, scrunched up in a rictus of hurt feelings and fury. "He said people like us have to aim low. I tried to pretend I didn't know what he was talking about, but I did. We come from a long line of ugly. Do you know people used to think our mom was our grandma? Our dad wasn't anything to look at either; he baled hay from the age of sixteen until we buried him. We weren't pretty — we knew that. We accepted that. I did, anyway . . . until . . ."

She trailed off, picking an object up off the sofa table and holding it absently in her hand. It was an old-fashioned metronome, the kind with the arm tucked behind a hook, ready to tick off the beats for whoever came to practice. Stella had a sudden vision of Alana in this room, practicing in the mornings, the long stretches between lunch and that first glass of cheap wine. Leaving for rehearsals with a hopeful slash of lipstick, wondering if there was still time to meet someone who would love her for who she was.

And watching her brother — no more

finely made than she, no cleverer — bring home a beautiful woman. Yes, one from another country, one he had to purchase, but a gorgeous woman nonetheless. Had it felt like he was showing off a trophy? Like he was judging her somehow, the sibling who couldn't even hold on to a man like Jeffers Javetz? Stella supposed she didn't understand the social intricacies of second-tier American symphonies, but she had to guess that Jeffers was not quite the lothario that a younger and more romantic Alana had dreamed about when she put her viola away for the day.

"You're saying that your brother took out this policy, with no input from you," she summarized gently.

"That's what I'm saying." Alana folded her arms across her chest and waited, no stranger to the indelicate moment. "If I had to wait around for Benton to die on me, that wouldn't do me much good. The foreclosure notices I'm getting aren't going to wait."

Exactly what Stella had been thinking, but she didn't say that. Quick cash required a quick death, and Alana's hatred of Natalya seemed to be sufficient that maybe she wouldn't mind hanging a murder rap on her.

"Besides," she continued as if listening in on Stella's frame of mind, "if anyone would be happy if my brother died, it would be Natalya."

"I thought the way the law worked she had to be married the full two years . . ."

"Yeah, sure, long as INS can find her. If she scoots out of town and passes that two-year mark in another state somewhere, then she can marry her new fancy man and *he* can be her ticket to stay. In case you haven't heard, they're kind of booked these days with all the hoopla at the borders — I don't suppose they have a whole lot of extra agents to be sending on errands out of state to bring back wandering housewives."

"Huh," Stella said.

Natalya was certainly not stupid, and she'd already proved she was calm under fire. Not too many women could have gotten through the dismembering interlude without a whit of evident distress. Could she have really planned such an elaborate scheme? If so, she could be planning to run right now.

Wait, wait, Stella cautioned herself; she was getting too far ahead.

"I think that's a pretty wacky scenario you're spinning. I know your brother and Natalya didn't get along so well, but suggesting that she'd kill him and run off and hide out with her new man, well, that all sounds a little too Bonnie and Clyde–like for the woman I know."

"Maybe you don't know her as well as you think," Alana said darkly. "You haven't seen how she can be when she wants something."

"What's that supposed to mean?"

"Oh, she's as sly as a snake, that one. They had a justice of the peace wedding, but Benton bought her this whole getup, dress and veil and slutty shoes and the whole nine yards — but even that wasn't enough for her. I offered to have a dinner here after, it was me and Benton's friend Topher that were the witnesses, but I guess Little Miss Have-Her-Way had a talk with my dopey brother, because next thing you know, she's dragging us all to this horrible Russian dinner club where I can't understand a single thing anyone says and they're all singing and carrying on — and these are people she has *never met before* and she's ordering shots for the entire place. All on my brother's dime, mind you. And the food — I mean, I didn't know what half that stuff was, and neither did Topher, and here we are starving and we can't even get a basket of rolls. But she's got Benton wrapped around her finger and — oh, and what about the ring? Oh yes. The *ring.*"

If she rolled her eyes with any more vigor, Stella feared they were going to spring free of her head. "What about the ring?" Stella asked gently.

"For the ceremony they just had simple gold bands. *Tasteful.*" By way of illustration, Alana held up her own boney, misshapen hand, and Stella saw that sure enough, it was decorated only by a plain narrow gold ring. "But a few months ago, after they sold off the patent, there she is, dragging Benton to the jewelry store to trade up. And that thing he bought her — simply the tackiest ring you could imagine. More of a *dinner ring* than a wedding ring, the sort of piece one would wear to a cocktail party, *maybe,* if one's taste went that way, but *never* for everyday."

Alana looked like she was just about to go into convulsions at the horror of it all, but Stella, whose own engagement ring had been a simple little solitaire that she took great pleasure in throwing into the brackish waters of Nickel Pond not long after Ollie was buried, wasn't sure she understood the distinction. "What do you mean?"

"Oh, it was so over-the-top — it was a heart-shaped ruby literally surrounded with a million tiny diamonds. The thing was just knuckle-to-knuckle, enormous."

"Ahh." Stella thought it sounded kind of pretty. "So you're saying Natalya picked this thing out and browbeat your brother into buying it for her? With the proceeds from the sale? Or are you suggesting she encouraged him to sell the patent in order to buy it, or . . ."

"I wasn't there," Alana sniffed, "but I'm simply pointing out that's a woman with ravenous tastes, a woman who will never be satisfied. She takes a man for everything he's worth and then — only then — does she move on to the next one."

Stella thought about the fact that Chip wasn't exactly, financially speaking, much of a trade-up, but she didn't see the advantage to pointing that out to Alana, who'd seen the couple's humble abode already and presumably could have come to the same conclusion.

"This has been fun and all," Stella said, snorting back a sneeze, the result of all that loose dust and tea leaves. She was anxious to leave the place, and not just because it threatened to send her into a wheezing fit. The energy around Alana was gloomy and angry — but could she be a killer?

Chapter Twenty-One

As Stella drove toward town, she thought about Alana's insistence that Natalya was a scheming, demanding, greedy opportunist. Was that possible? Could she have been hood-winked so thoroughly? Stella didn't think so, but it was true that she wanted to like Chip's sweetheart. It was more than that: After a lifetime of being a ne'er-do-well, Chip was finally showing signs of maturity, even settling down, something that would make Gracellen happy — and was that enough for Stella to overlook serious flaws in his choices?

Anyway, even if Natalya was operating on some whole other level of motivations and goals — hell, even if she was a murderer — Stella just couldn't get her mind around the idea that she was the trashy gold digger that Alana made her out to be. Stella hated to think ill of any wronged woman, but Alana was just plain bitter, a spinster whose own man had run for the hills, who'd let both her home and her looks go — and who lost the one man who was still dear to her, her brother, to another woman.

So that left Stella squarely on the fence, right where she was before, about Natalya's potential guilt or innocence.

On the subject of Alana herself Stella was no more certain. Oh, she was convinced that Alana hadn't taken the insurance policy out herself, but was there some other way she could benefit financially from his death? A will, perhaps, that left her his house, maybe savings, investments? She'd have to have Chrissy get on that.

Alana was certainly an angry woman, but she would have been more likely to kill Natalya than the brother she seemed to genuinely love. Which brought Stella right back around to square one.

By the time she was halfway back to Smythe, it was afternoon, and her hunger pangs would not be put off any longer. She pulled over at the CheeseHaus, a barnlike structure on the side of the road. WATCH US MAKE IT! was painted on the side of the building. Stella suspected there was little on offer that was likely to enhance her training for the half marathon. She wondered what her training plan was for today — she vaguely remembered she'd given herself a light schedule for her birthday, probably stretches and a short jog around the neighborhood. Meaning that yesterday was probably a killer, a nine-miler, and tomorrow would be the same.

Instead she was getting ready to eat a cheddar sampler, and she hadn't worked out in days. Which was okay if you were twenty. Or even thirty-five, like Camellia Edwards, who was probably tackling her own training today with her usual zeal, in one of her coordinated spandex outfits that showed off her tight little physique. Instead, Stella was fifty-one, and every day she didn't train would be three or four to get back her lost momentum.

The thought didn't cheer her. If she didn't wrap this whole Wisconsin situation up quick, she might wreck her chances for the half marathon entirely. Not to mention Goat might lose enthusiasm for his promise to take her out to dinner for her birthday.

Okay. Stella took a deep breath and marched herself up to the counter. "I'll have the *small* sampler," she said wistfully, "and a Diet Coke."

While she waited, she reviewed her problems. First, if she didn't figure out who killed Benton, Chip might end up being blamed for it, and his splotchy record, while speckled with mostly victimless crimes, would not endear him to any potential jury who might be asked if he had what it took to off his girlfriend's husband.

Then there was the possibility that Natalya really had killed Benton. Stella had a slightly different outlook than most people when it came to abused women taking the law into their own hands and ending the cycle in a decisive fashion, and not only because she herself had done it. She'd seen the damage that abuse could do, not just to the bodies of the wives and girlfriends who got smacked around but to their hearts and minds — damage that might not be apparent to the casual onlooker but would shape the rest of their lives. So there were certainly circumstances in which a woman was justified in killing.

The problem was that nothing Natalya or Chip or Alana or Topher had said had given Stella the idea that Benton was abusive enough to warrant killing. He sounded like a schmuck, it was true; and Stella certainly didn't like the sounds of his belittling and controlling Natalya, nor did she think it was his place to hire out any nipping and tucking that she herself did not think of first.

If a woman came to Stella with tales of a

319

marriage to such a man, Stella would consider taking the case — but with the understanding that what she was being hired to do was adjust an attitude, not end a life. Stella never killed for work, of course, but she did have a variety of more extreme measures that she saved for the worst offenders, including those that generally resulted in hospital time and vows to leave the state and stay gone.

Benton didn't qualify for that sort of handling. So if Natalya had killed him, that was the sort of error of judgment, an overkill of an extreme nature, that would lessen the woman in Stella's eyes, to put it mildly. She wouldn't intervene and try to get Natalya arrested or punished — that was outside of her purview — but she couldn't stand idly by and watch her nephew pledge his life to such a woman.

Stella's ethics were clouded and complicated, but they still had a "right" side and a "wrong" side. She figured it was no different from anyone else — say, the Missouri state supreme court — who was called upon to walk that line every day.

There was yet a third problem. If Chip managed to stay unprosecuted, and Natalya ended up being innocent, that still left the problem of Luke. He was temporarily out of the way, down in Prosper nailing up siding with Dale Savage, but there was no way to safely bring him back here to Smythe or, given the way the Chicago and Detroit gangs were infiltrating the rural northern Midwest, probably anywhere in Wisconsin.

Even if Luke turned out to be the best tradesman apprentice in the world, and she could find someone in Prosper willing to take on a hired hand, there was still the issue of his age. Until he was eighteen, he legally needed to be housed and educated and fed and his own residence status pursued. Plus it wasn't right to separate him from his mama, and despite her confusing tangle of issues and feelings around Natalya, Stella would lay odds she felt exactly the same way.

Of course . . . there was one neat way to tie up the last situation. One that helped out just about everyone involved, even if it would take a little convincing to make them see it that way. Stella thought about the idea from all angles as she nibbled her way through the pile of cheese slices and wedges and curds, washing them down with a second serving of Diet Coke.

She thought some more while she washed up in the spacious ladies' room, nodding and smiling at her fellow travelers, satisfied folks whose own tummies were full of cheese, and who were going on their way laden down with bricks and slabs and wheels of Wisconsin's finest.

By the time Stella was back in the little Subaru, letting it idle so it could cough out all the crud that had built up in its engine while she was having lunch, she figured that the idea was worth pursuing, at least in a very preliminary fashion.

She dialed Gracellen's number.

"Stellie!" Her sister answered halfway through the first ring. "I've been wanting to call you all day but I figured I better leave the line open. I know how you are, always coming at things from eight directions at once."

Stella didn't correct her, but Gracie had come surprisingly close to the truth. "Well, I've made a few calls, trying to see what I could do," she said carefully. Having shielded her sister and brother-in-law from some of the dicier revelations about their son so far, she would hate to accidentally spill the beans now.

"You've already done so much! Just letting us know that Chip is all right and that he's on the right path — well, you just don't even know the world of good you've done. Chess is out there on the rider mower right now. He's practically bouncing off the walls he's so happy. He wants to go out to his favorite restaurant tonight. Stella, he hasn't wanted to go there for just ages, not since our anniversary . . . we always have a few glasses of wine and then we come home and get naughty."

"Gracie!" Stella, who ordinarily was not particularly shy about the idea of folks enjoying their carnal sides, did not in the least care to hear about her sister's.

"Oh, relax," Gracie said happily. "Our family could use a little good news, what with Chester Senior so upset about the business and the economy and so forth."

"Well . . . that's kind of what I wanted to talk to you about."

"It is?"

"Yeah. See, I've been thinking . . . I mean, I still need to look into a few odds and ends about . . . immigration law and whatnot, but if it does end up where Natalya gets her residence status and she's free to be with Chip — I mean, you know, once things get sorted out with her divorce and all —"

Stella forced herself to stop and take a steadying breath. Outside the car in the next parking space over, a couple were wrestling a large golden wheel of cheddar into their trunk, the husband with one hand clapped to his foam cheese-head hat to keep it from blowing off his head.

"Oh, I do hope Chip doesn't rush into anything foolish," Gracellen interrupted. "Now that he's just getting the rest of his life sorted out, he doesn't need a woman complicating it."

"Well, see, I think you might be a little late for that. I mean Chip really seems to love her. And Luke? What a great kid, you're going to love him."

As the silence stretched out between them and Stella imagined that Gracellen was trying to come to terms with the idea of an unwanted stepgrandson, Stella realized that she actually meant what she'd just said — Luke *was* a great kid, or at least had the potential to be, if someone or more likely several someones took a firm hand and set out to show him how things are supposed to work in this country. The Golden Rule, for instance — she doubted they ever got around to teaching that in Russian grade school. That would be a good place to start. Then they could move on to the Pledge of Allegiance, the whole liberty and justice for all thing, and capitalism and helping out your neighbor just for the sheer pleasure of doing the right thing. Heck, Todd had all kinds of hellion tendencies that had been tempered by his mother and Stella and his teachers — if they could calm his savage spirit, why, they could do the same for Luke's.

Thinking of Todd pretty much sealed the deal. "I've been thinking — I mean, like I say, if the citizenship thing gets lined up — that maybe Chip and Natalya and Luke should come out and live with you guys, and Chip could take over the warehouse job."

This time the silence was distinctly shocked. That was a sister for you — you could sense the quality of her silences, could read between the lines of conversations as easily as if she were holding up a large-print book and you were wearing your cheater specs.

"We aren't exactly set up for guests," Gracellen finally said. "I mean we'd love to have Chip, of course, and maybe that would be a good idea, a sort of reentry into society arrangement, almost like a halfway house —"

"You live in fucking six thousand square feet!" Stella exclaimed. "You got what, six bedrooms and four baths? Four garage stalls? Hell, you could take in an entire displaced village and hardly notice."

"Well, it's not only the space issue, though.

I mean, Chess and I are set in our ways, it's been just the two of us ever since we got together —"

"Well, maybe that's part of the problem," Stella said. "I mean, you guys — and I don't blame you, Gracie, please don't think that's what I'm saying — you never had Chip living with you. I know Ilona would have made it tough, but that boy could have used a dad. You know I think Chess is a fine man, and he's done a lot to repair what's gone undone and unsaid between them, but you don't want that to repeat a generation, now do you? Not when you could do something about it —"

"But Luke isn't Chip's son!"

"Not yet he's not, but those two are talking about marriage and the boy doesn't have a father figure, I don't think anyone even knows who the father is, and even if they did, he's all the way on the other side of the world."

"You can't ask Chess to take in a boy that's no blood relation to him —"

"Gracellen Carol Collier!" Stella barked out her sister's full name for the second time in two days and realized only after the syllables hung in the air that she sounded *exactly* like her mother, who reserved their full names for when she was very, very disappointed in her girls. "I mean, Papadakis. Whatever. You should be ashamed of yourself. You know darn well that blood ain't the only thing that ties family."

This time the silence was even longer. Finally, Gracie sighed, a long pained exhalation that Stella could hear very well over the phone, and one that signaled that she'd won. "I don't have any *idea* what we'd even *do* with a little boy," she grumbled.

"He ain't all that little," Stella pointed out, realizing she'd never got around to telling her sister much about Luke. "He'll be in his senior year of high school in the fall. You wouldn't even have him under your roof all that long, he's practically grown."

"You don't say. But wouldn't that make his mom kinda older than —"

"How about putting him to work on Chester Senior's house, for a start," Stella interrupted hastily. "You yourself said he's got to unload that place and move to somewhere smaller, somewhere more manageable now that he's old. You get Luke to fix it up and put it on the market, that would keep him busy all summer."

"And then he'd start up at school? Does he speak proper English?"

"Oh my yes, probably better than most of the kids in the senior class."

Stella willed Gracie to come around with all her might. Luke had the potential to blossom, she was convinced of it, and cute girls and fast food and civics class and football games would certainly help. A lot could happen in a year. With a passel of concerned adults on his case, among them a father figure and grandfather figure and even a great-grandfather figure — and the occasional visit from Stella, if necessary — they might be able to keep him away from the lure of the wrong road.

"Oh, Chess is just gonna have an absolute fit," her sister sighed.

"But you're going out tonight," Stella reminded her. "You can make all kinds of magic happen, I bet. Anyway, don't get too far ahead of yourself, we still don't know if Natalya's going to be in the picture."

Because she might be in jail, Stella thought darkly, wondering how she would explain *that* to her sister.

CHAPTER TWENTY-TWO

Stella had jotted down the name of the jewelry store where Benton had done his shopping, and it was easy enough to find, just a couple of blocks from the drug deal she'd interrupted yesterday. As she cruised around the block looking for a parking place, Stella kept her eyes out for thugs who looked like they'd been imported from the city, but the streets were empty except for a few midday shoppers.

Hawthorn Jewelers was a sleepy affair, with its old-fashioned sign hanging over the door, but its windows were full of beautiful rings and pendants and watches. Expensive, classy stuff, at least to Stella's eye.

The gentleman behind the counter was bent over a watch on a square of dark velvet, doing something to the case with a tiny tool. When the bell attached to the door jangled, he pushed his loupe up onto his forehead and gave Stella a ready smile and hopped off his stool.

"May I help you?"

"Mr. Hawthorn?"

"Oh no, my dear, I'm Fred Nandedkar, but my dad started Hawthorn Jewelers in 1954 and it's been in the family ever since."

"So nice to meet you. I'm Alana Parch-Javetz." She shook the man's hand and found it warm and pleasant.

"What can I do for you today, Ms. . . . uh, what was that again?"

Stella smiled. "Please, just call me Alana. I'm here because I'd like to surprise my brother and his wife with an anniversary gift."

"Oh, delightful, just delightful!" Fred said, his entire face lighting up as though Stella had suggested the most fabulous and original idea. "We have lovely sterling frames, all manner of crystal accessories . . . so many things . . . Can you tell me what the couple might like?"

"Well, you see, I came here because Benton bought Natalya a ring from you just last year, a special piece, and I thought you might remember them, maybe she pointed out something she liked . . . ?"

A surprising change came over Fred's face. The florid good cheer drained away, leaving him looking crestfallen and chastened. "Oh, dear . . . that would be Natalya Parch?"

"Yes — yes, exactly."

"Well, I don't know how to tell you this, Ms. . . . I mean, Alana. It's certainly — well, it's not my place to conjecture, of course, but Ms. Parch returned that ring last week."

"She *did?*"

"Oh, indeed, yes. We have a generous trade-up program, you see, where fine gemstone pieces can be exchanged for items of greater value. The customer just pays the difference. In fact, I have the ring right here, I've already got a customer interested in it . . . such a gorgeous piece . . ."

He rummaged under the counter and pulled out a tray of glittering rings. Stella knew instantly which one had been Natalya's: Nestled in the center of the tray, among all the solitaires and eternity bands and three-stone rings, was the flashiest ring she'd ever seen. The heart-shaped ruby was large and perfectly clear, and the diamonds had a thousand-megawatt sparkle. Fred picked it up and tipped it this way and that, under the lights, sending brilliant beams to every corner of the shop.

"Did Natalya say . . . I mean . . ."

Instead of answering, Fred frowned and set to vigorously polishing the band with a cloth, and Stella realized he would never stoop to conjecture about a customer.

"I'm sorry. I just meant — did she already choose something new?"

"Well, that's just it, you see. I'm afraid that our policy does not allow a refund, and Ms. Parch is . . . considering her options, at the moment. She has a generous balance here in the shop, and of course it is my hope that she and —"

He blushed so furiously that Stella actually felt bad for him.

"That she will come back and choose something more to her liking," Fred finished in a rush.

Cash. So Natalya had come back hoping to get cash for her honking engagement ring. Could be innocent — after all, what was she going to do with a piece like that after the relationship ended? — but it was also rather curious, seeing as she'd come in only days before Benton's death.

Stella sighed. It just could never be easy. An hour earlier she'd been trying to strong-arm Gracellen into allowing Natalya and her boy into her heart and home. Now the woman's innocence was more uncertain than ever.

"Is there something I could show you . . . for *you,* Alana?" Fred had returned the tray under the counter and regained his composure. "With your lovely coloring and that red hair of yours, you really ought to be in sapphires."

Before Stella could politely decline, he'd pulled out another tray with a flourish. His hand hovered over the gems for a moment, and then he plucked one decisively from its slot.

It was an earring — a twinkling oval sapphire surrounded by tiny diamonds. Fred turned it this way and that, nestled in his palm, catching the light — one of the most beautiful things Stella had ever seen. It was set on a delicate white gold post, perfect for her pierced ears, and when Fred offered it to her, she couldn't resist. She picked it up between her thumb and forefinger and rested it next to her cheek, peeking in the mirror he gave her.

He was right — the color was perfect for her. The blue was deep and clear, like a moonlit night over Prosper, and the diamonds' sparkle seemed to reflect in her eyes, making them seem greener than usual. "They're beautiful," Stella said wistfully.

"One carat each in the center stone, point-two-five carat total diamond weight. Those are near-flawless diamonds, by the way, VVS clarity. A beautiful piece that would be

333

cherished by many generations."

"Well, I don't know about that. If I had something like this I expect I'd want to be buried in them."

Fred laughed heartily, and Stella decided she liked him. She handed the earring back. "Just out of curiosity, how much are these?"

Fred consulted a tiny tag tucked into the tray, squinting at the numerals. "One thousand seven hundred and thirty dollars."

Stella nodded. She hadn't really expected a bargain, and though she'd been tempted for a moment — it being her birthday and all — there were a lot of other things that she could do with that kind of money. Pay Potter's Auto to get her Jeep out of hock, for one. Add it to her carpet fund, for another — the carpet in the bedrooms of her house had not been changed since Noelle was a little girl, and it showed.

"Well, I sure do appreciate your time."

"Come back and see us again sometime. And if you, ah, should happen to see Natalya, do let her know that we've received some lovely new pieces."

Stella sat in the Subaru for a moment, thinking. It was nearly six o'clock, the springtime sun still high above the horizon as people strolled past, enjoying the evening.

Smythe was a nice town the way that Prosper was a nice town — there was nothing really exceptional about it. No historical significance or architectural marvels. No garden club had busted its butt beautifying the public spaces, and no wealthy benefactors had left fortunes for fancy renovations, but the citizens of the town were doing their part in small ways, tending front lawns and sidewalks, setting out pots of flowers, freshening up paint, and polishing brass.

The hospital complex where the surgery center was located was a recent appendage, much as the Prosper Office Park had been built at the edge of town in the eighties, a clumsy addition at odds with the rest of the town's spirit. Prosper's office park remained largely vacant, the hordes of high-tech businesses who found themselves itching to settle in the heart of Missouri having never materialized, to the consternation of the chamber of commerce. St. Olaf's, on the other hand, appeared to be thriving. With the money it brought into the community, it might make the difference for Smythe's future, allowing it to attract even more business and becoming, perhaps, an attractive commuter town for Madison residents who couldn't tolerate the hustle and bustle.

If it turned out that Natalya wasn't a

murderer — and if Gracellen and Chess could be talked into inviting the couple out to stay until they got on their feet — Stella figured there would be things they would miss about Smythe. Sure, Natalya was a recent transplant, but surely her nearly two years in the Midwest had endeared the place to her. Stella didn't know much about Russia, but she imagined lines of freezing women in black coats and woolly scarves and fur-lined hats, waiting for hours in snowy cobblestone streets for a string of fish or a loaf of stale rye bread.

Sure, she'd seen the CNN folks talking about commerce coming to Russia, technology and capitalism and so forth, and she was willing to believe that there were people driving sports cars and opening nightclubs and building banks all over the place. In her experience, though, the ladies who raised the kids and kept the houses and took care of the elderly were the last to benefit from an influx of any kind of good luck. She'd had too many clients whose husbands received windfalls only to spend them on mistresses or fast cars or wide-screen televisions.

Had Natalya had an experience like that with Luke's father, whoever he was? Had he left her pregnant and alone in some tiny grotto to fend for herself and her baby? Stella could understand how that might leave a lady feeling unrepentant about any manipulating and tricking she had to do to support her child after that, how such a lady might figure that the male gender owed her big-time. A mail-order wedding might look mighty appealing to such a woman, what with its clearly laid out expectations, its mutual benefits.

Could a woman like that — a user, an opportunist — ever again feel real love?

Not your business, Stella's conscience chastised her. She wasn't here on a matchmaking or even a match-un-making mission.

Her phone rang. Speak of the devil — the display read BENTON PARCH, and for a moment Stella had the jarring sensation of being summoned by the dead. But of course it was Natalya's, and now that Benton was a corpse and hence unable to pay any of his bills, presumably it would soon be cut off.

"Hello?"

"Stella? You are coming home soon?"

Was it Stella's imagination or was there a new opaqueness in Natalya's voice? Had Fred, perhaps spurred by Stella's visit, given her a call to try to talk her into one of his expensive trinkets — and mentioned the visit from Benton's sister-in-law?

Natalya was a shrewd woman. Stella had no doubt she would figure out instantly that "Alana" was really Stella . . . and draw further conclusions from there.

Like the possibility that she was under suspicion, for instance.

"Yeah, sure . . . soon. Ish. I'm, um, I'm following up on something out, ah, out of town a ways."

"What is this you are following?"

Stella's mind raced trying to come up with a convincing yet innocent possibility, but she stalled. "Uh . . . I'd rather finish following it up and then tell you about it."

"Okay." Natalya sounded displeased. "I am hoping you are coming home before dinnertime so I can cook for you something before I am going to have late dinner with Chip."

"Oh, I already ate. Anyway, you don't have to cook for me, I can take care of myself, and Chip gave me a key. I can let myself in and watch some TV or something."

"Oh." Natalya's disappointment seemed to deepen. Was she hoping to have a little one-on-one time with Stella — and if so, why? Stella wasn't naive enough to think she was looking forward to another knitting lesson; the only thing Stella could figure out that would inspire this sort of urgency would be if Natalya's self-preservation instincts had been piqued.

Could the woman be planning something even more dramatic than a heart-to-heart? If she'd already killed once, would it bother her terribly to kill again — especially if she was convinced that Stella was threatening the future she had so carefully built?

"Did you have . . . something special in mind? You and Chip?"

"No, not special. Sometimes we like the Thai food, sometimes we are trying new things. Chip is big eater for skinny man. Is lucky."

"Well . . . tell you what. Don't plan around me. I'll come by when I finish up, but I won't expect you to be waiting up for me or anything."

Natalya was clearly not happy to leave things loose, but Stella hung up after a cheerful signoff. Let Natalya wonder; if she was considering anything cagey it was better not to let her get the upper hand in advance. Meanwhile, Stella figured it was time to do a little further research into whether Natalya could have pulled off Benton's demise in the first place.

Ordinarily she'd get Chrissy to come over and prowl the Internet for her, but Chrissy was undoubtedly out with her secret lover.

Besides, Stella had a better source than the Internet for what she needed to know.

CHAPTER TWENTY-THREE

Doug was not happy to see her.

Stella stepped to the side of the front door after she rang the bell. The easiest trick in the world — any eight-year-old could have managed it more nimbly than she — and yet Doug fell for it, leaning out into the dusky evening with some sort of sandwich in one hand.

Stella stepped smoothly in front of him and basically startled him back into the house, pulling the door shut behind her and giving him a gentle shove with her palm on his chest.

"Why don't you stop right about there," Stella said, as he stumbled backward. "I thought I told you to get rid of those ugly-ass girl-pants."

Doug looked down at his drawstring hemp trousers as though surprised to discover them slung low on his hips, under the sort of faded river driver shirt that Stella's dad

341

had worn on winter weekends to fix his truck.

"Yeah, those," Stella sighed. "Look, this is just pathetic. I'm going to have you write down your address and then I'm going to have JC Penney send you a pair of pants. All's I ask is you take a picture of yourself in them and text it to me."

"I can't believe you came back here over *that*," Doug moaned. "I mean, I didn't think you were serious."

"I'm always serious. Once you get to know me better you'll realize that."

"So are we doing the kitchen table again?" he asked resignedly.

"Well now, I don't suppose that's necessary, if you promise to behave." Stella didn't bother to point out the fact that she'd come unarmed, seeing as this was a friendly call. "I'm not here to bust your chops. I just needed a medical expert for a few questions I have about a . . . case I'm working on, and I thought of you. Seemed a shame to let that expensive education of yours go to waste."

"I should have you talk to my dad," the young man said glumly. "He seems plenty happy to let it all go down the drain, won't even consider the bigger picture."

"Oh, lemme guess, you asked him for

money."

"Well yeah, after you-all came out and scared the shit out of me the other day, I've been trying to get Benton's cash together."

"Oh . . . I don't know if I'd be in any kind of terrible rush over that."

"But Mrs. Hardesty, he doesn't seem like the second-chance type, not like you are."

"Don't go tryin' to butter me up. I'm here 'cause I got to find out about something, and I got a couple of things I need to say first."

"Yeah?"

"How about if you make some of that French drip coffee before we start?"

That seemed to energize the young medical student. He set down his sandwich and offered her a chair — at the same table where he'd been so unceremoniously shackled — and started lining up supplies. Stella watched with fascination. First he filled an electric kettle with water and plugged it in. Then he took a brushed-aluminum canister out of the freezer and set it on the counter. Finally he took a fancy lidded glass carafe from the cabinet.

"Humor me here," Stella said. "Just what the hell are you doing there?"

Doug glanced at her in confusion. "Making coffee, like you said."

Stella had to admit that the aroma was heavenly, but if she ever started carrying on this way in her own kitchen, say for Chrissy or Jelloman or Goat or Noelle, she was liable to get laughed out of her own house. Only Sherilee, with her perfect manners, might let her slide.

Something to think about.

"Here's how this is going to work," Stella said. "I'm going to ask you a question that might or might not, depending on how curious you are, get you to wondering. Your job, though, is not to put your own what-ifs or whys into the picture. Just tell me what I need to know, and when I'm done, you forget all about this conversation. We clear?"

"Yeah."

"So what I want to know is, how you could go about killing a man without leaving any marks on him. This would be a . . . let's say a man in his fifties, average height, stocky. I'm not sayin' that a CSI team couldn't figure it out, just tell me about a situation where the average onlooker wouldn't be able to tell. No marks on the body, no bruises, cuts, that sort of thing."

Doug raised his eyebrows. "Well . . . all kinds of ways, really. Suffocation, that would be the easiest, though depending on if the guy was conscious, you're nearly always going to have a lot of fighting back and I guess that would leave marks. You'd have to ask a forensic guy —"

"I don't have a forensic guy. I have you."

"Yeah, all I meant was if you wanted to ask about victim behavior and what, ahhh, self-harm and so forth might result. But sure. I see what you're saying. So, suffocation, strangulation, depending on what was used. A cord, wire, whatever, that's gonna leave a mark . . . Now you could inject or inhale a poison, ingest it, absorb it through the skin. All kinds of possibilities there, depending what your . . . uh . . . your hypothetical person could have on him or be forced to consume."

"Just give me a for instance or two."

"Well, if this is a street drug setting, you got your GHB, though that can involve vomiting and convulsions . . . Barbiturates are good. Tricyclics, if you take enough. Really, there's lots of options."

Stella felt her spirits deflate. It wasn't going to be simple — it might not even be possible ever to know how Benton was killed.

"Gimme a sec here to think."

She half-watched Doug puttering with his fancy supplies, pouring a cup of the heavenly-smelling brew into a cup that looked like a talented third grader had made it in ceramics class and forgotten to glaze it before firing. It had probably been made by aboriginal craftspeople somewhere, which Stella could appreciate, except it was just so ugly. Still, when Doug handed it to her and she inhaled the fragrant steam, she no longer minded.

"Damn, this is a hell of a cup of coffee."

Doug beamed with pride. "Thanks, Mrs. Hardesty."

He really wasn't such a bad guy, Stella thought, relenting. Just irresponsible and immature. What was it with today's young people — they refused to grow up, to accept responsibility, until later and later in their lives. Stella couldn't imagine being nearly thirty and still calling home to be floated for loans. Noelle and Chrissy, both roughly the same age as Doug, had been providing for themselves — ineptly at times, scraping by and relying on elbow grease and the ingenuity of desperation — for a decade. Maybe a little hardship — the very thing every parent, including Stella, worked so hard to shield her children from — was actually the secret to reaching adulthood.

Maybe getting caught with the on-the-side scalpel job was actually the best thing to happen to Doug. Having the fear put in him, the threat of losing everything he'd worked for — maybe that was what would now make him a little more grateful, make him take his life a little more seriously.

Stella took a sip of the hot brew and smiled. She was glad to be a part of the young man's education. "Okay, so I hear you saying you couldn't really detect a poisoning, not as a, what do you call it, lay observer. Anything else? Any other ways you could off someone, maybe a little more creatively?"

Doug thought, extending his legs and crossing them at the ankles, his hands clasped behind his head. "Well, there's compression. They used to torture people by putting stones on their chests until they couldn't breathe."

Chest compression. Something clicked in Stella's mind. "Could a really tight shirt — I mean a really, *really* tight-fitting shirt do the trick?"

Doug frowned. "Probably not on its own. Although if the person was already having trouble getting enough air into his airways — like if he was having an allergic reaction — then sure."

"What kind of allergy?"

"Well, any, really — pollen, ragweed, dust mites . . ."

Stella stared into the swirling black mists of her cup. Natalya, if she really had been responsible for Benton's death, obviously had not done it herself, since she'd been out with Chip at the time his corpse was delivered to the door. Of course, she could easily have paid someone to drop him off, after engineering the simplest of "accidents." By Chip's admission, Benton had been wearing a ManTee — but how could she find out if he had allergies? She couldn't very well ask Natalya without provoking her suspicions.

"You've been real helpful, Doug," Stella said, getting up from the table, anxious to follow up this new direction.

"Sorry I couldn't do more. It's a tough question."

"Yeah, I know. I just thought it was worth checking into. But hey —" She picked up her half-full mug and toasted him with it. "It wasn't an entirely wasted trip."

Out in the car, she dialed Alana. It was a risk — if she was the real killer, this line of inquiry might tip her off that Stella was getting close, but maybe then she'd get nervous and give herself away.

"I'm on a rehearsal break," Alana said after Stella apologized for calling so late.

"What do you need? Has Benton turned up yet?"

" 'Fraid not, but I'm helping Natalya sort out her health insurance."

"Which my idiot brother is no doubt paying for."

"Well, that's the problem, actually. She's switching to private coverage, but since she's still legally married, she has to list Benton as an alternate insured, and there's a few things on the form we need to check off. She could wait until he turns up, but if we get this in before the new policy period, it'd save Benton some cash."

"Yeah? What do you need to know?"

"Okay, let's see . . . smoker?"

"No, which she could have told you —"

"I'm just being thorough. History of heart disease?"

"No."

"Allergies?"

"Dander and feathers — severe."

Bingo.

"Okay, I think that's all I need for now. Have a nice rehearsal, hear?"

Alana hung up without saying good-bye.

Chapter Twenty-Four

It was nearly eight o'clock by the time she got back to the house. The windows were dark, as she had hoped they would be; with Natalya and Chip off to dinner, Stella could search the house without raising suspicion. She didn't really expect to find a hidden cat or duck that had been used to send Benton into the allergic fit that killed him, but you never knew what you'd turn up when you went looking.

Stella dug in her purse for Chip's spare key, which was attached to a key chain bearing another of his Gamblers Anonymous tokens. She'd barely picked it out from the disarray in the bottom of the bag when a movement from the left caught her eye, a flash of white against the brown brick of the little recessed entryway.

A year ago Stella had made a grave miscalculation and gone to meet an informant in a dark, isolated area without sufficiently checking out her surroundings. She'd had time in the hospital afterward to stew and regret and reconsider sufficiently that she'd taken precautions to make sure such a thing never happened again. Specifically, she asked her Shaolin kung fu instructor, a certain Mr. Hou who owned a Chevy dealership in Independence, to teach her a few effective responses to use in situations where an attacker had the advantage.

Mr. Hou did a brisk business turning over Silverados and Impalas, but his true passion was the martial arts he'd learned as a boy five decades earlier in Changzhou. Stella had never met Mrs. Hou, because her husband's basement studio had a separate entrance for his students — if there were any; she'd never seen anyone else coming or going from the house. She had met Mr. Hou when a former client, Marjorie Peng, had made the introduction as payment for Stella's services. Marjorie was Mr. Hou's niece, and the only reason she hadn't engaged Mr. Hou himself to take care of the ex-boyfriend who'd cleared out their checking account and dislocated her shoulder was that Mr. Hou, who was nearly seventy, had been on crutches at the time after suffering a fall.

Mr. Hou had defied his doctor's expectations and recovered from his injuries, and soon returned to his daily two-hour workouts. During the months he'd spent on crutches, he barked orders at Stella until she was panting with exertion only to demand, in his broken and nearly incomprehensible English, that she approach his chair so that he could demonstrate hits that left her nearly doubled over with pain and surprise, all while seated.

When he was back on his feet, he was a terror.

Which was why Stella made the hour-long drive every couple of weeks for a lesson. In between, she practiced her "homework" as zealously as she could without an actual attacker to approach her from the left or right or behind. Her friend Jelloman Nunn had set up a couple of stinky old punching bags from his fighting days in her garage, and Stella did her best to imagine that they were the bloodthirsty members of the Chinese triads that Mr. Hou had battled in his youth, and beat as much of the crap out of them as she was able.

All of which was terrific preparation for when the hooded figure, all five foot eight of him, came charging out of the corner where he'd been hiding and tackled her. Or rather tried to tackle her, because Stella spun and met him with her rake fist. The man had miscalculated on a number of fronts, judging from the lackluster speed and force of his attack, and Stella's fist, her fingers folded and rigid in classic leopard form, easily connected with his throat, dropping him to the ground, where he made a strange bleating sound and clawed at his neck, kicking his feet and rolling against the brick.

Stella rubbed her knuckles — she'd have a hell of a bruise tomorrow for sure — and stared at the man in disbelief. Either the jerk had unscrewed the porch light or Chip and Natalya had neglected to turn it on before they left, but enough light from inside streamed out the narrow window that flanked the door that Stella could see that the fellow was wearing a too-big sweatshirt with a furry sort of hood cinched up around his face. Light glinted off his mouth, and Stella saw that he had metal on his front teeth. With his fur-trimmed hood, he looked like a supersized Christmas elf who'd been snacking on tinsel.

Whatever he was, Stella didn't have a whole lot of time to lollygag about before he became a threat again. Though short, he looked young and strong, and those were two distinct advantages he held over Stella.

She left him gagging for air and jogged back to the Impreza, where some of her own advantages were stored. Popping the trunk, she rooted through her Tupperware containers and was back on the porch by the time the young man had made it to his hands and knees, sucking air like a gutted coyote and trying to crawl toward the street.

"Don't waste your breath," Stella said. "Oh. Ha. No pun intended, sorry. You'll be okay, best just not fight it. Only we don't want folks wondering what you're doing crawling around like you want to play horsie on the front lawn, now do we?"

She kept up a steady chatter as she worked. First she put a Ked-clad toe to the guy's rib cage and gave him a gentle shove, enough to land him on his back like a stuck beetle. Then she got the front door open. She cuffed the guy's hands temporarily in front of him with a pair of metal cuffs — really, she preferred the plastic for just about everything, but this was only temporary and she didn't see the point in wasting a set of the disposable ones — and suggested he come on in the house.

He declined.

Stella sighed.

"I know you ain't feeling so hot right now," she said, "but if you don't make a bit more of an effort to get on in there, I'm about to — well, hell."

She had a sudden inspiration, no doubt suggested by her subconscious because of the very events that had first brought her to Wisconsin. She'd noticed the sizable diamond studs in his ears, and since he was immobilized, she crouched down and looked closer. The earring had to be a couple of carats. "Is this real?" she asked, flicking it with her fingertip. "Ah, don't bother answering, I ain't planning on believing you anyway." She dug in her pocket for her folding knife and popped it open. "Now there aren't a lot of nerves in the earlobe, which you prob'ly remember from when you first got your piercing, so just hold still and I'll see if I can slice this off clean."

She didn't really intend to separate the man from his flesh, but she had a steady hand from all her shop-floor practicing with her knife. Stella had discovered she had a particular talent for throwing. On one amusing occasion — amusing in retrospect, that is, not so much at the time — she'd been practicing throwing her Spyderco police knife at a square of orange wool felt that was left over from a Thanksgiving-theme needle-felting class. One of the ladies had left it on the design wall, and Stella had hit the blob of wool dead center six times out of nine and was winding up for her tenth attempt when Francie Cage popped up from under the table, where she'd been hunting for a needle threader she'd dropped. The old lady had been down there so long that Stella had forgotten she was there, seeing as all the other students had gone home and only Francie had stayed behind to finish her cornucopia wall hanging, since she meant to give the homely thing to Pastor Dewey at the Share Our Bounty dinner that evening.

Stella only saw the steely permed top of Francie's head rising up from under the table after the steel knife had left her hand and gone winging through the air, end over end, toward the wall. There followed the longest slo-mo moment of horror of Stella's life, as she imagined how Francie, who had designs on Pastor Dewey, only six years her junior and widowed, would look with a rakish black eye patch after her milky blue eye was put out by the flying blade.

In a stroke of great luck, Francie feinted left after spotting a nickel that had rolled under a chair leg, and the knife whizzed past her ear and embedded clean in the center of the wool tuft. Since then Stella had been more cautious, abandoning the showy but rarely useful throwing techniques for good old-fashioned close-in handling. Francie and Pastor Dewey had enjoyed a brief, mad fling before Francie was friended on Facebook by a fellow from her senior class — Prosper High Class of '56 — and her affections made a lurching hairpin turn.

All of Stella's knife practice made it possible for her to nick only the tiniest notch in her captive's ear, enough to draw blood and sting a little but nothing that couldn't be covered up with a nice silver hoop or cuff. A less experienced hand would have risked slicing or stabbing the man when he yelped and jumped, but Stella was able to slip her knife away and deftly twist the diamond stud free while he recovered from his fright.

He held still while she took the other one. She rolled them in her hand for a moment, admiring their fiery brilliance, then popped them in her pocket along with the knife. They weren't nearly as beautiful as Fred's sapphire and diamond earrings, but they might be worth something.

After that, the man preceded her meekly inside.

He was silent while Stella got him maneuvered to the kitchen floor and shackled up nicely to the pipe under the sink. Up close, she could see that he was older than she first thought — in his twenties, probably a shotcaller or lieutenant. They usually sent the higher-level guys on missions of intimidation.

Stella removed the rubber gloves and dish detergent and Windex and Brillo pads from the sink and made sure that her captive could rest more or less easily, with his head in the cabinet. He didn't complain, not even while Stella was getting his leg cuffs on, or when she went through his pockets and took a cheap handgun and a handful of plastic packets off him. This went in a Ziploc bag in her purse, after she made sure to roll his fingers all over them. But he still didn't have anything to say when she started asking him questions.

"Now I know you're feeling better, and I didn't do anything to you's gonna even hurt tomorrow," Stella said in exasperation. "I also know you're disappointed that Luke couldn't come out and play, and that I took your toys away. But I kind of need to know the scope of what we're looking at here. I'm not so much worried about *you,* seeing as I have a nice little package in there that I can drop off with the police on my way out of town, but I figure where there's one of you guys there's probably more, plus a little line of ants leading back to your anthill down in

Madison. Am I right?"

The fellow looked like he might actually be considering answering her. He opened his eyes wide and worked his mouth, though nothing came out, and then he kicked out with his feet and made a gasping sort of sound of surprise.

"Hey, there, easy, we don't want to go ripping the pipes out. Chip's got enough on his hands to — hey!"

The young man had made the very ill-advised decision to try to lunge toward her but, given his restraints and awkward wedged-in stance, succeeded only in cracking his forehead hard against the front of the cabinet, and Stella had bent down to try to push him back where he couldn't hurt himself when there was a loud cracking sound.

The idiot had managed to dislodge something, a pipe joint or disposal unit perhaps. The sound of it breaking was magnified so loud it echoed in her ears. Even worse, he'd hit himself so hard that — shit, was that — Stella reached out and touched the man's forehead, where a neat little hole was blooming with blood.

That was no —

It was —

Stella hit the floor and rolled just as the

second gunshot was fired. She didn't see where it went because she was frantically trying to propel herself out of the kitchen, but a tangle of dinette chair legs made it difficult. She'd been shot at often enough for her instincts to be sharply honed — basically the idea was to get yourself where the bullets weren't, which in this case meant out in the hall.

"Goddamn it, hold still," a voice hollered over the sound of more shots — Topher, to her surprise, who, thankfully, had remarkably poor aim. She dove for the hall and made it around the corner before she remembered that her own gun was in the purse she'd left on the kitchen counter. She pushed herself to her feet and careened off the walls. Down the hall were the bedrooms, two of them, and the bathroom. The windows were a possibility, but even as oafish a shooter as Topher was proving to be would probably be able to get a clear shot in before she managed to pry a window open and jump through it.

Which left the living room — racing across it, specifically, to the front door, then out into the indifferent streets of the worst neighborhood in Smythe.

Except that the string of cursing issuing from the other room was not being punctuated by any additional gunshots — it sounded, in fact, like the fury of a smited and quashed man, one whose best efforts were going awry. Stella, who knew a thousand times better, could not resist sneaking a peek into the kitchen before she escaped into the night.

"Damn it, damn it, *damn* it!" Topher was hopping around in a most unusual way, trying to kick the ammo clip that he had dropped on the floor, and succeeding only in sliding it along the slick vinyl flooring and lodging it beneath a cabinet. As Stella watched, fascinated, Topher tried to bend down and get it, but his man-girdle was hampering his attempts most cruelly. After his attempts to reach under the cabinet while on his knees failed, he gave up entirely and lay down on his stomach and inched toward the cabinet like a worm.

Stella knew she ought to run, ought to let the authorities handle it, ought to leave Smythe's finest to untangle the mess on the kitchen, which now included a pool of blood seeping out of the sink cabinet. The dead drug dealer would give them a lot to work with, but then again Natalya and Chip — even with the alibi the restaurant was sure to supply — might have more difficulty than they needed in explaining what he was doing there.

Most of all, she just couldn't pass up the opportunity to let a dumb-ass do what dumb-asses do best, which was to dig themselves deeper. She took her time walking back through the kitchen, pausing to fetch her own gun from her purse, then crouching down next to where he was lying on his stomach gasping for air.

"I got a few years on you, and yet look what I can do," Stella said cheerfully and did a graceful dip and lunge and plucked the clip from under the cabinet, just beyond the reach of Topher's grasping fingers. "Trouble with these crappy little Rugers, you only get six shots out of a magazine. Now I suppose you've noticed that the tables have turned, so to speak, and you ain't got any call to try anything tricky, or I'll shoot your hand off. I realize you have a, uh, limited range of motion in that getup, so I'm gonna let you make your own way into this chair, if you can."

It took a while, but eventually Topher grunted and panted his way into the chair. The bottom of his ManTee had somehow rolled up, revealing a pale band of puffy muffin-y middle that oozed out between his trousers and the shirt.

That just made Stella cluck sadly. "What

on earth were you thinking, anyway? I mean, you're not a bad-looking man. You're some ladies' kinda handsome, I'd be willing to bet, but I'll tell you one thing — don't anyone want to see the marks I bet that thing leaves on you once you take it off. And who do you think you're fooling, really? That there's like a — like a *comb-over.* There ain't anything in the world wrong with a bald man" — and she should know, given the fact that Goat Jones didn't have a single hair decorating his head — "but trying to cover it up with whatever you got left, well, that's just wrong."

Topher hadn't looked all that excited about the fact that he hadn't managed to kill her, but now he looked positively incensed. "That's nothing like —"

Stella, despite emerging unscathed from this latest threat to her life, was not about to have Topher hollering at her. She simply wasn't in the mood. "So what brought you here tonight, anyway? How'd you figure out I was onto you?" She hadn't really reached that conclusion on her own — the fact that he was trying to kill her was pretty convincing proof.

Topher looked disgusted, his scowl deepening the lines around his eyes. "I actually thought you were *interested* in me," he sputtered. "I looked you up. Only guess what, there isn't any state intellectual property department. And the only hits on any Stella Hardesty in Wisconsin are for a woman up in Muskego who's running for city controller — and she's a *blonde.*"

"I've been a blonde," Stella shrugged.

"Yeah, well, it was pretty clear you were lying to me, so I figured out that Chip and Natalya had hired a private investigator. I bet that isn't even your real name, is it?"

"Damn, you're good. What were you gonna do, make them admit they were onto you?"

"What ever I had to do," Topher said darkly.

"Huh." Stella didn't care for his attitude, a point she made with a gentle tap of the SIG's barrel against his temple. "So let me guess, you invited Benton over to your place. Pretended you wanted to kiss and make up —"

"I told him I wanted to show him a new design. I had to practically beg him to come, it's like he didn't even care anymore, even after he realized Natalya was never coming back."

"So he came over and . . . how'd you get him in that T-shirt, anyway?"

"I asked him if I could take a picture. For

the Web site."

"But — I thought you sold the patent."

"I sold *one* patent. For *one* product. Trust me, I've got thousands of ideas. The shirt I showed him was the one I had on the other day. It's meant for the gym."

"Huh. So he puts it on . . ." Stella thought of Benton changing clothes in Topher's apartment and remembered something. "In that room you just happened to have tricked out with down pillows, a down comforter. What did you do, lock him in?"

Now Topher smiled, cruelly. "From the outside. I just changed the lock, took me ten minutes. I could hear him knocking around in there forever. Got so bad, I went out for a latte — I didn't want to listen to it."

"That's — wow. And then how'd you get him into your car?"

"Hey, I work *out*," Topher said, looking wounded. "I just waited until midnight and drove my car around, and it wasn't too hard to get him in there. Dropped him off at the house and then waited until I was pretty sure janitor boy would be home from work, and then I called the cops."

"That was *you* who called?"

"Yeah." Topher frowned. "Should have known it would get fucked up. Man, I just can *not* catch a break."

"What I don't get is what turned you into an indiscriminate killer in the first place. I mean, Benton was your friend. You worked together for *years*. From what I hear you two would go out on Friday night and then get up on Saturday morning and go Roller-blading. Heck, it sounds to me like you were closer than most married folks. So what happened?"

"It wasn't *just* about the money," Topher said. "Even though that was bad enough. Selling the patent was stupid. The real money's in licensing. If Benton would've held out like I told him to, LockeCorp would be sending us a check every time one of those shirts rolled out of the factory, and it would have added up to a hell of a lot more than a few thousand bucks."

"So you two disagreed about how to proceed? And since his name was on the patent, you couldn't stop him from selling?"

"Yeah, but it doesn't matter. I've got a lot more planned than ManTees. Shaper tees have flooded the market, anyway; every major manufacturer's bringing them out. But I have other ideas men are going to love. The hidden-panel shirt, with customizable pectoral enhancement — no one's doing that yet. And the panel undershort I'm working on now, I've got a patent pending on a sling I designed for the front so it compresses the waist area without diminishing a man's other attributes at all. That's revolutionary, that's going to take the industry by storm —"

"Wait a minute," Stella said, holding up a hand. "I'm sorry, but I gotta stop you there a sec. 'Cause I got a picture in my head that just can't be right. You're saying you've got tummy control underpants that somehow let a man's johnson swing free so it can, ah . . ."

"It's nothing tawdry or lewd, like you're implying," Topher retorted. "It's a more natural profile, and I'm hardly suggesting anyone 'swing free,' to use your words. A man's preferred undergarments are easily accommodated by the —"

"Okay, okay," Stella said. "Back to the subject. So you got all these other . . . irons in the fire, let's just take you at your word that there's a market for all these designs a yours, let's say you got a income stream lined up there — so what's one patent? Why get all heated up over it, especially when Benton gave you half of everything?"

"Because he gave up on the vision!" Topher exploded. His face went purple with rage and he was half out of his chair before

Stella gave him a little reminder shove with her foot and waved the SIG in his line of sight. He lowered himself to the seat but remained agitated, twisting his hands in his lap. "Benton and I were out to change the entire men's undergarment industry, it's true, but it went further than that. We were going to change the way men see themselves. When we met, neither of us was successful with women. We kept getting turned down by women who didn't have anything on us in the ways that truly matter — steady job, good values, goal oriented. Women only go for guys who *look* the part."

"All women?"

"Well, the ones we wanted, anyway. The ones who took care of themselves."

"Ah. The hot ones. Isn't that always the way — an average guy wants to trade up, and if he gets shot down it's *her* fault she can't see his charms?"

"Well, that's what I'm trying to tell you. We set out to change all that. See, both of us were a little overweight, and a woman had said something about it to Benton on a first date. Needless to say, there wasn't any second date."

"He got his feelings hurt."

"We were working on an elastic fiber at work that they were going to use in industrial applications, but one day this gal at work picked up a piece of it and said it reminded her of what was in her minimizer bra. I took a couple of yards over to my mom and she measured me and sewed one up, and one for Benton. The first time we wore them out, I'm telling you the ladies couldn't get enough."

"So those were your magic ticket, is that right?" Stella doubted the women noticed any difference at all; if anything, they responded to an increase in confidence, even if it had come from something as ridiculous as a T-shirt. "If they were that great, how come you're still single?"

Topher glowered. "It's one *piece* of the whole *package.* I mean a guy's still got to have resources, good grooming, conversation skills — but yes, a control undergarment can be a big first step. I was committed to making that journey with Benton, working our program, letting it all happen in good time. But he got impatient."

"I see." Stella thought she might be starting to understand the true picture. "So let me guess — when Benton started hunting for girls online, you saw it as him abandoning you?"

"He stopped wearing the ManTees!" Topher exclaimed. "One day he comes in to work, tells me he wants to bring this one girl over. Natalya. He's never even laid eyes on her and he's ready to marry her. By then he'd let himself go completely, right back the way he used to be."

"So what you're really saying is that he called off this bromance of yours and you got your feelings hurt."

"*Bro*— No, that's not —" Topher sputtered in rage.

"Come on, you even had the matching outfits. People said you guys were joined at the hip."

"I'm *not* gay. Neither was Benton!"

"I never said it was a gay thing! You just had a special, special friendship. Women have them — no reason men can't, too, so good for you. Just sometimes people move on, you know? What I want to know was, if Benton's picking Natalya over you put you in such a murderous frame of mind, why did you wait so long to kill him?"

"I never planned to kill him! Not at first, anyway. I was his best man, for cripe's sake! I bought them a damn *juicer.* But the minute he married her, everything changed. I had to listen to Benton go on about her at work all day, and then he was always running home right after. He was sure she was cheating on him."

"Did he ever happen to mention that he was a little nuts on that subject? The crazy jealous thing?"

"I know, right? And she never even appreciated it!"

Stella tried to interject, to explain that it was hard to appreciate a man's devotion when it took the form of being locked in one's own home and forced to suffer screaming rages whenever one so much as looked the wrong direction in a restaurant, but Topher plowed on.

"Natalya, Natalya, Natalya, all day long. He brought her son over, did he tell you that? Even that wasn't enough. Then he decides he needs more cash, like buying her shit's going to make a difference. Makeup, jewelry, clothes. And the whole time he's completely abandoned our fitness program, the walking club, the tanning salon."

"So back to the murder part —"

"He came over about a month ago to tell me she'd left him, that Natalya had met this guy and was moving in with him. And get this, oh, this is rich, he wanted to know if I thought he could get away with killing the two of them."

"Now there's an idea," Stella said dryly.

"I told him she wasn't worth it, and he gets all bent out of shape. He tells me — he said —" The emotion threatening to burst forth from Topher had him tongue-tied.

"Deep breaths," Stella urged. "Stay with me now."

"He said that I could never understand true love. That it wasn't about the way you look or, or, what you wear. He made fun of me, called me 'fancyboy' — and told me I'd better never say anything against Natalya again. Well, I was just so angry, I, I . . . I said she was just a damn gold digger and he was a pathetic fool for falling for her. And so he — he *hit* me."

Topher's incredulity seemed as fresh as the day it had happened. Stella sighed. "You know what, it's a shame I didn't meet you before all of this."

"Why's that?"

"I know my way around violent men. I know what makes them tick. The thing you should have known is that abusers always go after the ones they love the best."

Topher paled.

"Benton must've loved you, otherwise he would never have tried to hurt you. And then you went and killed him." Stella gave him a sad smile. "See, I guess you just loved him more."

EPILOGUE

"When's Ian getting here?" Stella asked, as she doled out Popsicles to Tucker and his cousins Tater and Evvie. The sun was hot on the sprawling deck of the house Chester Senior had rented, overlooking the beautiful Lake of the Ozarks, for the Papadakis-Hardesty family reunion.

"Soon's he gets off work," Chrissy said, flashing Stella a can't-wait grin. "I told 'im I bought a new bikini."

Stella had already seen the swimsuit in question, a fire-engine red number that struck just the right balance between showing off Chrissy's generous figure and keeping parts of it tantalizingly hidden. She'd bought it with the bonus Stella paid her after pawning the dead gangbanger's earrings, which did not approach the fine quality sold by Hawthorn Jewelers but were worth a nice chunk of change nonetheless.

Chrissy had burst into the Paper Piecing

Posse last week to show everyone the spoils of her day-off shopping spree, so Stella had also seen the red cork-wedge sandals, the flirty dotted sundress, and the watermelon-flavored edible body shimmer.

"Fourth of July just says 'watermelon,' don't it?" Chrissy'd asked the giggly quilters, some of whom peered over their bifocals to get a good look at the tube of lotion.

In private she confided to Stella that it was more of a treat for Ian Sloat, the sheriff's deputy she'd finally confessed to dating.

"Y'all *still* ain't done it?" Stella had asked. It had taken Chrissy a while to make her peace with the idea of dating a lawman, given her checkered family history.

"After the fireworks, is what I'm thinkin'," Chrissy said. "I've been holding out for something special."

Stella had toyed with holding out for her own bit of sheriff's-department special, and Goat had apologized all over the place for having to delay the promised birthday outing once again, but he had been called away to teach a firearms refresher up at the Regional Training Center in Independence. After tamping down her disappointment, Stella had invited BJ over for the family barbecue. She'd had the notion that the fireworks would sparkle a little brighter if she had a man's hand to hold — and if between the flashes of silver and red lighting up the night sky she found herself wishing it was Goat's large and sun-browned one, well, she could sort through all those feelings later, after she'd had her well-deserved bit of fun with a man who was actually available.

Tucker submitted to a smooch from his mama before chasing after his cousins to the little beach down the slope from the big rental house.

Gracellen came out of the house carrying a big tray of frosty glasses. "Look what Chess and BJ been up to! These here are called May Days and I ain't got any idea what's in 'em."

"Well, I imagine it's five o'clock somewhere," Chrissy said, helping herself. "Now we got rid of the kids, we can get back to the game."

Chester Senior was presiding over a spirited game of Monopoly. Out of deference to Chip's gambling recovery, they'd left the poker chips in the closet; he and Natalya were playing as a team and had amassed a fortune in property already.

"Ooh, yum," Chrissy added, after taking a sip. "Y'all coming?"

"Nah, I think me'n Gracie are gonna talk for a while."

"Suit yourself," Chrissy said and took the tray from Gracellen, padding off on her bare feet to join the little knot of partiers on the deck.

Stella led the way down the steps to a pair of beach chairs shaded by a big sun umbrella, and she and Gracie stretched out luxuriously. In the ankle-deep water off the muddy beach, Todd and Luke splashed and hollered with the little kids.

"Luke sure is good with kids," Stella said, sighing contentedly. Since her disappointing finish in the Bean Blossom Half Marathon, she'd stepped up her training, and her muscles ached from yesterday's punishing workout.

"Oh, you should see him with the kids in the neighborhood," Gracie said. "Chester Senior's sponsoring a U-10 soccer team this fall, and he's got Chip and Luke running practices with the boys."

"Does Chip have time for that?" Since starting on at the warehouse in June, Chip had been putting in long hours getting up to speed, while Natalya spent her days helping Luke and Gracie fix up Chester Senior's place.

"They practice in the evening, after work.

Nat and I take sandwiches over and cheer 'em on. It's so nice, the way Chip and Chess are getting along."

They enjoyed a contented silence for a while. Up above, they could hear the adults' laughter; out on the lake a boat pulled a skier across the sparkling water. A mosquito buzzed by and landed on Stella's arm, and she nailed it on the first try.

"Eww, Stellie," Gracie said. "You got its blood all over you."

"I ain't afraid of a little blood. Better his than mine."

Which was a fitting thought for a reunion with Chip and Natalya, Stella thought to herself. Topher had confessed to shooting the drug dealer who broke into his condo — a scenario that had taken considerable effort and coordination to set up, with Chip and Topher transporting the body to Topher's place and calling the cops, and Natalya and Stella conducting a crime scene cleanup for the second time in a week in Chip's kitchen.

Stella guaranteed Topher's continuing cooperation by recording his confession to the other murder, that of Benton Parch. If all went well, the recording would stay hidden forever in Stella's safety deposit box, but meanwhile the knowledge of its existence kept Topher meek and compliant. The ongoing investigation into his home-invasion case was keeping him busy, which Stella figured was just as well, since she doubted the world was ready for his man-enhancing inventions.

"So I have to ask," Gracie said. "Are you *seeing* BJ, or, you know, just — seeing him?"

Stella blushed. "I don't know, we go out now and then. He's a lot of fun. I mean, sometimes we mess around a little, if we're drinking or whatever. But I don't think it's going to be any big thing, you know?" She didn't add that she still found his kisses to be a little mushy for her taste, or that it was still Goat who showed up in her dreams, usually in some state of partial department-issue uniform dress, and often suggesting she do something scandalous while he watched or, in her favorite dreams, participated.

"What about that sheriff of yours? You seen him lately?"

"Uh, well, we're supposed to go out for my birthday."

"Stellie, that was more than a month ago!"

"I know, I know. It's just . . . well, we've been busy." Plus there was the whole matter of Luke and his unofficial employment at the paint store and Chip and Natalya's visit to pick him up on their way to California.

Now all that had wound down, and there was still plenty of summer left for a fling. Or . . . whatever.

"Busy, huh." Gracie's tone said she didn't believe it for a minute, but she seemed content to let it go.

Summer afternoons at the lake were like that, a time for letting things go, for taking it slow and reconnecting. The Papadakis-Hardesty clan had taken up residence in the big house for the week, and every day brought visitors, from Chrissy and her family to the Groffes and Noelle's friends and Jelloman and his girlfriend. Noelle would be coming after work, and so would Ian, in time for the fireworks over the lake. Chester Senior had sprung for the house and everyone chipped in with the groceries, and already there was talk of making it an annual event.

"You know who I was thinking about today?" Gracie asked sleepily. "That dumb old cat. Sprinkles."

Stella smiled to herself. When the cat showed up one day forty-some years ago — not quite grown, half starved, its ears torn in a fight, infested with worms and hissing at everything that moved — Pat Collier had wanted to take it to the pound. Stella couldn't get close to it, not even by offering it bits of her hamburger.

Only Gracie — six years old and shy as a lamb — could not be convinced to give up on the cat. She named him Sprinkles and spent an entire summer following him around the backyard, talking and singing to him, leaving out food every morning and night. By that winter, Sprinkles had grown sleek and fat and ate out of Gracie's hand and slept on her bed, where he more or less lived for the next twelve years.

"He was a good cat" was all Stella said.

"Mmm. I don't even remember when he showed up. After a while, it was like he was always there."

Before long, Stella felt herself drifting off to sleep, the breeze tickling her hair and the sun warming her legs. Summer at the lake might not be paradise, but it was close enough.

ABOUT THE AUTHOR

Sophie Littlefield is an Anthony and RT Book Award winner and Edgar Award finalist. She lives near San Francisco, California.